Secrets of the Shingle

Emma Batten

First published in Great Britain by Emma Batten 2016

This edition 2020

A catalogue record of this book can be found in the
British library

ISBN 978-1-9995820-7-4

Edited by Maud Matley and Michael Golding

Proofread by Wendy Watkins and Maud Matley

Cover design from a painting by Zoe Beardsley

www.emmabattenauthor.com

To my friend Maud Matley, with thanks for the boundless enthusiasm you have shown for my writing since being the first person to read an early edition of *Secrets of the Shingle* in 2016.

Your passion for my author adventures have encouraged me to write and promote myself far more than I could have ever imagined possible.

About the Book

Secrets of the Shingle was first created as a paperback in July 2016, with the intention of displaying a copy on my bookshelf, and not as a book to sell or promote. Encouragement from friends in a writers' group led to a few copies being printed, and then offered for sale in a local visitor centre. The novel was well-received and was edited further as my unexpected author journey progressed.

Four years and six novels later, *Secrets of the Shingle* remains my bestseller, has been followed by two sequels, and has two prequels planned. I felt it needed a thorough rewrite and edit; this included adding a further eight thousand words, as I discovered scenes needing more detail. I enlisted Michael Golding from Dungeness to read my first draft and gave him free rein to comment on local detail and the plot – a task which he fully engaged in. Thank you, Mike. You did a fantastic job!

The manuscript was then passed to Wendy Watkins for proof reading, before having a final check from Maud Matley. Thanks to Wendy and Maud.

This Dungeness-Ashford series now needed covers to complement each other, and I commissioned local artist, Zoe Beardsley, to create a painting in the style we had used for *The Artist's Gift*. Finally, this edition of *Secrets of the Shingle* was born with new content and a stunning new cover!

As with all my novels, this book places fictional characters in real places. The main location being a remote, shingle peninsular called Dungeness, on the Kent coast. Within Dungeness the school, lighthouse, lighthouse keepers' cottages and railway station are based on actual buildings and only the exterior descriptions are accurate. There was not a vicarage at Dungeness. In real life a curate travelled from Lydd.

The settlement Denge no longer remains but was formally a small group of fishermen's homes, coastguards' cottages and a pub. It has been deserted since the Second World War and only a memorial stone remains.

I have researched historical details and tried to make the local area as authentic as possible. Descriptions of the lifeboats are based on the two boats at Dungeness during the period (1894-95). The incident where the lifeboat is called out in icy conditions in February 1895 is based on a true story. The rest of the plot is the product of the author's imagination.

Please note any opinions expressed in this novel are those of the fictional characters, not the author. Any resemblance to actual persons, living or dead and their homes is purely coincidental.

Emma Batten – June 2020

References: *Nanny Goat Island. Dungeness Then and Now*, by Keith Swallow (2019)
Wrecks and Rescues off the Romney Marsh Coast, by Edward Carpenter (1985)
www.theromneymarsh.net
www.dungeness.org.uk

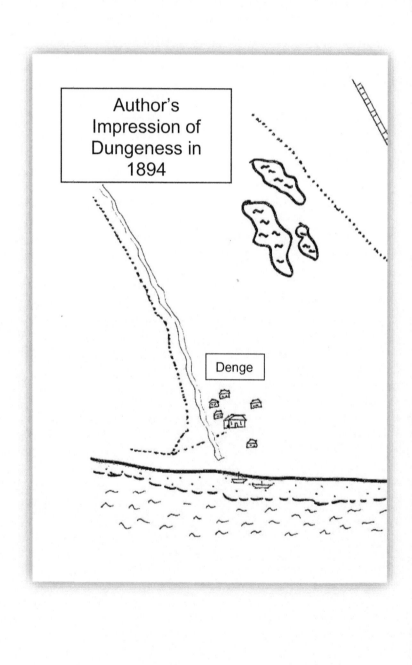

Author's Impression of Dungeness in 1894

Denge

Chapter One
1894

"Lydd, Lydd. All alight for Lydd. Next stop Dungeness." The station master called out with all the importance he could muster. It may be Lydd, but to him it was just as important as Paddington or Charing Cross.

Alice peered out of the grimy window as best she could. The grey drizzle was steady, and it seemed, even though it was mid-afternoon, dusk was not far away. There must have been half a dozen people stepping out onto the platform, pulling hats or shawls close to them, juggling shopping bags and scurrying through the red-brick station building. Porters stood by, stepping forward when needed, and within seconds the platform had cleared.

Next stop, Dungeness. Alice reflected on the words. *What a shame I'll be arriving at the seaside on a day like this.* The coach door had been left open and she looked towards the porter on the platform, hoping he would think to close it and then smiling to herself as she saw him step forward. As he reached out, a strong breeze gushed along the platform, wrapping itself around the engine as it went and filling the coach with soot laden steam, smarting Alice's eyes and leaving a repugnant taste in her mouth.

It seemed no one was going to join them on this last leg of the journey. There was to be just Alice and the friendly woman who had been her companion for the last few miles and whom she now knew as Bess Stevens, wife of a lighthouse keeper. They had exchanged a few friendly words and Alice was interested to know something about the life of people tending the light.

The coach doors had been slammed shut, the whistle had been blown and the flag waved, when the integrity of the staff at Lydd, and all the rules they stood for, were compromised by a latecomer. A shout alerted the guard, who turned but could not bring himself to assist whoever disrespected the Lydd Railway Company timetable. He turned his attention back to the train, determined that nothing and no one would prevent the smooth operation of the service. But the young man flung himself at the door of the coach, grabbing and turning the small brass handle, then opening the door as the engine made those first slow turns of its great wheels. Belches of smoke were being released through the chimney as he threw himself into Alice's compartment.

"I just saved myself a long walk in this damned miserable weather." His voice was cheerful but rough. Dark blond hair was ragged and there was no sign of a hat to lend him some degree of respectability. Sitting heavily on a seat, he took a bag from under his thick, grey coat and placed it beside him. Then he dropped a couple of flat rectangles of wood with leather straps across them, and they slapped upon the floor. Alice looked at them and frowned a little. Her companion had a similar pair. *What a very odd thing to be carrying about*, she thought. *I was curious about them when there was just the one pair, and now there are two and I can't possibly ask what they are for.*

"Good afternoon to you, Mrs Stevens. Been to see your sister? How is she keeping?" The newcomer spoke to the lighthouse keeper's wife.

"Oh, she is very well, and I must say the latest baby is bonny."

"Another babe? Life in Appledore must suit her, but I'd have liked it better if she had settled for Dungeness."

"I think we both know you would have led her a merry dance, Tom. I'd rather see her married respectably even if she is all the way over in Appledore." Bess Stevens spoke with good humour, but it appeared Alice's first impressions of this man were not unjust.

"We don't often see strangers on the line to Dungeness," Tom remarked, as he gazed at Alice with open curiosity. "And none as pretty as you!"

Alice chose to ignore his bold manner and kept her eyes firmly lowered. On her left hand she wore a thin gold band inset with a small diamond; she moved her hand a little, so the ring was clearly visible and twisted it to and fro. As a nearly married young woman it was prudent not to encourage the attention of a young man who was clearly in want of manners.

"She is our new school mistress, and you can treat her with respect Tom Barton, or you'll have the vicar to answer to," Mrs Stevens told him firmly, but the twinkle remained in her eyes and then she turned to Alice; "Miss Tibbs, this is Mr Tom Barton, fisherman at Dungeness. He'll be a neighbour of yours and a little familiar he may be, but he'll keep you well fed."

"Pleased to meet you Mr Barton." Alice raised her eyes to his and gave a brief smile before turning her attention to the view, which was all but obscured by the mist, the grime and the steam blasting past.

"The pleasure is all mine, Miss Tibbs."

Alice didn't reply, seeing no need to engage in further conversation. As an unmarried fisherman he wasn't at all the type of person with whom she would be striking up a friendship over the nine months she planned to stay at Dungeness.

The train had eased away from the station and, with a full head of steam, it made a steady pace, soon leaving the town and then the fields behind. Now vast stretches of shingle and scrubland stretched as far as Alice could see, melding with the misty rain until they became one. She struggled to see any landmark through both window grime and constant drizzle, so turned her attention yet again to her hands on her lap. Twisting her ring, she wondered if Albert was missing her yet. Had he called in to see her parents after work to enquire if she had left without incident? Would her mother have fussed at his soiled clothes, as he came straight from the engine shed, and given him one of her lesser quality cups in case he left a trace of oil on the handle?

On the Dungeness headland, the train progressed, and Alice felt calmed by the rhythmic sound of the wheels jarring over the joints. After a few minutes, the pace eased, and the newcomer could just make out the shapes of various buildings scattered in a disorderly fashion not far from the track.

"End of the line for us, Miss Tibbs." Bess Stevens began to gather bags and fasten her shawl. She picked up those slabs of wood and Alice's curiosity was renewed.

Tom Barton stood up as the train ground to a halt, belching a final, defiant blast of steam. He made his way to the door and opened it; then, stepping out, he held it open against the prevailing winds for the women to alight. Without pausing further to see if any help was needed with bags or cases, he was gone, vanishing into the misty rain.

Alice knew Dungeness to be remote and when she looked back on her time spent there, which she often did over the years, she couldn't remember what it was that first struck her about the place. Stepping down from the coach, she was assaulted by the strong winds driving the drizzle straight into her face; it settled on her skin and she brushed it aside, to no avail. Then there was the smell of the sea riding on the wind, and the taste of salt and seaweed when she licked the droplets of rain from her lips.

But the landscape! How could it be so different from all she was used to? How could it be that the orderly streets of Ashford, gardens with neat hedges, flowers and trees, were only an hour away by train? Here, shingle ridges rode out in all directions, and any greenery was ragged and sparse. The ripples went as far as Alice could see, presumably to the sea which she knew to be there, not just due to the smell but because she had been told she was coming to the seaside.

Alice stood for a moment on the platform and pulled her shawl as tight as she could around her head and shoulders. It wasn't much of a station: no red brick building with scalloped canopy. This was more of a… she wasn't sure what it was, but certainly not what she expected to find at her destination. The structure behind her was made of wood with a curved roof of corrugated iron. One of the signs fixed to the front wall directed passengers to a waiting room, and a window was topped with the word tickets. A man in an oilskin cape stood in the open doorway. Alice fumbled for her ticket, but he merely waved her on.

Through rain-laden eyelashes she couldn't quite see the village of Dungeness, but somewhere there must be a small green with neat cottages and, as it was at the seaside, perhaps a row of terraced houses and a promenade. She would see it all if the rain eased tomorrow and looked forward to exploring the area. The tearooms may be closed in October, but if not, then a pleasant hour could be spent with a pot of tea and watching the local people.

The railway line had no turntable, leaving the small but powerful little engine to slowly make its backward journey to Lydd. Salty rain and soot-infused steam mingled to make an unappetising taste as Alice licked her lips. There was no going back now. Besides, she had a commitment to be here and so this is where she would be for the foreseeable future.

"Were you expecting anyone to meet you?" Mrs Stevens asked. She felt compassion for the young woman who looked quite lost standing there with her smart suitcase and a carpet bag at her feet, slim white hands clutching at a leather handbag. She would be drenched in minutes; that shawl was no match for the fine rain sweeping in from the sea.

"I… I was to go to the vicar." Alice looked around as if there was a vague hope that the comforting figure of a friendly vicar might appear.

"Best come with me then dear, and I'll see you in the right direction."

Bess Stevens slipped her feet into those slabs of wood while Alice wrestled with her shawl. The women stepped off the station platform, not onto a path but on shingle and it was now Alice saw the reason for the pieces of wood, which acted as some kind of board, enabling her to move over the shingle without sinking in.

'You'll have to get some of these backstays commented Bess, noticing Alice's downward glances.

"Yes, I must," Alice attempted to respond, hindered by the rain driving straight into her face.

With the wind and driving rain, Alice thought it best to avoid the sight-seeing for that day and to just make do the best she could. So, with a case in one hand and carpet bag in the other, she hunched her shoulders, put her head down, fixed her gaze on Mrs Stevens' back and followed the older woman across the shingle.

It must have been ten minutes of slipping and sliding in her neat buttoned-up boots before they paused. All that time, the wind whipped at her shawl and the rain seeped through the back of her good winter coat. To Alice it seemed as if she was walking through an alien landscape, where the uneven forms of buildings came and went, yet none offered her comfort. No words were exchanged between the two women; the weather and the landscape did not allow it. All their energies were taken by the effort of walking. At last there was some respite from the wind as they stood in the shelter of a wooden building which was not unlike her father's shed at the bottom of the garden, although several times larger.

"The vicar's house," Bess announced. "Just give a tap and go on in. He's a bit deaf – might not hear you in this weather." She was about to turn back towards her own home, aware that it had taken longer than usual to make her way across the shingle with the newcomer in tow. Her fire beckoned her, but pity made her pause for a moment. "I'm at the lighthouse keeper's cottage. It's the first stone bungalow with tall chimneys if you need me. The vicar lives here amongst the fishermen, the lighthouse workers live by the lighthouse. We rub along together all right."

Alice murmured her thanks and tapped on the door of the shed, home to the local vicar. When there was no reply, Alice pressed on the latch, and was thankful the door swung open; she stepped inside.

At her home in Ashford, the front door opened into a hallway with a high ceiling, decorative cornices and a tiled floor which was swept daily and scrubbed regularly. But this was not home, this was some form of shed and the front door led straight into a room. Alice's first impression was of warmth: a very welcome heat coming from a tatty black range, and the yellow glow coming from a couple of oil lamps. Then she noticed books and papers, lots of them, on the dark wooden shelves stretching from the floor to the low plank ceiling and in piles on the side tables and on the gate-leg dining table – simply everywhere!

There were a couple of armchairs, upholstered in an olive-green velvet and strewn with woollen blankets. It was from under one of these blankets that a pair of dark eyes peeped through round, metal rimmed glasses. The figure beneath the blankets looked to be slight and only a small portion of his face showed between the blanket and his night cap.

"Good evening… Miss…" the vicar raised himself a little in his chair. "I'm sorry my dear, do I know you?"

"Miss Tibbs, Miss Alice Tibbs," the young woman replied with as much confidence as she could muster.

"Tibbs?" A broad smile spread across his face and eyes twinkled. "Now there's a co-incidence, I had a great friend at theological college named Tibbs. Edward Tibbs – ever heard of him?"

"He's my father, sir," Alice replied.

"Dear God, now that is a surprise!" the vicar exclaimed, and standing up he took a step towards her, his hand outstretched.

They shook hands with great exuberance on his part and casting aside a collection of blankets he gestured for Alice to sit on the second armchair.

"Well, well, this is a marvellous surprise. What did you say your name was?"

"Alice, Alice Tibbs." She set herself down on the edge of the chair.

"Ah, of course. Miss Tibbs, I had a great friend at college named Tibbs."

"Yes, my father, Edward Tibbs." Alice was beginning to feel that she was in a comedy act at the theatre. She'd been to see a few shows with Albert, then back to her parents' home for a sweet sherry in the front parlour. Her mother hadn't approved of

8

comedy shows.

"Your father... I visited him in Ashford, must have been several years ago. He had a splendid young daughter."

"That must have been me," Alice smiled.

The vicar sat for a few moments looking intently at his visitor before finally admitting, "Yes, yes I suppose it was." Then he frowned and continued, "But whatever brings such a delightful young woman to Dungeness on this miserable evening?"

What had brought Alice here? She was beginning to wonder herself. This was not at all what she expected and suddenly it all seemed a bit too much to cope with. The shock of discovering the vicarage was a shed, not a fine brick building, confused her. And then to find the vicar was not a portly middle-aged man with a wife, and an afternoon tea set out on china plates upon a lacy tablecloth... It wasn't at all as she expected, and Alice had visited many vicarages in her nineteen years; some as far away as Canterbury or Tunbridge Wells. She began to shiver as she sat there, still in her wet coat, with her shawl folded neatly on her lap.

"Would you mind if I just hung my coat by the range? And my shawl too?"

"Of course, my dear, I can see you are soaked through." The vicar stood up and busied himself with arranging a couple of chairs to air the clothes on. "And tea? We must have tea; they say that many of life's problems are helped with a cup of tea, although I prefer a glass of port!"

So, Alice found herself sitting with a cup of tea beside her and a piece of fruit cake. She still hadn't told the vicar why she was there, and he had been so busy fussing over the tea and cake that it seemed to have slipped his mind.

"Sir... I came... it was my father, Edward Tibbs; he

9

suggested that I might be of some use."

"Edward Tibbs – your father!" The vicar leant forwards clapping his hands together. "That is a surprise. I had a letter from him only this week and here you are!"

"Yes, it was all arranged. You were expecting me?"

"It seems to have slipped my mind. I find that happens every now and then." The vicar began to search frantically through the pamphlets and papers piled up on his side table. "I'll tell you what we'll do, my dear. I'll find that letter and then I'm sure it will all make sense."

Alice saw the thick cream-coloured envelope with her father's neat writing on it and part of the rectory's headed notepaper peeping out of the top. For a moment, tears threatened as she felt overwhelmed with homesickness. What would they be doing at home now? Would Albert have popped in straight after his morning's work in the engine sheds, or might he have gone home to change his clothes and might he still be there with them now, enjoying the comforts of the rectory? Would the three of them be seated around the table with its deep-red, fringed cloth and overlay of lace? Might they be eating scones or rock cakes and sandwiches? Would all the talk be of their Alice and how they would miss her, but what a great thing she was doing?

After much sighing and nodding, umming and ahhing, the vicar placed the letter on his knee and looked at Alice. "So, here you are and of course it says all about you in the letter. Your father was replying to a letter of mine where I had told of our desperate need of an assistant teacher here in Dungeness, and he said you were coming to help us. I recall now that I took the letter to Miss Wilkie and she was very pleased, very pleased indeed."

"Here I am," repeated Alice. She was beginning to feel pleasantly tired with the warmth from the range wrapping itself around her and the fruit cake filling that gap between dinner at home, and suppertime.

"If I said we needed an assistant then I am sure we do, and you'll be very welcome."

"You said that I was."

"I did, didn't I?"

"I do hope so." Alice looked at the 'diamond' set in the thin gold band and added, "It's just until the summer, until the end of term. I'll be getting married in August."

The vicar ignored her mention of marriage; his mind was still on the school and her work there. "Miss Wilkie will be expecting you, perhaps wondering where you have got to, so I had better take you to the school."

"The school? Would someone be there on a Saturday?"

"Where else would Miss Wilkie be on a miserable day like this? She'll be polishing the slates or whatever the good woman does in her spare time. There will be a room there for you and a roaring fire. It's a fine building the schoolhouse. Exceptionally fine for a smart young lady like yourself."

Alice felt a surge of relief through her slim body. She had assumed, in fact her father had assumed, that she was to stay with the vicar. Now she learned that she was to set off into the wind and rain again, but this time to the schoolhouse. The very name suggested respectability and the vicar himself had said that it was a fine building.

Alice took her teacup and plate to the sink, then began to put on her coat and, as she buttoned it up, she was pleased to find it wasn't too damp. Her shawl had dried out nicely and she gathered it tight around her head and neck, knowing that the wind would do its best to whip it out of place. Turning back to the vicar

11

she found him fast asleep, glasses askew and the letter from her father slipping down the blanket towards the wooden floor.

Rather than disturb him, Alice made the decision to set out alone to find the schoolhouse. She could call in at the lighthouse keeper's cottage to get directions if necessary. Yes, she would ask for directions and then make her way to Miss Wilkie and the schoolhouse.

Chapter Two

Alice stood for a moment with her back to the door of the vicarage-cum-shed. She looked upwards, thankful the rain had eased, and was rewarded by a shaft of light flashing across the dusky sky. With hands gripping her case and carpet bag, she took her first tentative steps across the shingle towards the lighthouse.

There was no visible path, and although Alice's journey to the lighthouse was not far, it was clearly going to be a battle to stay steady on the shingle with the wind pushing at her from the west. However, she was sure of a welcome and good advice from Mrs Stevens, and the young teacher was filled with renewed optimism that she would soon be on her way to the order and comfort of the schoolhouse.

Dusk was rapidly giving way to night and, as Alice felt compelled to look at the guiding light, which flashed every few seconds, it made it harder for her eyes to adjust to take in her surroundings. A few homes, if that was what they were, came between the young woman and the lighthouse. Small, low and irregular, there was the hint of light behind heavily curtained windows and the whiff of a driftwood fire in the air. The shacks were scattered at random and as for the expected streets, there seemed to be none. Alice could see no building substantial enough to be a schoolhouse, but in a place where the vicarage was a shed she felt incapable of imagining what a Dungeness schoolhouse would look like.

Another flash of yellow-white and, temporarily blinded, Alice caught her foot on a piece of rope or perhaps a trailing plant. A dip in the shingle threw her doubly off-balance and she landed heavily on her right knee and elbow. The sharp smack of stone on her slim body caused pain to rip through her, triggering a loss of her new-found confidence. She lay for a moment, nervous that any movement would cause further distress, then shifted a little and used her left arm to push herself up. *It will be no more than a nasty bruise,* she thought. *Nothing to worry about, nothing broken, but a lesson to take more care.*

Reaching out to pick up the case and carpet bag, Alice prepared to push herself up from her shingle seat. The lighthouse beam flashed again and for a split-second Alice saw another figure on the stones, just feet away from where she had fallen. *But can I be sure it is a person? Nothing seems to be as it should be here,* she reflected. *It looks as if it could be but is most likely nothing more than a bundle of nets, or rags, or… whatever else might be left to lie about. Surely not rags when they could be put to some use…* Alice was never far from her mother's voice ringing in her head and was well aware of how most items could be reused, even when they had seen better days.

Another flash and it was confirmed there definitely was a bundle of rough skirt and coat. Heart thumping so hard that it could wake the dead… *What an awful thought... not the dead, please not the dead…* Alice crawled across the shingle towards the body. With the wind pressing across the headland, and not wanting to go any closer than necessary to the possibly dead body, Alice paused at arm's length and strung together a few inadequate words.

"Hello… I'm… I… Can I help you?"

No response. Alice stretched her arm out and gave

the body a small prod, ready to recoil if it turned to show a pale lifeless face. It didn't roll; it didn't respond at all. Alice shuffled forward a fraction and reached out to touch long hair, matted and sticky with salt-water. *This woman has come from the sea; perhaps she is the wife of a fisherman. Do fishermen take their wives to sea? Please God, if she is alive then she'll need help soon. If I hadn't tripped, then no one else would have seen her until the morning.*

There was a groan? Or was there? How could the faintest of groans be distinguished from the whistle of the wind and the creaking of the wooden shacks? Then a slight movement of the body. Relief flooded through Alice and her heart ceased to pound quite so much. She leaned forward to find an ear under the tangled heap of hair.

"Hello, can you hear me?"

Another flash of light, and although Alice heard nothing of her weak voice, she saw the woman's salt-encrusted lips move and her grey eyes fixed on Alice. The moment passed, but they had made a connection and Alice knew this stranger was in desperate need of her help. When the light moved across the woman's face again her eyes were closed, dark rings encircled them, and shadows settled in the hollows under her cheek bones.

She needed to get help and quickly, that was clear, and warmth… this woman needed to be kept warm. Alice decided she must use something of her own clothing. But as she began to remove her shawl, a new noise reached her through the relentless howl of the wind. It sounded like the pull of the tide as it drags the shingle back with it and then a thud – a pull and a thud in a rhythmic pattern, and possibly coming towards her. Alice concentrated on this noise, trying to separate it from all the other sounds that the wind created. Then there was a shout, carried on a gust.

Afterwards, Alice wondered why she hadn't welcomed that shout and battled through the wind towards its source. But somehow her instincts took over and, without even pausing to fling her shawl over the dying woman, she scrambled over the shingle and to the shelter of a woodpile. From her hiding place Alice peeped through the gaps in the driftwood and had only just got herself in place when the beam of light showed a group of five men hauling a great sack along with ropes. They were well wrapped-up with long coats, snug woollen hats and sturdy fishermen's boots reaching midway up their calves. Their hoods were pulled low over their faces, and their bodies were hunched as they took the strain of their load.

When the light shone again, Alice heard a curse and saw one of the men tripping over the body and then they were all huddled around the woman, whispering furiously. One man flung her over his shoulder and with that the group continued on their way.

"She'll be fine now," Alice muttered to herself. "They'll know how to help her." But the tightening of her throat and twisting within her stomach, came as a sign that deep-down she knew the woman was not safe with these men. Whatever they were up to on this stormy evening was something that Alice Tibbs, rector's daughter, could not even dare to imagine.

Alice remained motionless for a few minutes, crouched behind the log pile, watching the clouds race across the black sky. The rhythmic shaft of yellow light was mesmerising, but she knew she was becoming chilled, and must find her way to Bess Stevens' home. She could still see the shapes of the men and hear the movement of the sack on the stones, but the distance between them was increasing with every sweep of the light-beam and Alice felt it was safe to continue.

The lighthouse keeper's cottage was one of a pair: a

solid, square, stone-built, single storey property with a porch to the front and a small window either side. The chimneys were tall, and the roof was slate. Alice rapped on the door as hard as she could and was soon rewarded by its being opened a crack. The round face of a boy peeped out. His brown eyes were curious, his hair a mop of brown curls and his face had a smattering of freckles across his nose and cheeks.

"Who is it, Bill?" The voice of Mrs Stevens came from within the cottage.

"I dunno. A woman. She looks posh."

"Let her in, out of the wind."

The door was opened; Alice stepped into the porch which led to a square living-dining room. Bess Stevens was standing at the door to the kitchen with a teapot in her hand. The boy immediately sat back down at the large pine table and stuffed the last of his bread into his mouth. There were four other children, and a great deal of clutter on and around the table. The smallest child being a boy of perhaps three years old; he was having his face wiped by a girl who, at about eleven years, must be the oldest of the five. Another girl and a boy came between them in age. They all had the wild brown curls of their brother, Bill. Their freckled faces and brown eyes were fixed upon Alice.

"It's Miss Tibbs," Mrs Stevens announced. "Children, it's Miss Tibbs that I was just telling you about." She began to pour from a huge brown teapot into a variety of mismatched cups. "Victoria, another cup for Miss Tibbs." The flow of the tea continued without disruption.

"I'm sorry, I… I just …."

"No need to explain." Mrs Stevens pulled out a chair and placed the cup of tea in a space between the debris of the just-finished meal. "I was worried the vicar might leave you to fend for yourself. You did the right thing coming here. You shouldn't be out in this

17

weather, but we'll have to get you to the schoolhouse and then you'll be settled for the evening."

"Thank you. I didn't know how to…" Alice fought back tears. "I didn't know the way."

"Of course, you didn't dear; how could you? Bill here will show you when you've had your tea and perhaps something to eat?"

Half an hour passed, and Alice felt much better with a plate of fried fish, tomatoes and bread inside her. The Stevens' brood were a lively bunch of children and mostly kept her thoughts occupied with the moment, as they bombarded her with questions about herself and offering information about themselves. In the midst, was their mother, Bess Stevens, giving orders, breaking up squabbles, soothing the younger ones and at the same time cooking and tidying away. What a contrast to the refrained dignity of supper at Alice's home in the rectory.

"Poor Miss Tibbs, you must be so tired, coming all this way and not having a proper welcome," Mrs Stevens began.

"Oh, no… not at all… well, maybe a little tired but you've made me so welcome."

"I know for certain you were expected at the schoolhouse, so you'll find a bed made up for you, but I feel for you having to walk all that way in this weather, what with you not being used to the wind."

"It's not far is it?" Alice asked. For all her polite words, the thought of going out again into the night was daunting and she really was exhausted.

"It must be ten minutes' walk," replied Bess. "Bill will fix you up with a pair of backstays and he'll keep you safe."

"I put them outside, by the porch, Ma."

"Backstays?" Alice queried.

"Them bits of wood, you move along on," Bill informed her.

"Of course, I saw them earlier, but I'm not sure I'll manage..." But Alice's words were left unheard by Bill who had already stepped outside.

So, Alice left the warmth of the lighthouse keeper's cottage and, with her coat buttoned up and shawl wrapped tight, she slipped her boots under leather straps fixed to flat pieces of wood. Bill set off at quite a pace, seemingly unaware of Alice's difficulties. She could see the reason for using the shingle shoes, as they would spread her weight and were less likely to dig into the stones. However, it would take some time for the newcomer to master the art and be able to lift and move her feet over the shingle ridges with ease. For now, she constantly stubbed the toe of her stay and being weighed down by her suitcase on one side meant that she could not distribute her weight evenly. After a few minutes Alice concluded that to stumble along in just her smart buttoned boots would be easier than learning a new skill in her weary state.

"Bill, I can't manage," Alice called. "Would you mind... it's these bits of wood, and the stones... I can't possibly..." She flicked her feet, so the backstays fell off.

He turned and trudged back. "Sorry, Miss, I shouldn't have gone off like that." He picked up the wooden boards. "Don't worry, Miss. It's easy enough to reach the school because we can walk along the railway tracks. Here it is."

"The railway tracks?" Alice repeated; she could hear her voice was high.

"There won't be any more trains now," Bill replied. In some ways it was as if he were the teacher and she the pupil. At least he was when it came to the ways of Dungeness. Alice could almost hear his thoughts: *She may be a teacher, but Miss Tibbs didn't seem to know much.*

They were nearing the railway station; Alice could

make out the shape of the small building and raised platform. If only she had known the school was so near to where she had left the train, she could have gone directly there and avoided having tea with the vicar, then the discovery of the body on the shingle. Why hadn't the teacher, Miss Wilkie, been there to meet her from the train? To take her in, away from the wind and sea mist, to seat her by a fire and give her tea and cake placed on a table with a lace trimmed cloth?

They stepped onto the rails and Bill explained, "See Miss, nice and smooth, easier to walk on like them pavements in Ashford town."

Alice could see his point and yes, for Bill it was easier, to balance and run along the narrow rail in his sturdy boots, with only his backstays to carry. But she was wearing her smart town boots and weighed down by her suitcase; it was virtually impossible to balance on a single rail. She settled for walking on the wooden sleepers which, although mostly covered in pebbles, offered a more even surface than before.

Weary and grateful for her young guide, Alice was content to follow. Her back was to the wind, another thing to be thankful for, and she could just plod along without having to think about much at all until they reached the school. They had been on the train track for about five minutes when Alice realised there were no buildings in sight and they were now some distance from the lighthouse, the shacks and sheds of Dungeness village.

"Why are we walking away from the village?" Alice asked.

"Because the school isn't near the other places, it's on its own," Bill replied.

Alice made no further comment but thought to herself it was all very odd. The school was usually a central part of any village, along with the church, the pub and a few shops. But nothing about Dungeness could be compared to her experience of other villages and small towns.

Time passed, with Alice negotiating her inconvenient path, before a white-painted building loomed to the right. In the moonlight, Alice could see it was a substantial building compared to what she had witnessed so far, albeit a little irregular in shape, having several additions to the main structure which must be the classroom. The school and adjoining home was adorned with several chimneys, which indicated to Alice that this was going to be a comfortable home for the next few months.

A picket fence surrounded the school and ran alongside the track. Bill paused to open a gate leading directly from the railway line and Alice stepped through.

"This way to the teachers' house," Bill led the way along the shingle path. "I go the other way in the mornings, but this is your entrance."

They turned the corner and came across a plain wooden door set in the white wall. Alice was tired and the events of the past hours had led her to feel anxious as to what life would bring over the next few weeks. It was only as she stood, almost on the threshold to the teachers' accommodation, that it began to dawn upon her there was no light showing at the schoolhouse windows. Not a glimmer between drawn curtains or spreading out between the slats of a shuttered window.

The next thing she noticed was a carpet bag on the doorstep. It was hers and she hadn't put it there. Neither had Bill, as the boy was standing behind her.

Chapter Three

"There's a bag here, Miss." Bill gave the carpet bag a prod with his toe.

"Yes, it's mine," Alice replied. "I must have left it behind somewhere."

How had she not noticed that it had not been with her since… Alice reflected on the last couple of hours: she recalled holding the bag when she left the vicar, but not when she reached Bess Stevens' home. So, since she fell on the shingle? That was it: she had gone to look at the body… the woman, and that was when she had left it behind. How could she have done such a thing? Alice prided herself on having everything in order, from her neatly arranged toiletries on her dark wooden dressing table to always being on time for church. Miss Alice Tibbs did not go around leaving her belongings just dumped in any old place.

"Nice of someone to bring it here," Bill commented, as he opened the schoolhouse door and pushed it open.

"Yes, very kind." Alice said the words, but the shiver had grown to panic. A horror rose from the pit of her stomach and inside her head it screamed at her: *Someone knew you were there, Alice. Someone knew you were hiding behind the wood pile. You were being watched. They knew you were out there in the night and that you saw the men and their load. They knew you had seen the body.*

"It's a bit dark in here, Miss." Bill interrupted her

thoughts. "You'll need to find a lamp." They had stepped into a small porch and were pushing on the door leading to the living area.

But there was a lamp, albeit giving out a weak light, and Alice felt the warmth coming from the range. "No, it's all right," she replied. "Look! Someone has thought to leave a light for me."

"I wonder who that was," Bill replied.

"Miss Wilkie, of course!"

But there was no Miss Wilkie to greet Alice. No Miss Wilkie to commiserate over how late she was and to say how worried she had been, and how she must come in out of the night to be warmed by the fire. No Miss Wilkie to say how wonderful it was that Miss Tibbs had arrived to help her teach the children.

"She's not Miss Wilkie." Bill saw how confused the young woman was. "She's Mrs Stubbs now, since she married Mr Stubbs from Lydd last month. He's a policeman, you know."

"And she lives?"

"In Lydd of course," Bill informed her.

With Bill gone, Alice was left in an area that was both kitchen and living room. The first thing to do was to top up the oil in the lamp and to light another one. Alice took a taper from a pot on the side and put it to the weak flame, then to the wick in the second lamp. Thankfully, the range was alight, but it would need tending before she retired for the night. The Tibbs family had Martha to deal with the business of keeping the range going, and Alice had watched her enough times to feel confident she could add a few logs from the basket and warm the room up a little. As she took in the details of her surroundings, from the central table, dresser and kitchen sink to the armchairs and bookcase, Alice's attention fell on the inky blackness of the windows. She pulled at the heavy brown curtains, making sure that not one bit of the night sky was showing or, more importantly, that no unseen person could peer in at her.

Then, in a panic, Alice rushed to the outside door and pulled the bolt across, there was another, perhaps leading to the school room, which was already bolted. But there were two more doors and what if… what if the person who had brought the carpet bag was already here. She picked up a poker from beside the range and with her heart thumping, fit to explode, she opened one. A bedroom, unused. She must check under the bed, in the clothes press, in the chest. All fine. And the other room, the same: clothes press, bed (made this time), chest. All clear. Back to the kitchen and a smaller, narrower opening led to… the larder. Nothing there. She was safe… for now.

On her return to the bedroom which was to be hers, Alice noticed a lump under the covers. A clay hot bottle to warm her bed. The young woman began to feel a little less tense. Here was a sign that someone had thought of her comfort.

The bedroom was quite respectable. In fact, just as good as any room she would expect a schoolmistress to be given in Ashford, or even Canterbury. There was a thick rug on the floor, sturdy dark wooden furniture, a couple of decent landscape paintings and her bed looked comfortable. There seemed to be no gas lighting, but of course Dungeness was rural and couldn't be expected to have all the modern conveniences.

Alice opened her case and looked at her belongings, then took out her two good blouses, her tweed skirt, the dress she usually wore to church and the black dress with a white collar. She laid them out carefully in the clothes press. There was a cross stitch sampler at home which showed the value of order and tidiness; this was something Alice would always aspire to. Not today though, she had a feeling the same rules didn't apply here. Everything else was a bit disorderly in the suitcase and bag, but for once it would have to wait until the morning.

The next fifteen minutes were spent by first exploring the larder and looking in the cupboards. Alice was pleased to note that some fresh bread, milk, butter, bacon, cheese and eggs had been left on the cool slate shelf in the larder. There was tea too, sugar and some dry ingredients for baking. Again, someone had thought of her, presumably the former Miss Wilkie, now Mrs Stubbs of Lydd.

Finally, a small pot of tea was brewing, and Alice sat in one of the armchairs, her shawl around her for warmth, and read a few pages of a book she had brought from home. She soon realised that she may well have been reading the words but her mind was distracted by thoughts of shingle ridges, vicars in huts and, most of all, a body on the stones with tangled hair like a pile of tarred rope and the dark-ringed eyes that held Alice's own brown eyes for a moment, begging for help.

Ever practical, Alice knew there was nothing to be done about it now, but perhaps some enquiries in the morning? She stood up, wanting to physically shake off those invading thoughts and busied herself with filling the range and closing the damper for the night. Then, after checking all the doors and windows again, she prepared herself for bed.

Alice saw her coming; she came from the doorway and walked slowly towards the bed. She didn't speak and her expression was of nothing... not fear, not friendship and certainly not aggression. Her hair was thick, long and wavy; the colour was auburn. Her skin was pale. She stood by the bed and waited... just standing there. Terrified of what was to come next, fear

25

rendered Alice immobile, a scream stuck in her throat as she opened her eyes, and gradually the woman faded away. It was just a dream and no wonder after what had happened, but that knowledge didn't stop her heart from slamming against her chest, forcing her to crouch in a foetal position as she waited for the pain to ease.

How long had she been asleep? Alice didn't know. She recalled an hour or more of lying there, nervous to every sound. Then she had slept until... until this terrifying vision had come before her. Alone in a house with no other property nearby, how was she ever to find peace when night-time came? She forced happy thoughts into her mind: Albert, her parents and inconsequential things like piano practice and her collection of pressed flowers. Anything to make the fear go. Gradually Alice's heart settled and, although the image of the unknown woman stayed in her mind, she fell into an uneasy slumber.

The dreams returned: a vicar who sang his sermons and preached his hymns; a lighthouse keeper whose light only shone Monday to Friday; Tom Barton from the train walking in his backstays with a woman... a woman with auburn hair. Time and time again Alice woke, until finally falling into a deep, dreamless sleep for a few hours. When she woke for the final time it was still an hour before dawn.

At last the weak morning light crept through the gaps in the curtains. Alice got up, gathered her shawl tightly around her shoulders and pulled back the heavy window coverings. She wiped at the condensation, but it was just repeated on the exterior of the glass in the form of light rain, so the curtains were left to fall back into place.

It was Sunday and so the best blouse with delicate pearl buttons was taken from the clothes press and Alice dressed as quickly as she could. As she brushed

26

her hair neatly into a bun at the nape of her neck, her face in the mirror looked tired, skin dull and eyes nervous. She attempted a smile, but it looked false; it was false. "Come along, it's a new day and a fresh start," she told her reflection, but it stared back, weary and barely willing to give the day a chance.

Half an hour later, with the damper open and the range glowing, Alice sat at the table and poured her second cup of tea. The fruit loaf found in the larder had been excellent toasted and, as the young woman's fatigue lifted, her curiosity about the new life ahead was revitalised.

The rain had passed when Alice decided it was time to pull back the curtains. Weak sunshine tempted her to look outside, and she decided not to peep through grimy squares of glass but to go and have a proper look at the place. Her coat had been left in the kitchen-cum-living room for the night and had been thoroughly dried by the heat from the range. It might be sunny but would still be chilly. With coat on and hat firmly over her ears, Alice stepped out of the front door, scurried along the path and at the picket fence she turned to look back at the school for the first time in daylight.

The young woman couldn't help comparing what she saw with what she was used to. Her experience of schools was that they were generally red brick or stone, and this building was built of concrete block and painted white. It was small, but of course she had expected that, and modern, although not as fashionable in design as the Victorian schools in her hometown. The building looked quite respectable though and the main building even boasted a tiny cupola for the school bell. The roof was slate, and several tall, white painted chimneys protruded almost majestically. Alice hadn't explored the main school yet, but it was clearly in the larger portion of the building.

The living accommodation came out from the rear of the school with three extensions jutting out at right angles and each one just the size of her own room. The windows were wooden framed with glass in square panes. It was not a notable or imposing building, nevertheless Alice felt satisfied with her first impressions, adding to the growing confidence in her new venture.

The countryside was a different matter, in fact to call it countryside was an injustice to all that was lush pasture and rolling hills. No, this was not countryside but some form of grim, bleak scrubland. A desert of pebbles. Neither was it the seaside she had in her mind's eye when leaving home in Ashford, as there was no sea to be seen and no sign of it in the immediate area. However, Alice did concede that the coast was nearby; she knew this because the fresh smell of ozone and salt permeated the whole area and of course she could see the lighthouse in the distance.

There were ridges of shingle as far as Alice could see. She let her eyes follow the railway tracks towards the building that called itself a station and along the coast to the east where she saw the smattering of shacks that were apparently homes. One of these was the vicarage, which she could not recognise from this distance. Then back to the station, and just beyond it where, standing proud, was the lighthouse with its stout base which provided further keepers' accommodation and work rooms. There were other outbuildings in the vicinity, and two additional cottages, one of them being the home of the Stevens family.

Alice saw no beauty in this land; her expectations of the countryside were fixed and limited to her study of watercolours of country scenes and likenesses of wildflowers found in the books she had studied in her not so distant youth. The patches of short, coarse grass and woody broom failed to lift her mood and did not compare to cottage gardens or woods of oak and beech. She did not notice the beauty of delicate lichens nestled amongst the grass and stones. Neither did she marvel at the tenacity of the tiny roots that clung on regardless of the lack of earth and the strong winds.

Walking to the other side of the school, and looking in the direction of Lydd, Alice noticed the shingle gradually became less prominent and the greenery more abundant. However, the landscape remained flat and uninteresting, nothing caught her eye or inspired Alice to explore further, and the view was only broken by the small town of Lydd which could be distinguished by its church tower and cluster of houses.

Here, at the back of the building, Alice found some chickens, six of them all pecking and fussing around in a pen. In a brick outhouse she spotted a tin of grain and scattered a couple of handfuls in their direction. Whilst the chickens were absorbed, she checked their nesting area and retrieved a couple of brown eggs. Raised beds of soil had scrappy pieces of greenery within them. Perhaps it had been some time since Miss Wilkie had tended the plot to produce fresh vegetables for her dinner. Although satisfied with the chickens, there was nothing else to please Alice in this garden of sorts.

The kitchen door was still locked from the inside, so she made her way back around to the front door and, in the direction of the sea, some movement caught her attention. A bent figure in black scurried along, coat flapping in the breeze. She couldn't be certain, and she had only seen him in the confines of his small home but perhaps this was the vicar, and of course he must be coming to see her. Then it became apparent that there was quite a gathering following in his wake; in their greys and browns they blended into the landscape but as the minutes passed the figures became more distinct. It seemed that, for some reason Alice could not fathom, the vicar was approaching with some form of procession.

She stood waiting and as the vicar neared her, he extended his arm to shake Alice's hand. He did this with gusto. "Ah, Miss..."

"Tibbs, Alice Tibbs."

"Of course, of course," He nodded furiously and, with his thin head and pointed nose, Alice was suddenly reminded of a small bird frantically pecking at a worm. "Miss Tibbs, you arrived at church in good time. Splendid, did you come far?"

Chapter Four

Alice had planned to explore the school next: to examine the variety of books, study the maps and pictures on the walls, then count the desks so as to get a feel for the place. Instead she was ushered in with a dozen others and became a part of a change as school became church. This was something she had not been expecting and, shamefully, she felt the intrusion interfered with her plans for the day. But the guilt soon passed, and she was brought abruptly back to reality with a demand.

"Desks first," commanded a scrawny woman, her shawl bound around her with a piece of rough twine. She took one side and Alice, following the lead from those about her, picked up the other and they set it down at the edge of the room. "So, you're the new young school mistress."

"Miss Tibbs," Alice introduced herself, but couldn't hold out her hand to shake as they were on the second desk by then.

"Is there something wrong at the church?" Alice ventured to ask as they moved the fourth desk.

"Wrong?"

"I mean why are we here today? Has there been some… some storm damage… or something?"

"There is no church," replied her companion in surprise. "Only here, the school."

It wasn't polite to question this woman any further and it was becoming clearer that indeed the school was also used as the church. A small teaching platform did very nicely as a pulpit, kneelers were brought from crates and placed in front of the plain wooden chairs. Finally, the transformation was complete as a curtain was pulled back to reveal an altar in front of the eastern window. More people arrived and began to seat themselves.

"Curiouser and curiouser," Alice thought to herself, drawing comfort from the well-known words of her favourite children's book. This might not be Wonderland, but Alice was certainly bemused by it all.

Where should she seat herself? At home it was quite clear that as daughter of the rector she sat beside her mother at the front and a little to the side. Alice decided on placing herself at the end, four rows back as there were six rows of seats. This left space for any of the important families who perhaps had their own chairs. The hymn books were in a box at the doorway, so she made her way to them, feeling very conscious of being a newcomer and knowing all eyes were on her, although no one had introduced themselves.

As Alice went to pick up a rather well-worn hymn book, faded with age and barely legible gold lettering on the spine, another hand firmly held onto the same book. A huge, rough hand with unsightly brown hairs sprouting from it and short, neat but dirty, nails. She looked up at the owner of the hand, her own slim, pale hand still clasping one corner.

"Miss Tibbs," Tom Barton's mouth smiled down at her, but his eyes were hard.

"Mr Barton," she replied with a small nod. Why would he deliberately take the book that she was about to use and what was it about those eyes and that smile? As if he knew things... secrets... but she had none to hide.

"Settling in nicely?" he asked, hand still on the book, challenging her to back down. "It's a lonely place

out here. Just the wind for company at night-time…
just the wind and your thoughts and dreams."

"Oh, I'll manage very well, thank you, Mr Barton,"
Alice replied with bravado, lifting her sharp chin high.

"And you have all your luggage with you?" he
asked, as if with concern. "You wouldn't like to
misplace something else out here, would you?"

"I… thank you, I have all I need." Her throat was
constricted now, and Alice didn't think she could
squeeze out another word. What did he mean by that?
He was just being polite of course… in his own way.
That would be it. But someone knew, someone knew
she had mislaid her carpet bag.

His hand released the book and Alice swung
around, almost colliding with Bess Stevens.

"My, you look all nerves today, Miss Tibbs. I'm not
surprised, stuck out here all on your own. Come and
sit with me and the family." They occupied a whole row
of seats – the lighthouse keeper, his wife and children,
with Alice Tibbs feeling safe for that moment in the
heart of this family group.

There was a piano in the school which substituted
as a church organ and voices sang with gusto,
although lacking finesse. The sermon was more for
Easter than autumn and the vicar commented on
several occasions that he was sure he had picked up
the wrong notebook. But never mind, so long as the
Lord's message was heard, she was sure it would not
matter. The prayers were lengthy and with many
references to keeping the fishermen and lifeboat crew
safe, which was entirely appropriate. It was not at all
what Alice was used to, but nothing here was the same
as it was at home in Ashford.

After the best part of an hour, the vicar's gaze
alighted on Alice and he paused as if surprised to see
a stranger amongst the weather-beaten regulars.

"Ah, and of course… yes indeed we have a
33

newcomer to our flock and most welcome she is." A pause and a nod. "Yes, here she is Miss... Miss ... and of course we pray that she'll be very happy here in Dungeness."

Alice felt her colour rise as she forced a smile. Bess Stevens gave her arm a pat and all faces swivelled, relieved to have the permission to stare openly if only for a few seconds.

"May the Lord be with you. Amen." The church service was concluded.

Alice muttered, "Amen."

Then the congregation rose from their seats, exchanging a few words with each other, buttoning up coats and cramming on hats. Soon there were just half a dozen left and they were busy setting the schoolroom to rights, ready for Monday morning. One of those left was Tom Barton, lifting the desks with ease, carrying the heavy box of hymn books, and sometimes catching Alice's eye then giving her a look. He knew. Alice knew he knew – about the carpet bag and the body.

"Splendid to see you here," the vicar said as the door was locked behind them. "Did you come far?"

"Oh no, I was just..." Alice looked in the direction of the schoolhouse living quarters.

"Come on, Vicar, enough of your jokes. She's the new school mistress. Our Miss Tibbs," Tom Barton smirked. Alice tried not to scowl at his words, finding them to be a touch familiar.

"Of course, of course." The vicar nodded frantically. "Our Miss Tibbs, it seems that she is one of us already. I knew her father of course."

"Indeed, she is," agreed Mr Barton. "Not a day has passed, and Miss Tibbs knows the secrets of Dungeness and she will be one of us until the day she dies."

"How lovely to have settled in so well, my dear. But

please, Mr Barton, don't speak of her parting yet!" With a broad smile and a pat on her arm, the vicar turned his back on Alice and moved along the pebbles in the direction of the coast and his vicarage shed.

Tom Barton didn't catch her eye again. He pushed his boots into the backstays and off he went without a backward glance, passing the vicar with ease and soon his broad figure was indistinguishable amongst the other creatures of this wilderness. Alice shivered, suddenly aware of the cool breeze, and made her way back to the teachers' accommodation, firmly closing and bolting the door behind her.

As the milk hadn't turned sour yet, Alice was able to relax with two cups of tea. She then decided it was not right to be sitting in a chair all day, and a walk to the sea would do her spirits the world of good. Having decided on a cheese omelette for her midday meal, a third cup of tea, and an apple from the fruit bowl left her fortified for the trek. She would worry about her supper later and tomorrow she could ask Mrs Stubbs about where to buy her food.

Some of Alice's belongings remained in the partially unpacked case and bag on the floor of the bedroom. She had paused beside them several times, knowing that she really should put everything away in the clothes press or chest of drawers, but not yet able to bring herself to see this as her home. Alice thought about the cross-stitch picture on her bedroom wall in the rectory and recalled how her mother had fussed over every stitch. She imagined Mrs Tibbs standing in this room, scanning the contents until her gaze stopped on the handkerchiefs and face cream, and then the notebooks, all of which needed putting in a place of their own. "Very well, Mother, I'll do it later. After my walk," she murmured.

The backstays were propped up against the white

wall of the schoolhouse; Alice picked them up, finding they were not too awkward to carry and might be useful later. Presumably, no trains ran on a Sunday, she hadn't seen or heard one passing that day, so she decided to take young Bill's advice and walk the tracks towards the coast. In her sturdy boots, used for countryside walks, she could negotiate the uneven ground with relative ease, making good progress along the lines.

After five minutes, Alice paused and noted that the distance between schoolhouse and station building was about equal. The wind was still brisk and white clouds scurried across a grey sky, but the rain had subsided, and weak sunlight passed through the intermittent gaps in the clouds.

Shingle ridges stretched in all directions: grey stones with patches of short, tough grass and woody plants, bowing to the east. Alice saw no beauty in the subtle shades of white-grey through to charcoal, beige, fawn and taupe. Just stones, stone-shaped stones. She did not see anything of interest in the textures – rough, smooth, jagged – or the wonders of a broken stone with its centre of a richer colour and smoother quality. This land of shingle did nothing to captivate the young woman for one moment. She stopped for a while, looked at the landscape and sighed, aware she was being uncharacteristically judgmental about her surroundings. Alice had always been inquisitive about all things that surrounded her and rarely missed the opportunity to investigate something new.

The track came to an end just past the tiny station building, which was hardly bigger than a coach and similar in proportion with an arched roof. There was no more to it than she had spotted the previous afternoon, other than a water tower and some small extensions. Alice thought of the impressive brick-built railway buildings in Ashford, but of course she was being foolish in making a comparison; there was no need for such grandeur here.

"It's a different place altogether; no point in comparing it," Alice scolded herself out loud. "It's just for a year, so you may as well get used to it. In fact, not even a year; I'll be gone by the end of July."

Considering herself told off, Alice traipsed beyond the end of the track and straight by the lighthouse keepers' cottages. It would have been lovely, and all too easy, to be cosseted by the warmth and friendly atmosphere of the Stevens' family cottage, but Alice hadn't been brought up to call in somewhere uninvited, so she didn't linger. Besides, it was only a few more steps to the sea and she was eager to see it.

The English Channel rolled towards a steep shingle bank; it smashed against the land and recoiled, fighting with the next incoming wave, then surged onwards. The sea not only mirrored the grey of the sky, they both became as one, making it impossible to detect the horizon. Looking at this did nothing to improve the newcomer's first impressions of the area. Standing, almost on the point of Dungeness, Alice could see there were large bays on both sides. In the direction of Hastings, the land rose to hazy hills and cliffs. Much closer there were half a dozen isolated cottages, but not enough to give Alice any hope of civilisation being at hand. Out in the bay, a few small fishing boats, with their nets extending into the deep water, looked so tiny and vulnerable against the vast expanse of the open ocean.

The bank leading to a narrow strip of beach, was steep. A line of flotsam and jetsam from the sea had settled on it, tempting Alice to investigate. The tide was out, and Alice was surprised at how high she was above the area of soft sand, only visible at low tide – at least fifteen feet. *That could be dangerous for the unwitting,* she mused

She placed one boot on the slope, and then the next, before beginning to slip, and scrambling back to the ridge. *I'll walk along the top here, past the lighthouse, and towards the place I found the woman,* Alice decided. *I wonder if I'll recognise the very spot I fell? Not that it matters, as there will be no clue as to what happened to her, but it would be interesting to see it in daylight.* She slipped her boots back into her shingle shoes and plodded on. Despite finally having mastered the techniques of the backstay, she still found the effort of moving across the beach rather exhausting.

A few minutes later, and Alice kicked the backstays off. "What am I doing?" the young woman muttered to herself. Images of a proper Sunday afternoon slipped into her head. A stroll around the park, or along the River Stour with Albert. Afternoon tea with his mother or her parents. Holding hands and talking about their thoughts for the future: dreams for their own home, rather than living with one of the sets of parents, and plans for further time to be spent together. It was so pleasant and normal. In all her nineteen years, Alice's life had progressed exactly as expected.

"I thought it would be just the same," she spoke out loud again. Pondering on her words for a moment, Alice felt cross with herself for being so foolish. "Not quite the same of course… the same type of people… the same… oh, I don't know what I mean."

There it was, she had rounded the point and it was all just the same as the other side. Alice felt unreasonably cross about it and she didn't usually suffer from bad moods. She was tired of course after a poor night's sleep and the events following her arrival were still fresh in her mind. Alice felt cheated; she felt that she had not known that she would be coming to this… this odd, desolate place. Her legs ached and she still had to make her way back to the schoolhouse.

The lighthouse was now five or six hundred yards behind her, and another building was squatting on the shoreline. It was an interesting place, long and low with a curved roof. Both roof and walls were built of corrugated iron and supported a stumpy steeple, containing what seemed to be another revolving light. Also protruding from the roof was a horn, shaped like the end of a huge trumpet. Another day this would have captured her interest, but today Alice sneered at yet another oddity in this strange place and marched on by in the best way the shingle would allow her.

Continuing along the beach-front, the dispirited young woman turned inland and passed between a group of shed-homes. She saw the vicarage to her right. Was this where she had fallen last night? It was hard to tell, but it must have been nearby.

What had happened to that bedraggled young woman? She looked to be barely alive, but their eyes had engaged, and Alice knew she had failed her. She should have somehow ensured her safety. At the very least there was a duty to find out if she was alive and safe. Both strangers, they were sisters in this harsh, unforgiving land.

Alice, ever sensible, pulled her thoughts up short. "It's the exhaustion and no wonder," she excused herself out loud, and then started upon hearing a response to her words.

"Sit and rest a while, Miss."

There were three of them, sitting on a bench at the front of a long low shack. *Damn, it's that Mr Barton again and with a band of scruffy fishermen, most likely. Can I not get away from the man? Look at how he irritates me, causing me to… to use such language, not that I said it aloud, but I thought it, nonetheless.*

"Thank you, no, I am enjoying the walk," Alice lied.

"Nice afternoon for a walk," an older man agreed. His hair was a shock of white, his ruddy face deep with wrinkles but his eyes shone a clear, bright blue. "But if you were tired, we'd gladly make space for you."

"No, I am perfectly fine," Alice insisted.

"You're the new teacher," the next man stated. It wasn't a question, as news of the young stranger had reached every weather-beaten corner of the shingle landscape. He looked up at Alice and she saw the same bright eyes in a younger face.

"I am," she replied, determined to move on yet remembering she had been brought up to be polite, and so she wavered

"This is Miss Tibbs," Tom Barton announced. "We've already met."

Alice looked at him and said nothing. His eyes were on her, compelling her to keep her thoughts to herself and the secrets of the shingle silent.

"Nice to meet you all." The words sounded rude and Alice knew it. She turned her back on them and walked on. Exhausted when she finally reached the schoolhouse, a warm drink and something to eat was at the forefront of Alice's mind. Then perhaps an hour relaxing in the armchair.

The front door was locked, as it had been when Alice left, but as she stepped into the kitchen-cum-living area she was stunned to see someone sitting in a chair, which had been pulled close to the range so its occupant could make the most of the radiating heat.

Chapter Five

"I won't usually come on a Sunday, but with you being new here I've made an exception today. Only the once mind." Her tone was sharp; this was a woman who clearly made all the rules and expected to be obeyed.

"I… thank you."

"There's mutton stew in the oven. Fresh bread and milk in the larder." This was accompanied by nods of her head in the general direction of both oven and larder.

"That's very kind," Alice forced a weary smile. "I wasn't expecting..."

"No, well you only arrived yesterday. I'm Mrs Webb, but you can call me Peggy. I'll come and prepare a midday meal for you and Mrs Stubbs every school-day and the same for you on a Saturday. Sunday, you manage for yourself. That's excepting today of course. I'll bring your milk, it's goats' milk here, and bread too of course." The old woman got up from the armchair and began to gather her coat and wicker basket.

"Lovely. Thank you." Alice felt some relief that she would not be totally reliant on her own inadequate baking skills.

"I don't gossip. Don't offer advice. I do a job and I go on my way." Once her coat was buttoned up, she paused to look Alice straight in the eye. "Keep your opinions on what you see to yourself; it's Denge business."

"Denge?" Alice couldn't resist asking.

"Dengemarsh, Dengeness, Dungeness – it's all the same," Peggy replied. "Eyes down. Understood?"

"I see," Alice confirmed. So, she knew too. She knew what Alice had seen.

Mrs Webb, Peggy, made her way to the back door. So that was how she had got in, Alice realised.

"I'll let myself in and out this way," Peggy brandished a key and dropped it into her basket. "And I'll see you tomorrow, you and Mrs Stubbs, or Miss Wilkie as we used to call her."

Alice felt the teapot, it was still warm and even if the leaves were stewed it would do for today. There was time enough to resume normal standards tomorrow!

When Alice woke later, the room was almost dark. Her first thoughts on waking were of self-disgust as she felt the guilt of an illicit afternoon nap. She spent no time wallowing in the comfort of the old chair or savouring the heat of the range, instead leaping up to busy herself with lighting a couple of oil lamps.

"It doesn't matter… it's to be expected after last night… and the walk too…" Alice was quick to excuse herself and spoke out loud as she pulled the curtains. "It's not as if anyone saw," she added. Then as an afterthought, "Not that it makes it acceptable, under normal circumstances."

The mutton smelt appetising, and Alice realised that she was ravenous. Carefully removing the cooking pot from the oven in the range, she spooned the contents onto a plate. Bread and butter from the larder completed the meal. As she sat down, Alice thanked God for her meal and began to eat. Her eyes roamed about the room, and she recalled eating in the kitchen when she was a child; there was usually a nanny, and later the housekeeper, in attendance. The walls at home in the rectory were also cream, but a collection of still-lifes – fruit and flowers – adorned them. Here, in the schoolhouse, the paintings were a group of local scenes, created with amateur brushstrokes. Her attention moved to the colourful blankets folded on the back of the armchairs and she smiled to think of someone taking the time to crochet the squares; they made the room feel more like a home and less like a place where people stayed for a while. As Alice scraped the last of the gravy from her plate, she wondered what books were on the shelves, and if it would be a good idea for her to put her own small collection with them? She left the table and knelt on the floor to examine the titles embossed on the covers. Some of her favourites were there: the Brontës, Elizabeth Gaskell and George Eliot. Her own books would sit happily beside them.

Later, having checked the windows were secure and all three outer doors were locked and bolted – she thought of the door to the school room as an outer door – Alice prepared to retire for the night. The bed, warmed by the clay hot water bottle, beckoned and she was grateful to sink into the soft comfort of the mattress. Sleep came quickly.

Not a murmur came from her pale lips, yet her presence shook Alice from her sleep. The intruder stood in the corner, silent and still, grey eyes unblinking, auburn hair dulled by the darkness. With her heart pounding with such force that surely her ribs would crack under the strain, Alice cowered under her blankets. The visitor's eyes remained fixed on the young woman in her bed, until finally her features became less defined and then her body slowly faded away. She had meant no harm but, to Alice, it was a sharp reminder of the failure of one stranger to help another.

Pulling a blanket around her shoulders, Alice stumbled out of bed and to the kitchen table where she lit an oil lamp. She returned to the bedroom and placed it on the chest of drawers, a safe distance from the wall. *Now I'll know… I'll be able to see… there's no one here, not really.* The light would stop her confusion at the time where dreams and reality became blurred.

Alice thought of Albert and pictured the home that they might choose together. She thought of sitting in front of the bandstand on a Sunday afternoon or walking hand-in-hand along the streets of Ashford. Sleep was surprisingly dreamless and when she finally woke there was weak sunlight forcing its way around the gaps in the curtains and through the patches of thinning material.

When a brisk rap announced Mrs Stubbs' arrival the next morning, Alice's first thought was that the headteacher had come earlier than she would have expected. Her second was Mrs Stubbs was clearly a person in possession of good manners as she had knocked on the door. Knocking on the door was of course normal behaviour but in less than forty-eight hours the young woman had come to expect her neighbours to behave not quite as she would anticipate.

"Miss Tibbs, I am Mrs Stubbs." The teacher removed her coat and hat, placing them on the wooden pegs on the wall. "A pleasure to have you here."

"Thank you." Alice had risen from her chair and sat down again. "I wasn't expecting… I mean not that… would you… would you like a cup of tea?" Alice looked towards the pot and started to get up again, to reach for a cup from the dresser.

She is older than I expected, Alice thought, *not that it matters. Not at all.* She hadn't really had the time to

44

consider what the head mistress would be like. But, now here she was, sitting at the table and Alice was surprised that the newly-married Mrs Stubbs was not in her early twenties but was perhaps forty or more.

Mrs Stubbs was dressed just like Alice, in the unofficial uniform of a teacher: a long black dress, with pleats and a row of small black buttons down the front, and a white collar. Her hair was almost black, and streaked with grey, tied back in a knot at the nape of her neck. Alice's own brown hair had been brushed back into a neat bun which shone like a conker. Mrs Stubbs was a little taller than Alice and had a very slim figure: her back was straight and she held herself as if she were a person of some importance. As teacher and policeman's wife, she looked just the part.

"Thank you, Miss Tibbs. Tea would be perfect," Mrs Stubbs smiled across at her new colleague and appeared to like what she saw. "If I am a little earlier than you expected it is because I have to travel by train from Lydd and have no choice but to take the one leaving at half past seven. I think myself lucky though, as the driver makes an exception and allows me to step off here at the school."

"I heard the train, but it didn't register as to why it had stopped," Alice responded, as she busied herself with pouring the tea. Her bacon was in danger of becoming overcooked and she glanced towards it nervously, "Have you eaten?"

"I'll eat here with you before morning school, but I'll see to myself; it was my home for many years before I married." Mrs Stubbs stirred a spoonful of sugar into her tea. "You've met Peggy, I presume. She'll come along mid-morning and prepare our lunch."

"I've met, Mrs Webb, Peggy," Alice confirmed. "She was here yesterday when I returned from a walk."

"And how are you finding Dungeness? A little different from Ashford, I know." Her voice was brisk

45

and offered no chance for confidences.

"Very different," Alice agreed. "I'll become used to it though." Her reply was hollow; she couldn't force enthusiasm into her reply.

"Of course, you will," Mrs Stubbs agreed. "Normally, we will move through to the schoolroom at half-past eight and prepare for the children at nine, but today I suggest we go as soon as you are ready. You'll need to be a quick learner as you'll be in sole charge from half-past two until the children leave at four."

"On my own?" Alice repeated in alarm.

"I am at the mercy of the steam trains, dear Miss Tibbs, unless I care to walk miles across the shingle back to Mr Stubbs. The last train leaves at half-past two. Besides, I am the exception in being a married teacher; at the very least I must be home to prepare an evening meal for Mr Stubbs."

"Of course." Alice pondered on the unusual situation Mrs Stubbs was in, its being rare to be a married female teacher.

"His widowed sister lives with us," Mrs Stubbs explained. "It's a long-standing arrangement and there was no reason to make any changes on the event of our marriage. She does the domestic chores during the day and I help prepare the evening meal. It suits us all."

"How many pupils are there?" Alice asked, understandably concerned about the time she would be in charge.

"I have thirty-two now, their ages are from five years to eleven. Ruth and Hazel come to help me; they are fifteen and seventeen years old respectively. Ruth comes from the lighthouse; her father is a keeper there. Hazel is from one of the fishing families; I have found her to be pleasant and reliable. You'll find them to be a great support."

Alice pondered on what she had learnt. It was not

46

uncommon for a school to have sixty children in a class, not that she had expected it in this remote place. Her own time as a pupil was not that far off and she saw in Mrs Stubbs a woman who was well-organised. Alice was sure that with the headteacher, herself and the two older girls, the routine would run like clockwork.

Before long, the door between house and schoolroom was being unbolted and the teachers stepped through, ready to start the day. They stood at the rear of the classroom, with four rows of double desks in front of them, five desks in each row. Mrs Stubbs immediately started adjusting the desks slightly, muttering about them never being quite right after the disruption of the Sunday church service. There was nothing to show the school's role as a church: the curtain once again covered the east window, altar, and altar rail. Only the pulpit stood as a reminder of the school becoming a church and this now served as a platform for Mrs Stubbs to stand proud, looking down upon her pupils.

"Miss Tibbs, I see your duty as keeping a close eye on the youngest pupils, those who sit in the first two rows. If you could place slates and slate pens on those desks, please."

The head teacher pointed in the direction of the long, low shelves running the length of a wall, only parting to accommodate the two entrances into the school. One for the boys and one for the girls. Alice pondered on the reasoning for two doors when both boys and girls learned together. In her own school, the children had been taught separately with classes for infants, upper infants and juniors. Dismissing her idle thoughts, she lifted a pile of slates and set them neatly on the desks, then returned for the slate pens. Mrs Stubbs placed copy books, ink and dip pens on the remaining spaces for the older children.

"If you could help me with the sand trays, Miss Tibbs, we'll place them over there."

They carried shallow sand-filled trays and placed them on the floor. Alice remembered her own early school days when letters were traced by her fingers in the sand before she progressed to a slate.

"It's all about repetition, of course," stated Mrs Stubbs. "Most of these children have little need for any more than being able to sign their name and perhaps keep a record of the amount of fish caught."

"We have to try our best for them." Alice firmly believed all children should have the opportunity to better their prospects. There would always be one or two pupils who aspired to study further, perhaps become a teacher themselves or a clerk. Alice saw it as her duty to encourage all pupils to do their absolute best, whether they were rich or poor.

"Indeed, but most will have little use of a good education in these parts." Mrs Stubbs' tone was pessimistic.

Alice's thoughts now turned to the time when she would oversee the school, and she asked, "What will I do in the afternoon once you have left?"

"Nature study, drill, singing, reading and all with help from Ruth and Hazel. You'll soon become used to our routines and we can discuss it during our lunch break. The rest of it you will find familiar from your own school days and you'll learn as the days progress." Mrs Stubbs' reply was brisk as she began to pull a huge blackboard in a wooden frame to the front of the altar curtain. "Miss Tibbs, I suggest that while I start on today's copy writing, you familiarise yourself with our modest selection of learning tools."

"Of course." Alice went to the old pine shelves and explored the familiar trays of weights and measures, bibles and story books, pens, paintbrushes, papers and inks. None of it any different from those she had used in her own schooldays. On one wall there was a vast map showing the great British Empire – from her own small country to the frozen lands of Canada in the north and the sun-baked countries of South Africa, India and Australia. It fascinated Alice that her own Queen was monarch of so much of the world. There she was: a young Queen Victoria, displayed on a copy of the very same painting that had been on the wall of Alice's classroom when she was a junior. The other prints showed religious scenes.

Alice moved across the room to study an area of the pupils' own work. Images of the grasses, lichens and wildflowers found in the area around the school were created in pen and paint, and displayed on thick, rough paper. Shells and small creatures from both land and sea had also inspired the children. Rough sea and moody clouds were shown in charcoal, and the lighthouse was displayed with its beam shining bright. On a wooden plaque, in the centre of the wall, amidst the paintings, the school motto was displayed: 'Play the Game'. Alice pondered on this for a moment.

While admiring the detail in some of the pictures, Alice became aware of the scattering of shingle and the voices of children, scurrying towards the school. They came in a trail, like ants, and as they passed through the gate in the picket fence, they turned to the right and went around past the altar end of the building and into their play area.

Mrs Stubbs kept a close eye on the clock and at exactly nine o'clock she opened the girls' door and rang the school bell. Two young women, whom Alice presumed must be Ruth and Hazel, each stood by a doorway and the children lined up in two neat rows: boys and girls, from the smallest to the tallest. When the lines were silent Mrs Stubbs gave a nod, then Alice opened the boys' door, and the pupils were ushered in by the assistants.

49

They moved to their desks, with girls the furthest from the doorways and boys nearest. Alice recognised Bill Stevens and his sister Victoria, who both gave tentative smiles. She searched for brown curls and freckled faces amongst the younger children and picked out their younger brother and sister.

The children settled and morning register began with Mrs Stubbs reading the names, and a 'Good morning, Miss' in return. "We'll start with a short passage from the bible." Mrs Stubbs reached for the thick tome and, looking towards Alice, she continued: "Our new teacher, Miss Tibbs, will read to you today."

Alice walked towards the pulpit-cum-teaching platform and took the place of the headteacher. Standing tall and taking care not to rush, she read the passage slowly and clearly, but barely comprehending the words. Her thoughts were on the children before her and she wondered how she would fit within her new role.

On their return from lunch, the pupils lined up again and this time it was Alice who welcomed them back into school. They settled at their desks and Mrs Stubbs had started the afternoon register when the boys' door was flung open and a child darted in, allowing the door to shut with a bang behind him.

"'Ere Miss, you'll never believe... you'll never believe what me Ma... what she found on the beach this morning..." Young Fred's breath was ragged and his cheeks pink from exertion.

As the whole class turned to Fred in anticipation, Mrs Stubbs visibly grew an inch and her lips became pinched as a sign of extreme disapproval.

"Fred, you will leave the room now, knock on the door and enter quietly." The headteacher spoke slowly and firmly. "There is no excuse for being late and no reason ever to speak without raising your hand at the appropriate time."

The whole class slumped in disappointment. Fred did as he was told, but on his return to the desk he sat there with his cheeks still rosy and eyes darting about the room.

"Fred." Mrs Stubbs read his name from the register.

Fred flung his arm in the air and, without being given permission to speak, the words burst free: "It were a body, right there on the shingle."

There was a gasp from the class. Alice felt the skin on her throat tighten and simultaneously her mouth went dry. *Another one, another body just lying there to be found on the beach... or was it another? Could it be? Yes, of course it could be the very same one, just casually discarded, or another new body...* Alice's heart began to pound at an uncomfortable pace, and she leant for support, just very slightly, against the bookshelf. *What type of place have I come to where bodies lie strewn upon the shingle?* Her thoughts raced. *And where boys get such pleasure from retelling the news?*

Mrs Stubbs was not to be deterred; she showed no sign of either curiosity or concern. Her position as upholder of discipline and order was clear for all to see.

"Frederick Brown, go to the corner and stand in silence."

Fred's step was jaunty as he moved to the back corner. His moment to tell would come and all the time he stood with his back to the class he could relive the story, perhaps adding in a few details. By the time school ended and his peers were crowding around him, the story would be all the better for having waited another couple of hours.

"This afternoon we'll be drawing with charcoal, taking special care with the shading, by rubbing gently with our fingertips. You may go outside and find a large

51

pebble with an interesting shape or texture and bring it in to draw." And so, the afternoon continued in an orderly way, just as Mrs Stubbs intended. All the pupils, excepting Fred, had chosen their stones and were absorbed with the task. Ruth read to the youngest ones as they worked.

"Continue with this task until three o'clock and then the class can practise their singing. The music is on the piano." The instructions were given to Alice when the steam train was heard passing the school on its journey to Dungeness station. "You can finish the day by reading to the class."

"Very well." There was no time for Alice to seek further details. It was clear the teacher was eager to leave.

Mrs Stubbs then raised her voice to the class: "Good afternoon boys and girls. Good afternoon Miss Tibbs, Hazel and Ruth." She left through the living quarters, no doubt gathering her coat and handbag before leaving by the schoolhouse door. Alice imagined the headteacher striding to the track as the train could be heard on its return.

In time, the artwork was finished and stacked on the shelves. Alice was aware Fred (now slumped) had been in the corner for an hour and she had been given no instructions about how long he was expected to remain there. She was now teacher-in-charge and decided to approach the boy.

"Fred."

The boy looked up at her with hope in his brown eyes. "Yes Miss."

"You may sit back at your desk now and join in with the singing."

"Thank you, Miss." Fred didn't move but looked intently at Alice. "It were true, Miss, what I said."

Alice had never considered to doubt him and now she felt able to ask: "Was it a man or a woman?"

"A woman, Miss. It were a woman, dead on the beach," Fred's voice was low, his gaze unwavering.

"I shall pray for her soul," Alice replied calmly, whilst her stomach twisted with the horror of it all.

"That's very kind, Miss Tibbs." Fred turned away and strolled back to his desk.

Alice moved towards the piano, thankful her mother had insisted on daily practice, and she was able to play *All Things Bright and Beautiful* whilst concentrating little on either the tune or the children's singing. She was just vaguely aware the piano was badly out of tune.

It was equally fortunate *Black Beauty* had been a great favourite when Alice was younger, and she could read the words whilst her mind was on other matters. The woman found on the shingle absorbed all her thoughts. Who was she and why was she there? Could she possibly… could she be the same woman Alice had found two days before?

Four o'clock came and with it the end of Alice's first day of teaching. Her new role had been a success, she felt. The only flaw being her interest in Fred's news. She had been eager to learn more, whereas she should have remained unmoved and disinterested as Mrs Stubbs had done. It had gone well, but much as she tried to reflect over the day, with a cup of tea, back in the schoolhouse, all Alice could remember was the flushed face of Fred and his announcement of there being a body on the beach.

Chapter Six

Head down, shoulders hunched, Alice moved, in her own unique way, across the shingle. The toes of her backstays were constantly stubbed, and she lacked any form of rhythm. It wasn't dark, but the sky was turning grey and the sun softening in the sky towards the west.

Curiosity drove her onwards: she had to know if the woman found by Fred's mother was that of the auburn-haired young woman. Was it that she had not survived, and her lifeless body was an inconvenience? Did the men who picked her up want to avoid explaining her presence? If she had simply hindered their plans, then it would be easier to abandon her on the beach; she could become a body washed up on the tide and not many questions would be asked. Or perhaps the woman had survived – for a short time – until they put an end to it.

What was the woman doing there on the beach? This person with whom Alice had made a connection when grey eyes looked into brown, and wordlessly begged for help. Who were the men who had walked from the beach dragging a heavy load, and scooped her up as if she were nothing? There was no doubt that Tom Barton was involved, and he knew about Alice; he knew she had been there cowering behind the wood pile. It was this which made her the most nervous. If something had happened on the evening of her arrival, something which she shouldn't repeat, then her own life could be in danger. No one would hear her screams if the men who took the auburn-haired woman chose to seek out Alice as she lay in her bed in the remote schoolhouse. The thoughts rattled about in her mind.

She saw no one on her trek from schoolhouse to vicarage. The only sign of life being the smoke spiralling from the chimneys of the lighthouse keepers' stone cottages and the shacks the local fishermen lived in. Alice took off her backstays and leaned them against the plank wall, then tapped on the door before raising the latch.

The heat inside the vicar's curious home was quite unbearable for Alice who had become accustomed to the damp air of the late afternoon. The vicar was seated in his chair, a blanket on his knee and a book in his hands. His metal-rimmed glasses were askew, and Alice suspected he had been snoozing rather than reading.

"My dear Miss… Miss?" He rose from the chair and put the book on his side table.

"Miss Tibbs, sir. Alice Tibbs," Alice reminded him. "We met on Saturday and again at the school when it was the church. I mean on Sunday when you took the service."

"Ah, yes indeed, how kind of you to visit an old man. Do sit down." He had a broad smile breaking through the deep wrinkles on his face and his eyes sparkled a clear blue. Clearly a visitor was very welcome, and Alice suspected his life was quite lonely. "Some tea? Yes of course you would. I just made a pot … if you wouldn't mind?"

"Of course not."

Alice took cups and saucers from the dresser and set them on the gate-leg table. A jug of milk was keeping cool on a slab of stone in a cupboard, but she still lifted its cloth cover, weighted with a circle of beads, and sniffed to be sure it was fresh. The pot radiated heat through its cosy, confirming that the tea was indeed freshly brewed. While Alice busied herself, the vicar watched her every move and commented on her progress.

"Now this is very nice, dear. Most kind." He sat with the cup cradled in long, thin hands. They were clean and white, Alice reflected, not like those of the fishermen who laboured in all kinds of conditions.

"I came because I heard something rather upsetting at the school today," Alice began. "You recall that I came to be the assistant teacher?"

"Indeed, I do," his head nodded furiously. "In fact, I had a letter informing me of your arrival and here you are. The letter was from... it was from... It will come to me shortly."

"It was from Reverend Tibbs," Alice supplied.

"How very clever of you!" the old man marvelled.

"Not at all," Alice admitted. "He is my father and arranged for me to be here."

"So, you are Miss Tibbs and your father is Edward Tibbs, such a dear friend. Delightful, absolutely delightful."

Alice had been brought up to be polite and especially respectful to her elders and betters. However, it was clear that this conversation could go on enthralling the vicar until the time he needed a nap, and so she must forge onwards with her task.

"It was terribly upsetting at the school this afternoon." Alice put down her tea and tried to fix his gaze, to ensure her words were not misunderstood. "One of the pupils returned from his lunch-break and reported that a body had been found on the beach." She paused for a moment and her companion's furious nodding assured Alice her words had been heard. "A woman, a body of a woman, here on the beach."

"Indeed, there was, my dear Miss Tibbs. I am so

56

sorry it caused you upset. Did you know her?"

"Know her?" Alice was momentarily lost for words, seeing the woman with her tangle of salty auburn curls, pale skin, and grey eyes. "No, I just wondered, that is to say, I wondered if it could be true."

"Sadly, it is."

"And was it someone local? Did she have an accident? Perhaps whilst helping with the fishing?"

Alice knew nothing of fishing, only of the sedentary Sunday afternoon activities on the banks of the River Stour. She knew nothing of sea fishing, of hauling the boats back across the shingle and unloading the catch. Were women involved with this kind of work? Surely not, but it hadn't taken long to realise that the rules of Dungeness differed from those of the civilised streets of Ashford.

"Was she local?" The vicar repeated her words. "Oh no, my dear. I think not."

"Where could she have come from?" Alice wondered aloud.

"Why, the sea of course."

"The sea?"

"Washed up on the tide. It happens, you know."

But had she been washed up? He said it as if it were a regular occurrence, as if it were perfectly acceptable, which of course it wasn't. For someone to be drowned and washed up on the beach was a horrific, devastating incident. It affected people, turned their lives into disarray as children lost a parent or a husband lost a wife. Alice's thoughts lingered over the enormity of such grief. Still, the question remained: was this a new body or was it that of the woman who she had found crumpled on the shingle just two evenings before?

"Have there been any other bodies?" Alice asked cautiously, hoping for a clue.

"Any other bodies?" The vicar leaned forward in his

57

chair and stared directly at Alice over the top of his glasses. "My dear girl, do you think that you have come to a place where numerous bodies lie strewn upon the shingle with no thought of dignity?"

"I… of course not… of course that isn't the way we behave at all." *Not in Ashford at least.* "I was just wondering if..." Alice allowed her voice to trail away.

"Living by the sea, we do have a body from time to time, but no others recently my dear."

"How incredibly sad… I mean to say, how sad about this young woman." But Alice didn't know if she was a young woman, so she asked, "Was she a young woman?"

"Why my dear Miss Tibbs, bless you for your concern. Why don't you see for yourself? It would be rude not to as you are here?"

"As I am here?" Alice squeaked.

It was only then she noticed a long low bench at the far side of the room, at the furthest point from the range and not within the comfortable circle of armchairs and book-covered tables. The bench had something, a body, upon it, covered with a white sheet. At one end (the head, no doubt) was a single candle burning low.

Alice felt horror shimmer through her body, but not the same degree of shock she would have felt just two days before. She was already becoming accustomed to the fact the rules were different here. There was almost an acceptance that the vicar had the body in his living room, and Alice had sipped tea and talked with the vicar whilst the unknown woman lay in her final sleep.

"Yes, indeed. I shall just go and… and perhaps light another candle for her." Alice began to rise from the chair. This was what she came for, although she hadn't expected to find out in this way.

"Perfect, my dear," the vicar approved.

Slowly, Alice moved across the room and forced her leaden arms to pull back the cloth. It only took a glance to see that this woman's hair was brown, streaked with grey. She was not the woman of two nights back. She was at peace, despite her face being bruised by a pounding upon the stone beach and showing all the tell-tale signs of being a mature age. Alice needn't linger, her question had been answered. Or at least one question had!

A candle was lit, and a prayer hastily muttered before Alice turned to retrieve her coat and shawl from the coat stand. She turned back to the vicar who had been sitting quietly all this time, eyes closed as if not wanting to intrude.

"Thank you for your time; she is at peace now."

"Thank you dear, thank you for coming to see us." He began to close his eyes, but then opened them and leaned forwards, looking at Alice with urgency in those blue eyes. "Miss Tibbs?"

"Yes?"

"You work at the school? Here at Dungeness?"

"I do."

"Then I have an important message for you to relay." The old man rose from his chair and took a step forward. "The headteacher, Miss Wilkie, could you please tell her that the funeral must be tomorrow."

"Tomorrow?"

"Yes, tomorrow. We can't leave her here like this. Tell Miss Wilkie it will be tomorrow, in the afternoon."

Alice frowned for a moment, but then she understood. "You mean to say that it will be at the school, that the school will become a church on a weekday?" She thought for a moment and continued, "At what time? There are the children. We must think of the children."

"I believe the usual is at two o'clock," the vicar informed her. "Morning school only. The children will be pleased!"

"Yes, yes I suppose they will," Alice agreed. Then, as she buttoned her coat, she continued, "Miss Wilkie has married. She is Mrs Stubbs now. But I will pass on the message and no doubt she will understand."

"We learned yesterday, in a somewhat ill-mannered way, that a body was found on the beach." Mrs Stubbs addressed the class from her headteacher's platform-cum-pulpit. As her words rang out clear for all to hear, the class sat in silence and she was sure of their attention. Even the youngest ones were rapt. Fred had a broad smile on his face and sat with his back straight, his chest puffed out with pride. It was he who had first told the news and it was worth an hour in the corner.

"I have prepared a short prayer which I shall read aloud, while we reflect on the sad death of this woman: Dear Lord, as we sit in the shadow of death, let your light shine on those who mourn for the loss of an unknown woman and for her family and friends who suffer, unknowing of her fate. May we rejoice in your holy comfort and be grateful for the good life you have bestowed upon us. Amen."

The class solemnly repeated 'Amen' and waited in anticipation for Mrs Stubbs' next words. Unlike Alice, they were well-versed in the traditions of Dungeness and knew what was coming next:

"Sadly, the school will be used for the funeral service at two o'clock this afternoon. I am sorry to say that school will be closed at lunchtime."

Nods and half-grins of approval rippled through her enthralled audience. Fred felt, as yesterday's reporter of the news, his status should not go unforgotten and with no thought other than immediate gratification he piped up with: "That were my news that gave us a half-day And I say we play bat and ball, girls versus boys!"

"Frederick, go to the corner immediately," the

60

headmistress's voice was rich with fury.

Fred bounced along the well-worn track between his desk and the corner of the classroom.

Lunchtime brought with it Mrs Webb, and a tasty fish pie, followed by stewed apples and custard.

"Mrs Stubbs brought them apples from her garden in Lydd," Peggy volunteered the information as she dished up the fruit.

"Very nice, what a treat," Alice replied, looking up from her book. She found it a little uncomfortable, just the three of them in the kitchen-cum-living room and followed Mrs Stubbs' lead by picking up a book rather than making conversation.

"You'll take some home, won't you, Peggy?" Mrs Stubbs looked towards the wicker basket which she had brought in from home that morning.

"Thank you, Mrs Stubbs, I don't mind if I do." The apples were already snug in her own basket, protected by an old cloth.

Alice excused herself and went to her room. It was from her bedroom window she spotted the small funeral procession moving slowly across the undulating shingle ridges. Six stooped men carried the coffin and, gathered in a small group behind, were another dozen men and women. They were well wrapped up and it wasn't until they entered the gate at the picket fence that Alice saw that most of the mourners were elderly. As the vicar led the group into the building, Alice turned away from the window and returned to the living area.

"We'll be going through then," Peggy had her hand on the door leading through to the school. Mrs Stubbs and Alice followed.

"Will you have time?" Alice asked, knowing the train to Lydd would not wait for the teacher.

"It will be a short service," Mrs Stubbs informed,

"with no family or friends to attend, and besides, she'll have to catch the train to Lydd."

"The train to Lydd?" Alice repeated. She must have misunderstood, the headteacher must be referring to herself as 'she'.

"The dead woman," confirmed Peggy. "We don't bury 'em here in the stones, she'll lie more peaceful in a bit o' earth."

They went through the doorway and into the school; already some of the desks had been moved aside for the small congregation. The unknown woman lay in a coffin on a long, low table and the other local people were seated. Alice and Mrs Stubbs placed themselves at the back, and Peggy sat next to a man with a forest of hair on his face, who presumably was her husband.

"We are here today to give our respects to this woman whom we found amongst us." The vicar paused and gazed at the small congregation. "The boats have gone out with the tide… I mean to say that many of us cannot be here this afternoon, but their prayers are with us. We know nothing of this woman and of where she came from, but we can pray for her soul, nonetheless."

The service was short, and the dead woman made good time for her appointment with the passing train. She was placed unescorted into a luggage van and Mrs Stubbs stepped up into the carriage.

"She'll be met by the vicar of Lydd," the vicar reported. "Now time for a cup of tea I think."

Chapter Seven

Dear Albert,

On writing this letter, I have been here only three days, but already I miss you, Mother, Father and all that is dear to me. It is the silliest things I think of whilst I put pen to paper, such as the ripe fruit on the trees at the end of our garden and the autumnal colours on the trees. You see, it is all so different here, nothing at all like I expected. I have come to the seaside but there is no promenade, such as in Hythe, merely a very steep shingle beach. It is not only the beach that is shingle, but the whole area is also a mass of pebbles. The schoolhouse is perhaps fifteen minutes' walk from the sea, yet it sits on shingle, not earth. I write of walking but there are no pavements and certainly not a road. I slip and slide across the stones and am only grateful that I brought my stout walking boots, although I feared they were a little scruffy. There is no greenery here, just rough grass, broom and lichens, with the last of the seakale near the beach. It really is the most godforsaken place (may Father forgive me).

My work is satisfactory and the children pleasant, although I cannot imagine what prospects they have living here. The headteacher is a Mrs Stubbs, newly married and now living in Lydd. She arrives by train daily; it is the only form of civilization I see in this place. I live alone in the schoolhouse and a local woman brings me food and prepares a mid-day meal which is very welcome.

It is a very strange place, but I shall say no more because I would not want to cause undue distress on my account. I shall become accustomed to it, no doubt, and in no time at all we shall be reunited at Christmas when I shall welcome a two-week holiday from work.

With my fondest thoughts, your Alice.

Alice felt comforted having written to Albert. For a time, her thoughts were back home and her family a little closer. In a matter of days, there would be a reply and she would feel less distanced from her loved ones. Now to write to Mother and Father; she would tell them about the vicar and her work in the school, then they could compare letters and discuss them. She fetched a fresh sheet of paper and began.

Later, both letters were carefully folded and sealed in envelopes with a stamp placed in the corner. She would ask Mrs Stubbs if she could post them in Lydd tomorrow. Alice put them on the chest of drawers in her bedroom.

It was still only half-past three and Alice didn't feel inclined to spend the rest of the day sitting like an old woman in front of the range. No, that wouldn't do at all; she would stretch her legs and get some fresh air. It wasn't raining and the wind was slight, so best make use of the fair weather before the winter set in.

Alice checked that both the back door and the entrance to the school were bolted before closing and locking the front door behind her. She walked along the tracks rather than battle with her backstays and within ten minutes she was at the railway station. Feeling refreshed, Alice paused to consider which way to go next. She decided to veer to the east of the lighthouse and go towards the fishermen's cottages, some of which sat in clusters of three or four and others alone but none of them far from the sea. Amongst the cottages there was a variety of additional buildings, and she wondered what they held. *A privy of course, and perhaps a place for nets… and a store.* She frowned to see smoke seeping from a narrow chimney on some of them and considered it for a moment. *They must smoke the fish here so that would account for it.*

There was quite a gathering of children playing chase or tag. They shouted out in glee. *What freedom they have,* Alice pondered, *not enclosed even by the fence of a park or their own back yard.* For the first time she considered the restrictions of her own childhood: always watched by an adult, never free to explore or to play. *The children of Dungeness have no gardens,* she observed. *Or at least no fence or hedge to define them, just the beach and the open ridges of shingle, as well as the abandoned remains of fishing boats. How lucky they are on a day like this when the wind eases and there is no rain.*

"Here, Miss!" one of the young girls called out.

Alice waved back.   As she approached the children, a girl of perhaps eight or nine ran over. Her hair was dark brown and somewhere amongst its curls were the remainder of plaits woven just that morning. She wore a long brown dress with a badly stained white apron over the top. Her eyes showed enthusiasm for life although her skin was already coarse beyond its years. When she spoke, her voice was rough:

"Miss Tibbs, let me show you around." Dora offered her hand. "I'll show you me 'ouse."

Alice smiled down at the little girl; she really was endearing. "That would be lovely, thank you. It's quite different to my home you know."

"You came from Ashford," Dora stated. "It's a big place."

"That's right."

"It's not near the sea though?"

65

"No, it's not."

"Poor you," Dora looked up into Alice's face. "At least you came here."

Dora led Alice past three wooden homes, all different with a ramshackle collection of outhouses beside the main cottage. She gave a commentary about who lived in each one and who they were all related to; the names meant nothing to Alice, so she just smiled and nodded.

"That's a lifeboat over there, up on the shingle an' another one in there," the girl pointed to a building on the last ridge before the sea. "The boat's inside. The other boats went out on the tide, except those old ones that are all broken up and no good now. They'll be back after dark, me dad, me uncle and the others and we'll pull the boats up here."

"Does the lifeboat go out much?" Alice asked.

"It were out Friday night," Dora replied. "Ma twisted her ankle and Grandma had to bind it up."

"Why was your mother out?" Alice asked, "Did she go to see your father off on the lifeboat?"

"They launch the boat Miss, the women do." Dora looked at Miss Tibbs with pity – a teacher who knew nothing about life!

"Oh, I see," Alice replied, but she didn't at all.

"An' that's where Alf and Peggy Webb live; you know she does your cookin'." Another wooden shack. Quite small and on its own.

"Very nice," said Alice. How very silly. Nice? They weren't nice at all.

"An' that's the Britannia, back over there. They'll go for a drink when they come in later with the fish."

"Oh, a pub. Yes, I see."

"An' there's another pub, a bit further along – The Pilot. Pa goes there too. See over there Miss, that's my place and my nan, she lives with us now. Pa built a room on the side for her. An' that's Ma over there, she's gone to get water from the pump."

All those homes with extra little sheds and extensions. All those places where a body – alive or dead – could be stored and maybe no one need even know about it. Where a community could hide a secret because strangers rarely passed by.

"Do you get many new people come here, Dora?"

"Oh no, Miss. Sometimes they come over from Lydd or Denge way. But no one new excepting …."

"Excepting?" Alice repeated.

Dora looked up into Alice's face, as if she wanted to please. "Excepting you of course, Miss Tibbs, cos you're new, aren't you?"

Alice smiled down, "Yes, I am."

"Do you want to meet me Ma, Miss?"

"It's going to be dark soon, so I think I had better get back to the school and you can have a little longer with your friends." They turned back towards the group of youngsters. "Say 'good afternoon' to your mother from me and I will meet her properly at church on Sunday. How does that sound?"

"That's lovely, thanks Miss."

It was dusk by the time Alice reached the schoolhouse. She felt invigorated by her walk and cheered by talking with Dora. It was fascinating to see the area through the eyes of the girl. For the first time Alice felt that she might just be able to become used to her new life.

She came again that night. Alice knew the auburn-haired woman was there before she opened her eyes. Someone was watching, looking down on her; she could sense it. As Alice's heart began to slam upon her ribs, instinctively she shrank back in the bed, arms tight against her chest, hoping to ease the pain. There was nowhere to go, no place to back into. Then the vision began to fade away.

There had been no malice in the woman's face, nothing to fear in her eyes. She wasn't going to cause harm, so why haunt the young teacher? Yet she didn't come, didn't stand there really. It was all conjured up in Alice's troubled mind.

The earlier feelings of acceptance had gone. Alice knew as long as the sea produced unknown bodies and the fate of the bedraggled woman remained unresolved, she would never settle in this desolate place and the night would continue to bring terrors for her. It was another hour until Alice fell asleep but then she slept soundly and when she woke the time was just past seven o'clock.

A light misty rain came with the following morning. It looked as if it was set to last all day and further dampened Alice's already low spirits as she began her third day teaching at Dungeness. The air in her bedroom was chilly so she opened the door through to the kitchen-cum-living room, hoping warmth from the range would seep through.

Once she had dressed and braved the privy, Alice pushed the kettle onto the hotplate and pulled back the bolt on the door leading to the school.

"Good morning, Miss Tibbs. Through to the schoolroom already?" Mrs Stubbs stepped into the teachers' accommodation; her cheeks flushed a little after her train journey.

"Yes, I thought I'd get the fire lit and then have my breakfast." Alice tied the strings of a coarse apron. The day before it had been suggested that she took the regular task of sweeping out yesterday's ashes before laying out a new fire. Resentment still simmered in Alice's usually mild demeanour; it was the job for a maid, not a teacher. However, there was no maid, only Peggy and she came mid-morning to prepare lunch.

The chore only took a short time, the worst of it

being the dust raised as the ashes were gathered and then tipped into a bucket. Later, they would be used as nutrients on the vegetable plot. Once the fire had taken hold, she put a guard in front of it and returned to share a pot of tea with the headteacher.

"All done for today, Mrs Stubbs," Alice reported with false cheeriness, as she stepped back into the living area.

However, on her return to the classroom, Alice discovered the fire still lacked spirit and she had to spend more time tempting it to burn. Mrs Stubbs remained with her tea, while Alice took her turn to write on the huge blackboard. Every day, one of the teachers wrote useful sayings to improve both the minds and handwriting of the pupils who laboriously copied them. Usually she had some pleasure in creating long loops, and lines standing tall. Today it was just words on a board and Alice felt quite defiant in not wanting to ponder on those sayings.

'Least said, soonest mended'
'Say well is good, do well is better'
'The devil makes work for idle hands'

The morning went smoothly but Alice found, like the misty drizzle that lingered, her lethargy would not lift. The windows dripped condensation and damp coats gave off a stale odour from the coat pegs by the doors. With spring still five months away, Alice could see that this was the way it would be for much of the time over the coming months and the image was disheartening.

Lunchtime came and with it a cottage pie made by Peggy. As they finished eating, Alice remembered the letter she had written to Albert and the thought of him replying brightened her up.

"Mrs Stubbs, I wrote a letter to Albert and one for my parents, I don't know if there is a post-box nearby, so I wondered if you would mind posting them in Lydd, if it's no trouble to you."

"No trouble at all, Miss Tibbs, I pass the post office on the way home."

"I have stamps on them." Alice stood up from the table and went to get the letters from the chest of drawers in her room. They were not on the side where she had put them, perhaps they had slipped off... or had she left them elsewhere?

"I can't seem to find them; it's very odd, I'm sure I put them in my room, but perhaps ...." She looked on the bookshelf in the living area. "No, I definitely put the stamps on and put them safely in my room."

Peggy came back in from giving the vegetable peelings to the chickens and started filling the sink with hot water from the hob.

"What's that you've mislaid, Miss Tibbs?"

"My letter... my letter to Albert and one for my parents too. I just don't understand."

"No need to worry, Miss Tibbs. I've got them right here, ready to put in the post for you." Peggy patted the pocket of her apron.

"You have my letters?"

"They weren't going to get posted stuck there in your room, were they, dear?"

"Is there a post-box?" Alice queried. "I would like to know, so as to post them myself..."

You leave it to Peggy." The daily help dismissed the question. "They'll be on their way as soon as I'm done here, and on the last train to Lydd. Now, who's for a nice cup of tea?"

With Mrs Stubbs not making any further offer to take them and with Alice unable to snatch them herself she felt powerless to demand her precious letters back. If her bedroom were not a safe place to keep

70

them, then she would ensure any other letters were put away and she would find a way to post them herself. Alice settled down to read a book but couldn't concentrate as a bitterness settled upon her and her thoughts were occupied with the knowledge that her private belongings had been moved.

The day continued with Alice dogged by feelings of depression and general dissatisfaction with her new life. In the afternoon, the rain had eased but the clouds lay low above the shingle landscape and when they went outside for drill, neither the lighthouses to the south nor Lydd church tower to the north could be seen. After fifteen minutes of *Black Beauty*, Alice's school day had ended, and she stood at the front of the building watching the backs of the departing children.

Sitting down with a pot of tea, Alice couldn't shift the feeling that something terrible was about to happen. The curtains had been pulled tight shut and all doors to the school and house had been locked and bolted where possible. The windows were securely shut. There was nothing more to be done but sit and wait.

Chapter Eight

It was about six o'clock when Alice was startled by a frantic banging on her front door. The handle was being turned and the door shook. Then, before she had tentatively made her way to the door, it was her bedroom window being rapped and surely a pane of glass would break at any moment. No sooner had the thought crossed her mind, there came the sound of glass cracking under pressure. It was at this point that Alice called out:

"I'm here, come to the door and tell me what you want."

There was nothing to do but face whoever had come across the shingle in the darkness, their anger not abated by the walk. She heard the stamp of boots on the stones as the stranger stormed back to the door.

"Who is it?" Alice called, "There's nothing here of value; it's just the schoolhouse. I have nothing to give you."

"I've come from over Denge lookin' for my wife and I'll not be givin' up until she's back where she belongs. You're hidin' her, one of you are. So, let me in and I'll have a look for myself."

"I'll not let you in until I can be sure you'll do me no harm," Alice spoke with bravado, but her slim body shook with fear. "I don't know of your wife. Why would you think she could be here?"

"This looks like as good a place as any. Out of the

way. You'd think I wouldn't come searchin' all this way. An' as to why she'd be here? Not by her choice, but they've hidden her away somewhere, you can be sure of that." He pushed on the door again, rattling the bolts.

"And if I show you she is not here, will you leave me in peace?"

"I'm not out to cause trouble for them that haven't harmed my Emily."

Alice slid back the bolts and opened the door; he would have broken it down within minutes if hindered any longer. He came in, barging past her and stood by the range, eyes scanning the room for signs of someone else, who had perhaps been secreted away when he made his presence known. His clothes were coarse and patched in many places, and his boots were like those of a labourer: sturdy with thick soles and frayed, knotted laces. Tall and broad, with curly black hair and a wild beard, the stranger's eyes settled on Alice.

"It's just me here, as you can see." Alice hid her shaking hands behind her back and held her pointed chin high.

"I'll be lookin' around rather than take your word for it."

"But why… Mr…?"

"Ed… Ed Brooks."

"I'm Miss Tibbs… Alice Tibbs. Why, Mr Brooks, would I have your wife? What would I want her for?"

"You'd not want her for anythin' I'm sure, but they've made you keep her here to teach me a lesson… to teach us a lesson to keep to our own side of the bay. I can see you're not one to make trouble, but you got caught up in it maybe." He was beginning to calm down now, seeing Alice was ready to listen.

"You've lost your wife or are you saying she's been taken?"

"Taken, yes that's exactly what I'm sayin'. She's

73

been hidden up somewhere, but I'll find my Emily, by God, I will."

He looked at the various doors leading to the school, bedrooms and back outside again. Then stepping towards the schoolroom, he said, "This goes through to the school, does it? I'll take a look there, although I was thinking of a shed or storeroom."

Alice was no longer feeling threatened by the stranger and although she would prefer it if he left peacefully, she could see that if she gave him no difficulties then he would have a fruitless search and move on into the night. She watched as he looked around the room, checking in large cupboards and especially behind the altar curtain. She said nothing and he searched in silence.

Once back in the schoolhouse, Alice's curiosity got the better of her and she was tempted to ask more about the missing wife:

"Your wife… how long since she… since you last saw her?"

"It were last Friday night, she went out and didn't return."

"And you knew she was coming this way?"

"Oh yes, I know where to come looking. They think I'll keep away, but I won't." He moved towards Alice's bedroom door. "I'll just look in here."

Alice looked down at her hands and twisted her engagement ring. *What if Albert were to hear of this… of a man being in my bedroom? He won't of course… how very silly… but if he were to learn of it…* She heard the movement of cupboard doors in her bedroom. *What is most important is that he wasn't invited, and I won't follow… won't be in there at the same time. He forced his way in… that's exactly what he would have done if I had tried to prevent him.* Ed left the room and Alice felt some of the tension flow from her body.

"I only came here on Saturday, in the afternoon,"

74

Alice offered the information. "So even if I had seen her, I wouldn't know… I wouldn't know she wasn't from here, would I?"

"You've got a storeroom or an outhouse? She could be there, and you'd maybe not even know." He moved to the back door.

"I had a good look, there's the chickens…"

But he had already gone, and she heard doors opening and closing, chickens squawking in alarm, logs being pushed aside, then the stamp of his boots on the pebbles as he returned. All she could do was stand and wait.

"There's no sign of her and if you've only been living here a week – and I have no cause to disbelieve you – then you can't be much help to me."

But Alice stood there knowing of two women who had been found in just the few days since her arrival. One she knew to be dead and the other, well she didn't know what had happened to her, other than she looked close to death lying there on the shingle. One she knew was a nameless stranger and the other? Was she known to whoever picked her up as if she was nothing better than an old sack?

Alice knew nothing of this man. Had his wife been fleeing from him? Was that why her eyes had looked so desperate for help? However, if his wife were the dead woman then it was too late to help her and all he could do was visit the fresh grave in Lydd.

"There was a woman…"

"I knew it!" Yellowed teeth showed in a snarl of a smile.

"But I don't know… I can't say if it was Emily."

"You can't, but they can. Those that took her knew what they were doin'. It was my Emily for certain."

"No, they didn't. I'm sure of it. You see…" Alice knew she should tell but she had a feeling that he wasn't ready for the news. "It was a woman's body, brought in by the sea. I'm sorry. She was buried yesterday, Tuesday. They didn't know her name or surely someone would have said."

He paused to consider the news for a moment and then responded with: "No... no, it can't have been Emily. She swam like a fish and could battle the strongest current. I remember the first time I saw her in the sea, with her hair come all loose, dark red all down her back. It was her mother who insisted she learned to swim." He took a step towards the door. "Thank you, Miss Tibbs, it's not over yet and I'll find her, by God I will. I know she's alive because if she wasn't... I'd feel it here in my heart."

As he stepped through the doorway, Alice called out, "The woman, she had brown hair, going grey. She wasn't your wife."

"No, she wasn't," he confirmed, but he hadn't needed to hear it; he was that sure his Emily was still alive.

Now, she had a name: Emily. This young woman with the raggle-taggle auburn hair and the grey eyes. She had a husband too, who was desperate to get her back. Alice thought about Emily all evening and she couldn't say (not even to herself) why she hadn't told Ed Brooks what she knew. Perhaps it was because of the temper he had been in and if she had told him then he'd be back at the fishermen's cottages, shouting and raging. He would tear them down if he had to, nothing would stop him once he had the scent of Emily in his nostrils. Alice was beginning to know the pupils now and those little ragamuffin children didn't deserve to be terrorised whilst they lay top-to-tail in their beds.

Emily. The name thundered around in Alice's head and she could find no peace. Her husband had such a temper. Had she chosen to face the desolate shingle-land of Dungeness rather than spend another day with him? Had her eyes begged protection from her husband or from those who picked her up and carted her off? There was no way of knowing.

There was one thing Alice had learnt in her first days here at Dungeness: They had their own rules and way of life. Standing together, they would hold their secrets close. Alice was sure of it. They whispered their news from fishing boat to wooden shack and there was not a thing that went on they didn't all know of. They knew the young teacher had seen the body of Emily Brooks and she feared what it would mean for her.

There was no peace for Alice once she huddled up in bed that night. Dreams were vivid and muddled; Emily with her salted, auburn hair and her eyes begging for help appeared in them all. Sometimes there was a whisper: a barely audible 'help me' and Alice was left not knowing whether she was sleeping or awake. Was the whisper in her dreams or did it come from an unsettled ghost?

When morning came, Alice brushed her hair back in a tight coil at the nape of her neck. Looking in the mirror, she saw tired eyes in grey sockets and dull, pale skin. Another night of disturbed sleep. A heavy cloud settled upon her as she considered the fuss they would make if she were to return to Ashford as a weary shadow of her former self. Would Albert regret the promises made when he placed the ring on her finger after so many months of deliberation?

"Good morning, Mrs Stubbs, Miss Tibbs. It's a nice day out there, don't you think?" Through the back door came Peggy with a jug of goats' milk and the basket she usually carried.

"Good morning, Peggy," Mrs Stubbs replied. "It's a little earlier than your usual time."

"Yes, you are right there, Mrs Stubbs, but I had to come and check on Miss Tibbs. I was so worried about her." Beady eyes turned and looked intently at Alice.

Alice looked down at her tea, "I didn't want to worry you, Mrs Stubbs. There was a disturbance last night."

"And so I came along to see that she hadn't got upset or hurt."

"That's kind of you Mrs Webb, Peggy. I am absolutely fine; no harm done at all." Alice looked at Peggy directly and continued, "How very kind of you to come all this way to check on me. I do appreciate it." Then turning to Mrs Stubbs: "A Mr Brooks came along, not very late, just after supper, and he was a little distressed as his wife has gone missing. She clearly wasn't here, so he went on his way."

"Brooks," Mrs Stubbs paused, frowning as she thought about the name. "It doesn't sound at all familiar. Poor man, what an odd thing to do, to come here looking for his wife. I do hope she wasn't… could she have been the woman who was found on the beach?"

"No, I thought of that," Alice replied, "but he said she had long, red hair and the other woman had brown hair."

"That's good news for him, but it would be good to have given her a name."

"You told him about the dead woman then?" Peggy asked. "You asked if it were his wife, did you? Her with the brown hair found washed up by the tide?"

"It wasn't her." Alice turned to her book.

"And did you get talking about any other bodies?" Peggy persisted.

"Other bodies?" Alice looked up in surprise.

"Did you maybe think that his wife had been washed up before?"

"I merely assured him that the dead woman was not his wife." Alice kept her voice steady. Mrs Webb was looking for a reaction; she was looking to see fear and discomfort. Alice would not reward her probing by giving away any of her emotions. "We spoke of no other dead bodies because he is looking for his wife whom he believes to be alive."

Alice stood up and moved away from the table. She went to her room to tidy her bed and closed the door behind her, although she felt Mrs Webb would have no qualms at all about opening the door and continuing the conversation if she wanted to. A tight knot of anger settled in her chest. Peggy Webb had been sent as a spy from the fishermen's settlement; who was she looking to protect and why?

Having tossed the sheet and blankets into place, Alice left her bedroom, and shut the door firmly behind her. She had come here to teach and that was her sole purpose, so she marched past the kitchen table and into the schoolroom to prepare for the day ahead.

Chapter Nine

Alice had been invited for afternoon tea. With the low autumn sun leaving a golden light on the stones and the wind barely a whisper, her fatigue had lifted, and spirits were high.

It had been after lunch break when Victoria Stevens had approached her. "Miss Tibbs, Ma says maybe you'd like to come back with us after school and stay for your tea. Nothing fancy but she thought you must be a bit lonely stuck out here."

The teacher found herself balancing on the railway sleepers, with each hand held by a young Stevens child, Lilian on her right and George on her left. Bill had gone ahead with other boys, but Victoria stayed with Alice and the younger children. Walking with them in this way made a game of there being no pavements, and their chatter alerted her to birds and plants which had previously gone unnoticed. In no time at all, they reached the end of the track and the lighthouse loomed high before them.

Since being in Dungeness Alice had walked with her body hunched and often shielding herself from the wind, now she was open to seeing the features of the landscape and paused to look at the lighthouse. "Is your father working there now?" she asked.

"Yes. He'll be back home at eight o'clock," Victoria replied. "He's lit the lamp, but someone will be there all night, keeping a watch. They take it in turns."

"And someone else will be at the low light," George

informed her. "It's like a steam engine down there. But it doesn't run a train; it makes the fog trumpet work."

"I've seen it." Alice recalled the oddity of a building on the beach. "But I must look again, and I'll think of the steam being pushed through the pipes. When I hear it, I'll wonder if your father is there working it."

The lighthouse was sturdy, with rows of small windows running from the base to the lamp room. It was painted in black and red stripes and, at the base, there was a ring of keepers' accommodation. *What curious homes they must be,* Alice thought. *Look at how they are circling the bottom. I'd love to see inside one.* But the Stevens family lived in one of two homes detached from the tower, and they were approaching it now. She glanced up at the lamp room and saw the light flash, then followed the children into their home.

"I keep thinking of you all the way out there in the schoolhouse." Bess Stevens sat down beside Alice at the table. "I just had the feeling that you didn't know what you were coming to and perhaps you are feeling a bit lonely, it being all on its own."

The children were busy with watercolour paints, having devoured cheese scones and teacakes. This was the first chance for Alice to speak freely, without constant interruptions. She liked Mrs Stevens, or Bess as she had been told to call her, and it was good to have the company.

"No, I didn't know what I was coming to," Alice admitted. "I thought it would be a village by the sea, a bit like Hythe but smaller, perhaps with a promenade and some shops..." Her voice trailed off as she pictured the perfect seaside village.

"Oh, my dear, it isn't a bit what you expected. It's bleak here and that schoolhouse... Well, there's not a neighbour in sight."

"I lock the doors and the range keeps me nice and

warm." Alice tried to be positive. "And as for being lonely, I have all the children and Mrs Stubbs."

"Mrs Stubbs is a fine woman, but not the type you feel you can have a nice chat with and come the evening you are a long time on your own. I'm just trying to say that it's bedlam here most of the time, but you know where we are if you want to call in for a chat. Just come along after school with Victoria and the others."

"Thank you, I really appreciate it. It would be something to look forward to. Perhaps once a week…?"

"That's all arranged then. Another cup of tea?" Bess poured freshly-made tea for the two of them and continued with, "We had some bother last night, some man from Denge, round the point you know, he came here looking for his wife. Thankfully, William was in and he dealt with him, told him we hadn't seen nor heard of her. They're an odd lot, those from round there. Dishonest. You can't trust them if you know what I mean."

"We are meant to have a few pupils from there," Alice told her. "Not that I have seen them. Mrs Stubbs says that they don't appear for weeks at a time. Then maybe they'll come in for a day or two and not for another week."

"That sounds about right. Anyway, he was in a temper, saying that we had her here. What would we want with his wife? It's hard enough to feed our own family without keeping someone else for no good reason."

"He came to the schoolhouse, banging on the door, and he broke a window."

"Oh Lord! Alice, I didn't realise. You really shouldn't be alone out there." Bess shook her head and took a sip of tea. "I just don't know of another way and Mrs Stubbs was there for years with no bother."

"He calmed down when he realised she wasn't

there and that I was new to the area." Alice tried to reassure her new friend. "He was just so worried; it's no wonder he was in a state. I do hope he finds her."

"I hope so too, if only to stop him coming round the point and bothering us. Who knows where she went; she could be anywhere."

Alice wondered whether to confide about that first night and what she had seen, or rather who she had seen, as it must have been Emily. But however kind and caring Bess was, something stopped Alice from telling her. Perhaps next week when she visited it would feel like the right time. Of course, Bess knew what it was like to come to Dungeness as a stranger and it would be comforting to exchange experiences. She was about to ask Bess where she had lived before Mr Stevens' work brought him to the lighthouse, when Bill burst in through the door.

"Hello Ma, Miss Tibbs," his cheeks were rosy from running. "Uncle Toby gave me this mackerel for tomorrow. He's just come in and I helped unload the boat."

"No wonder you stink of fish!" His mother laughed, "Best wash your hands before it's everywhere."

"I know Ma." The boy was already at the kitchen sink.

"I'm lucky we get fish most days from Toby," Bess told Alice.

"Your brother?" Alice was unreasonably shocked, "I presumed that you came here with Mr Stevens… for his work."

"No, I was born over there, where my older brother still lives with his family. One of my sisters is here, she married Bert from next door, and I went all the way off to the lighthouse! It was only our Rose who moved away; you remember I'd been visiting her in Appledore last Saturday?"

"Yes. Your sister from Appledore. I thought that

was where you came from."

"No, Dungeness born and bred I am. It's my William who isn't local. He came all the way from Whitstable. It was a bit of a change for him too."

Dear Albert,

I hope this finds you well. It has only been a few days since my last letter but writing to you gives me a sense of you being close by. I find myself in a lonely place. During the day there are the children and Mrs Stubbs, the headteacher, but I have many hours isolated from other people. I am sure you will think me foolish, so I must explain that the schoolhouse is fifteen minutes' walk from any other property. It sits away from the other homes and I cannot imagine why it was built here. By the time school ends, it is almost dusk and with the never-ending winds and misty rain, there is nothing to do but sit and read by the fire or do household chores.

On my first day of teaching, a body of a woman was found washed up on the beach. No one knew who she was or where she had come from. On the second day, it was a half-day at school so her funeral could be held. Did I mention before that there is no church building here and the school is used for the services?

Last night a man came banging at the door and he was searching for his wife. However, it was not the woman who had just been buried. It was another woman gone missing. I couldn't help him, so he went on his way. What sort of place have I come to where one woman is dead and another missing, all in less than a week?

My teaching goes well, and I find that I have a good rapport with the children. Some of them are very engaging, although they must be so solemn in school. It is only in the playground or out on a nature walk when I get to see their true personalities.

How I look forward to Christmastime and two weeks back at home with you, Mother and Father. Please tell them that I shall write soon and anticipate letters from you all.

Much love, Alice.

Alice felt soothed for having written; Albert and her parents were only a letter away and once she put pen to paper there was a relief in having shared some of her thoughts. Not all of them though, she couldn't, just couldn't, put to paper all that had happened. It would make it too real and feed the guilt that she should have stopped to help poor, desperate Emily.

Now stiff and cold, Alice realised she had been sitting at the table for too long. She stood and rubbed her arms to bring warmth to them and moved to stand by the range. Still not satisfied, she opened the door and added a couple of logs, then moved through to her bedroom to find a stamp to stick on her letter. Alice opened her soft leather pouch in which she kept her good, thick paper and matching envelopes. She reached into a small inner pocket to retrieve a penny lilac, one of a dozen she had brought with her.

The stamps had gone, yet they had been there just two days ago when she had written to both her parents and Albert. She had come into her room, just as she was doing now, taken them out and put them on the letters. Then she had left them on her chest of drawers to post later. Had she mistakenly left the penny lilacs on the side? Had they slipped down the back? Alice had a thorough search, pulling out the furniture, looking in the drawers, checking and re-checking the leather pouch.

While Alice searched, she remembered those other letters and Peggy patting the pocket of her apron to show she had them safe. Peggy who had been in her room and taken them, without permission, but under the pretence of being helpful. Was she interfering or was controlling Alice's life?

"You're being unreasonable," Alice muttered to herself. "She's just an old woman, just trying to help."

But the stone that sat heavily in the pit of Alice's stomach told her otherwise. She was trapped here, and not just by the distance from home. Stripped of any way of communicating with her family and Albert, Alice was now reliant on others to send her letters and buy her stamps.

Five days. Alice had been at Dungeness for five days. Five days and two bodies. Five days and cut off from any means of keeping in touch with her family. This was enough. No longer would she be timid Alice, yielding to what other people expected of her, dependable and reliable. This place – this grim, miserable place – was going to suck all that was good and moral from her being if she didn't leave this very evening.

Never mind how she was going to do it, Alice had to get to Lydd. And in the morning, she would be on the way to Appledore and then Ashford. She lay her suitcase open on the bed and started putting her clothes in it, barely folding the smart dresses, skirts and blouses. In the carpet bag went her good buttoned boots, books and the leather pouch. Then she scoured the living area, picking up her pens, more books and her shawl. The suitcase was put back under her bed and the bag in the clothes press; you never knew who might turn up uninvited.

It was too soon to leave; no point in waiting all through the cold, damp night at Lydd. Alice sat down with a fresh cup of tea and tried to relax in the armchair. It wouldn't hurt to have a nap, but she was far too agitated. At eleven o'clock, Alice tipped away the cold tea and washed out the pot and her cup. She took a wedge of fruit cake and wrapped it in brown paper, then a couple of apples which had come from Mrs Stubbs' garden. She put on her coat and wrapped her shawl around herself, then put on her hat and gloves. At the doorstep, Alice pondered for a moment about the key, then stepped back in, put it on the kitchen table, and closed the door without locking it.

Chapter Ten

Alice had no choice but to follow the tracks; she knew of no other way. They would take her to Lydd, that was certain, and from there she would wait for the morning train to Ashford. She would have to take care to avoid Mrs Stubbs in the town as she made her way, in her upright fashion, to catch the early train. Knowing she should apologise for her failure to stay, yet fearful of doing so, led to a tight knot of guilt settling in her stomach. The moon slipped in and out from behind the clouds and while Alice welcomed the silver light, it made her fearful of being spotted.

"Who is there to see you?" Alice asked herself out loud. "Who else would be foolish enough to be here?" She didn't know the answer, whether there were cottages along the trackside or if a farmer might be out at night. She had not ventured in this direction before and there had been no view through the condensation and mist on the day of her arrival.

The sleepers were never clear from a scattering of stones, so not one footstep was taken with ease. At best each step was awkward, at worst she slipped, her fall broken by the case and carpet bag, one in each hand. The case was particularly awkward to carry, making Alice hold one shoulder higher than the other, so it stayed clear of the ground. This lopsided gait caused a nagging pain in her lower back. But the effort and discomfort meant nothing to Alice when every step took her closer to home.

An hour had passed when the moon went behind a thick mass of clouds, and as it did so Alice's foot caught on a piece of twisted metal. She came down heavily, her knee hitting the track and her chest pressing hard on her suitcase. Lying sprawled across the case for a moment, the pain ripped through her body. Any feelings of exhilaration Alice felt, having made her decision to leave, were now long gone. They had been lost as she battled with every step taken. It was dark, really dark, and cold too. A need to curl up and sleep right there came over her, but the young woman wasn't going to be drawn into such thoughts; she knew she must force herself to get up and carry on. As Alice's brain told her to move and she willed her body to respond, she found herself being given no choice. Alice was lifted clear of the tracks and held upright. She didn't even attempt to scream. Perhaps because it was pointless or perhaps because her energy was spent.

It came as no surprise to see her rescuer was Tom Barton. No surprise at all; he seemed to turn up wherever she was and always unwanted. This was no different; she could have managed perfectly well without his assistance.

"So, here I am walking home after visiting my cousin and here you are... in the middle of the night!"

"You seem to make a point of turning up where you are unwanted." Alice's voice was high. "Take your hands off me and I'll be on my way. I'm going home."

"Home is the schoolhouse and as I am going in that direction myself, I'll escort you. You'll no doubt slow me down, but I can't leave you here like this." Tom's arm remained at her elbow keeping her steady.

"Don't let me hinder you, Mr Barton. I am quite capable of finding my own way." Alice pulled herself free from his grip and floundered on the uneven surface.

"Accept it, Miss Tibbs, you are one of us now." He took her chin for a moment and forced her to look at his face. "You're to come back home and we'll say nothing more of this."

"I'll not come back of my own free will," Alice replied, scowling up at him. "Who are you to tell me what to do?"

Who was he, this Mr Thomas Barton? Just some fisherman who appeared with the sole purpose of belittling her. He was tall and solid, not an ounce of fat on him, simply hard muscle from controlling the fishing boat, hauling in the catch, lifting the sodden nets and boxes of fish. At about thirty years old, he was at the peak of his game, experienced but still strong and healthy. He was, no doubt, on the lifeboats too. Brave and willing to go out on a steely grey sea to save lives. Did he think he was some sort of king around here, someone who was used to doing things his way?

"I've decided to keep an eye on you, make sure you don't get into trouble. Besides, I was one of the local people consulted by Mrs Stubbs and the vicar about employing a second teacher and I don't like to be mistaken."

"I've tried and I just can't stay in this miserable place," Alice's voice rose; she was desperate now to be on her way to Lydd. "Just let me go and you'll find someone more suited. Someone who will put up with all this."

She turned her back on him and took a step towards Lydd, but it took no effort on his part to hold out an arm and take a hold of her suitcase.

"You'll come back, do some teaching and within six months you'll be married to a Dungeness man and thinking nothing of those in Ashford with their fancy ways."

"I'd not marry you." Alice turned and spat the words at him.

"I'd not marry a prissy teacher!" he retorted, as the moon came out from behind a cloud and she saw he was laughing at her.

"You said..." She was uncertain. What had he said?

"Not me, but surely someone would have you." He stood back and looked her up and down. "You'll do for someone and then you'll settle down here and keep that pretty little mouth shut."

"How dare you," she screamed back at him. "I'm engaged to be married." Alice brandished the ring as proof. "I will not 'do' for some fisherman or... or... boulderman."

Tom Barton took her hand, looked at the ring and dismissed it. "Where is he now then? Back in Ashford? If you were my woman then you'd be with me."

"I thank God I am not your woman."

Tom lifted her suitcase and started walking along the tracks, back towards Dungeness. Alice paused for a moment, thinking of fleeing without her case, but then bent down to pick up the carpet bag and scurried along, slipping and sliding, whilst he strode along, at ease with the stony ground.

What was it he meant by saying I would do for someone? Alice scowled as she reflected on his words. *As if I were the only animal left in a market after all the prime stock have sold. Who is he to judge me, when he knows nothing of my real life and the things I do? He thinks he is too good for me. Well, he can think that if he cares to. His opinion is nothing to me. And... if being prissy means having good manners then that is fine and exactly as it should be.* But it wasn't. It was not fine at all. The thoughts continued to race through her mind.

They didn't speak for five minutes or so and his temper must have eased as Tom slowed to allow Alice to catch up.

"You have more grit than I thought!" he looked back at her with a half-grin.

"I just want to go home."

"Is our school not good enough? Does it not compare to an Ashford school?"

"It's a good school," Alice admitted. "I like it very much."

They walked on, Alice still slipping and sliding but it was easier with him carrying her case. He knew of the body she found on that very first evening. She was sure of it. He knew that she knew. He had found the abandoned carpet bag and left it at the schoolhouse; she was sure of that too.

"What happened to that other woman?" Alice ventured to ask.

"What woman?"

"She was lying on the shingle near the vicar's cottage. I tripped over her and I thought she was dead, but she wasn't, was she?"

"Keep out of it."

"How can I when I don't know if she is dead or alive? I saw her and I was going to help… she was asking for my help… but I couldn't do anything before she was picked up and carried off." It came out in a rush, all those words left unsaid for a week. "Did she die? She must have done; she haunts me because I didn't save her."

"If she died, she'd have worse enemies to worry about haunting than you, Miss Tibbs." His speed picked up as if to stall her words by putting some distance between them.

"She's alive then?" Alice called out.

"We need her alive."

"You need her alive?" Alice repeated.

He didn't reply, just carried on walking, eventually slowing down again and allowing her to catch up and then adjusting his pace to match hers. He offered her

92

his arm and, stubborn as Alice was, she was also bruised and exhausted, so she took it. When he spoke again, his tone was softer, and the subject had been changed:

"I can see it's lonely for you. You must miss your family and here you are stuck out at the school. You'd be happier with a bit of company, but you have got a decent house there, warm and dry. It didn't seem to bother Miss Wilkie, Mrs Stubbs that is, but it's not for everyone."

Alice appreciated his thoughts and decided to put her curiosity about Emily aside for a moment. "It's only until the end of the summer term, I have my books in the evening and company during the day. If I am to stay, then I shall manage."

"You'll stay," he confirmed. "You've had your outburst and now you'll settle down to the teaching."

"I would like to be able to write a letter home and one to Albert once a week."

"No harm in that if you keep to the weather and how your tapestry is going, or whatever else young ladies like to talk about."

"My stamps have been taken," Alice recoiled at the words, feeling his contempt for whatever hobbies may engage her time. "I mean they are missing."

"I'll have a word with Mrs Webb," he replied, his tone grim.

Again, they continued in silence, but this time it was more companionable. Finally, as the moon broke free of the clouds and Alice thought that the shingle looked quite beautiful under the soft blue light, they left the tracks and walked to the schoolhouse.

"Do you have the key?" Tom asked.

"I didn't lock it." Alice opened the door. "What's the point? If someone wants to get in here, they seem to manage without one."

He put the case on the floor. Alice lit one of the oil

lamps and the room looked as if she had never left. A quick look at the clock showed that it was past one o'clock.

As he went to leave, Tom turned and said, "You'll stay now." It was a statement rather than a question.

"Yes, I'll stay."

Alice meant it too. Not because of him and his bullying ways. No, she would stay because of the commitment that had been made to the children and Mrs Stubbs, long before she knew what she was letting herself in for. More importantly, she would stay for Emily, to find out what had become of her, and release her so she was free to go back around the point to Denge, or wherever she wished to be. Alice had a reason for staying and with it came renewed energy and determination to solve the mystery of the body found on the shingle.

Chapter Eleven

There were some changes over the next few days. The first happened on the Friday lunchtime when Peggy Webb spoke to Alice, looking directly at her with those beady eyes which saw and knew everything: "I hear you'd rather care for your own room. So, I'll keep to the kitchen and what some people might call common space in future."

"Thank you, Mrs Webb, I have plenty of time to clean my bedroom," Alice answered, managing to hold her gaze.

Later, after school time, Alice saw that her penny lilacs were on the chest of drawers in her room. She had her stamps but how to send a letter and be sure it would reach its destination? Nonetheless, standing up to Peggy was a small victory and Alice felt a shift of power in her favour.

The bigger change came when, at the end of that same lunchtime, Hazel returned to the school and announced that she would be moving into the spare bedroom.

"It was Tom Barton that suggested it to Ma," Hazel told Alice. "There I am all squashed up in the bedroom with my sister's little girls. She's got the baby in with her and Stan. Then there's my brother, Wilf, still at home too and sleeping on the floor. We're all getting under each other's feet and no space for ourselves and here you are with a spare room and maybe getting a bit lonely out here. We'll be company for each other, but I won't get in your way, I'll not be bothering you if you want to write a letter or read a book. I was that excited I ran on ahead to tell you about it. I hope you don't mind, Miss Tibbs… I hope it's all right with you."

"That's marvellous news, Hazel. A wonderful surprise. But do call me Alice, now we are to live together. Keep Miss Tibbs for the schoolroom." Alice couldn't help sharing Hazel's enthusiasm.

"Thank you, Miss Tibbs, Alice. Can I look at my room?"

"Of course!" Alice led the way. "We'll need to air the mattress." Hazel was a decent young woman and at seventeen years old she was only two years younger than Alice. They would soon become firm friends and the company would certainly be welcome over the winter evenings.

By ten o'clock on the Saturday morning, Hazel had appeared with a bag of clothes in each hand. She enjoyed arranging them in the clothes press and, after a cup of tea, the young women set out to get more of Hazel's belongings and some bedding from her parents' home.

The light rain of the early morning had passed, and the sky was a clear blue with patches of high clouds. The breeze carried a salty reminder that they were by the sea, but not the fishy stench of previous days. Alice was at last walking, in backstays, with some ease over the pebbles and looking down she saw a soft, understated beauty in the various tones of silver and dove grey to gunmetal, mingled with beige and fawn.

They took the path many of the school children used, leaving the railway track and lighthouse to the right and heading straight to where the fishermen's shacks stood in either small clusters or isolated from their neighbours. As they neared the settlement, children could be seen playing out on the shingle; they waved to Alice and Hazel but let them continue. For

96

Alice, there was a great deal of satisfaction to be had from having a purpose for the day, as well as a companion.

Hazel's family home was built from rough shiplap timber, liberally painted in black tar. They approached from the back and Alice noticed a pen with goats as well as a chicken coop. Wooden frames held precious earth, which nurtured hardy winter greens and root vegetables. There were various outbuildings and two additional extensions jutting out from the back of the original rectangular home. Its roof had a high pitch and, as they walked around the side, Alice saw a ladder leading up to a door in the loft space. To the front, it had a large porch facing the beach and, beyond it, the sea. There were two small windows to each side of the porch and Alice found herself appreciating its orderly appearance.

"We normally use the back door, but Ma said to bring you in the front," Hazel said, giving the door a hefty kick to loosen it from the frame.

The porch was empty except for a pair of wooden chairs. They stepped through and into the cosy kitchen-cum-living room. The range, Belfast sink, scrubbed pine cupboards and shelves ran along the back wall. A large wooden table was to the left, with a teapot and clutter of cups, saucers, plates and cutlery placed in the centre. Armchairs and a sofa draped with mismatched crocheted blankets were set around a large rag rug to the right. A dark wooden cabinet with glass doors displayed a collection of fine china and ornaments.

It was a warm, cosy room and although it lacked the formal style of the rectory, Alice was beginning to find a certain charm in unmatched crockery and furniture showing wear from a busy family life. When Hazel's mother offered her a cup of tea and a slice of apple cake, she was more than happy to stay for a while and curious to learn about the lives of the local families.

"How are you finding your first week teaching, Miss Tibbs?"

"I am liking it very much, Mrs Tanner. I can learn from Mrs Stubbs' experience and it is so worthwhile to be able to teach these young children." Alice replied politely, but her mind was really on how to divert the conversation to the fishing community and the missing Emily.

"It's wonderful for Hazel to be able to come and live with you. She's been so happy about it. Now, pass Miss Tibbs the sugar, Hazel." Mrs Tanner gestured towards the sugar bowl, and continued, "Not that I won't miss her, of course I will, but it's got a bit crowded here what with her sister and her three here. Wilf has to sleep on the floor." She pointed towards a roll of bedding against the wall. "They are saving up to build a cottage, Annie and Stan I mean, but it will take a while."

"And does Stan fish too?" Alice asked.

"He does, but he goes out in his own boat. They are out on the beach now, checking them over; we don't go fishing on a Saturday, but they'll be out a couple of hours before low tide early tomorrow afternoon."

"I saw a smart boat moored just off the beach. Is that the lifeboat?" Alice asked.

"That's Thomas Simcox," Mrs Tanner told her.

"No, a boat, not a man!" Alice laughed a little to cover her embarrassment.

"I didn't think you'd be talking about any smart young men around here!" Mrs Tanner smiled, "No, Thomas Simcox is the lifeboat and she does look fine out there. We've had her here, the last two years; she came in '92. Then there's the R.A.O.B, just came this month and she's at the lifeboat station."

"If Alice thinks Thomas Simcox is confusing, she'll never guess what R.A.O.B stands for," Hazel joined in. "Go on have a guess."

"R, maybe Royal ... A ... O ..., I don't know," Alice couldn't imagine, but she felt that this frivolous conversation was doing her good. "B? B for boat?"

"You got one out of four correct, now what do you think of this? Royal Antediluvian Order of the Buffaloes!" Hazel had a big grin on her face. "I can hardly say it myself!"

"Why?"

"It's some charity," Mrs Tanner informed. "They help people in need. This boat – the R.A.O.B – it came on the train, the same as you. My, that was a job to get her brought over the shingle! She's the second one they've given us, the other one was called the same!"

"It's not something I've ever heard of," Alice reflected, "but Antediluvian, that means 'before the flood', before Noah's Ark, so they must have been around for a long time. I'll note it down and when I am back at home for Christmas, I'll ask Father if he's heard of it."

"You do that, dear, and then you can come back and tell us all about them."

"I heard the lifeboat was out last weekend," Alice started on what she really wanted to talk about.

"She was, and I can't help thinking that's where the poor woman came from." Mrs Tanner poured a second cup of tea. "More cake Miss Tibbs?"

"Yes please, it's delicious." Alice pushed her plate forward. "You mean the woman on the beach? The one who was found washed up?"

"Yes, she wasn't from the boat our men went out to because they saved the crew and there were no passengers, but it was rough that night and I hear the Rye boat went out and maybe it didn't go so well."

Hazel was standing at the front window. "It's

coming over quite dark, I think we need to get back before the heavens open. I can't believe it was so lovely just an hour ago. Dad and the others will be back in a minute. No need to get wet if they're not at sea."

The young women put their coats on and gathered armfuls of bedding. Hazel strung her smarter boots around her neck and Alice welcomed a basket containing goats' milk, cheese and cake. They stepped out of the front porch and into their backstays. Goodbyes were said to Mrs Tanner, and Alice assured her that Hazel would be no trouble at all, then thanked her for the delicious cake. Hazel promised to visit at least once a week after school and at the weekend.

What a difference an hour had made: a mass of dark violet cloud hung over the distant sea, changing it to a steely grey. Looking inland towards Lydd, the day was just as it had been, the clear blue sky not giving a hint of what was to come. The darkening sky over the sea brought with it a change in depth to the colours of the landscape, the greens of the grasses and broom were stronger and the colours of the shingle more pronounced. The young women moved as quickly as they could, determined to beat the weather.

Hazel's home was one of three in a cluster but standing alone, and slightly inland, there was another cottage. This one was a natural wood colour with black painted window frames and doors. As they passed by, a woman was outside gathering the sheets from the washing line. Hazel gave her a wave.

"That's my Aunt Connie,"

The woman waved back and went into the house. There was another woman sitting on a bench by the back door. She was well wrapped up in a blanket or shawl, with only part of her face showing.

"Is that her daughter?" Alice asked.

"Her daughter? No," Hazel replied. "She doesn't

have any children. I heard her husband's cousin was visiting. A distant cousin I presume as we've not known of her before. Ma said she was there and not at all well, so we weren't to bother her. Poor woman, think of coming all the way to Dungeness and then becoming ill."

As they looked across, the woman stood up slowly and put her hand out to support herself on the side of the building. She looked towards Alice and Hazel and, as she turned, her shawl slipped away from her head and Alice saw the glint of auburn in her hair. The young woman pulled the shawl around her slim shoulders and stepped into the cottage. Alice stopped; her gaze fixed on the spot where the woman had been.

"Are you well, Miss Tibbs... Alice?" Hazel's words broke into her thoughts.

"I... yes. Sorry. I was staring, how very rude. What beautiful hair that young woman has; did you see?"

"A dark copper. Yes, it was lovely."

"I expect Connie's husband has the same colour, but it's truly lovely on a woman." Alice patted her own chestnut coloured knot of hair. "How pretty hanging in curls down her back; mine is so straight and always secured in this sensible knot."

"Perhaps you could let it down, just on a Saturday. You could try something different?" Hazel suggested. "But of course, you want to look proper for teaching and church."

"Yes, I could," Alice responded, her thoughts full of the young woman who must be Emily. "Does Connie's husband have copper coloured hair?"

"No, it's fair, like mine, maybe a little darker. I don't know of anyone with that colour hair from around here. I think she's come visiting from Hythe way, that's what I heard."

By now the two friends were some way past the fishermen's cottages and the storm clouds were catching up with them. They could see the first heavy drops of rain were falling on the beach and that the men had retreated to their homes or the pub. There was now a sharp chill in the air. Alice and Hazel hurried along, eager to be back home at the schoolhouse before the storm broke.

That night the wind came from the west, battering the wooden homes and boats, and sweeping across the shingle. It whipped around the solid schoolhouse, shaking the glass in the windows and buffeting the piece of hessian sack tacked in place over the pane of glass smashed by Ed Brooks. Alice lay cocooned by her mattress and thick blankets; she felt at peace to know Hazel was in the room beside her.

The next morning, when they opened the door between the house and school, Alice was beginning to feel comfortable with knowing the school would become a church for the next hour. It seemed quite reasonable to make use of a space which would otherwise remain empty on a Sunday. Alice and Hazel stepped through as the first families arrived. The area was soon filled with chatter and the scraping of table legs on the floor, as desks were moved aside, and additional chairs placed to fill the space. Rows were formed and the curtain covering the altar was pulled to one side. The teaching platform became a pulpit and the change was almost complete.

"I knew Ma would be here early," Hazel said, as she went to greet her family, whom Alice presumed must include her brother, sister and brother-in-law, along with the three children.

"Miss Tibbs, if you wouldn't mind..." The vicar pointed to a pile of kneelers and Alice, pleased to be kept busy, started to place them in front of the chairs.

The woman, Emily, was never far from her thoughts now and Alice kept an eye on the door. *How foolish of me,* she scolded herself. *If that was Emily I saw yesterday, then it's clear she is hiding away. But what of the family who she is staying with; will they risk leaving her in order to come to church? I doubt it, not with Ed Brooks prowling about.* Peggy Webb entered with her husband; Alice looked away. There was an unspoken truce between them, but she preferred to avoid the woman as much as possible. Then Tom Barton strode in; Alice picked up the last of the kneelers and turned her back on him as she placed them on the floor. She seated herself on the far side of the door and opened her hymn book, looking at the pages without seeing.

Afterwards, Alice couldn't remember the church service. She could sing along to all the well-known hymns and say the responses whilst all the time her mind was on Emily and the mystery surrounding her. Finally, the vicar gave his parting words, "...and peace be with you." Alice repeated the words and started moving the extra chairs to the side. She made brief comments and nodded politely to the people who introduced themselves as parents to her pupils, whilst having the excuse of still being very new to the school if they thought her a little vague.

It wasn't long before the desks needed putting back in place. "How are you today, Miss Tibbs?" Alice found herself partnered with someone who was not her ideal choice.

"I'm still here; I told you I would be." Alice replied in a low voice; she avoided eye contact with him.

"I've come to the church, not to check up on you."

"I thought…"

"There's no need for us to be enemies. I'm looking out for everyone here and doing what's best. We need another teacher, so here you are, and I hope you'll soon feel at home." Tom Barton made it all sound quite reasonable, while he picked up his end of the desk with ease and pulled her along in his wake. "Let's call a truce. I've upset you and I'm sorry."

They set down the desk and went for the next one. "Very well, but what about my parents and Albert? I want to write to them, or they'll worry." Alice tried to keep her tone friendly; people were watching. "My stamps have been returned, but I have no way of posting a letter."

"You've already written to them."

"One letter was taken from my room without permission and the second was not sent as my stamps had gone missing."

"You can send a letter home, but first I have a little job for you. A chance to show your loyalty to Dungeness and those who live here." Tom looked down at her as they stacked the second desk on top of the first. He must have been a head taller than Alice and his hands on the wood of the desk were huge with stubby fingers, although she had to admit they were clean, and his nails were neat. He had made an effort for church.

"A job? I'm here to teach and that is how I'll show my commitment. It will be to the children, not to you. A truce?" Alice felt a rage rise within her, and she could hear her voice was sharp as she continued. "You want to order me around. To make me grateful for anything you do to help me. Just keep away from me, Mr Barton. That is all I ask."

Alice turned away: she would not be a part of whatever he was planning. Her body was tense and shaking with anger. From the moment she first saw him, he did nothing but infuriate her with his bad manners and domineering ways. There he was, lifting the desks on his own, as if no conversation had taken place between the two of them. As if he could just wait until she came asking for his goodwill and protection.

Finally, when the school room had been restored,

104

Tom stood between Alice and the doorway through to the house.

"Excuse me, Mr Barton," Alice's voice was cool.

"You'll meet my sister by the station at noon. She'll tell you what needs doing."

"I'll be here preparing my lunch at noon," Alice snapped back at him.

Chapter Twelve

Shoulders rounded and heart heavy, Alice slid alongside the railway tracks. The cloud was low, and the breeze carried a sharp chill as swathes of sea-mist rolled inland. Alice's brown woollen hat was pulled low over her ears and her coat buttoned to her neck. Looking up, she saw the outline of the railway station and, as she did so, she stubbed her backstay on a stump of broom, causing her rhythmic pace to be lost.

"Damn and blast," she muttered, followed by: "there was no need for profanity, no need at all."

The young woman waiting in the shelter of the station gave a brief smile as Alice entered. She was well wrapped up with a tweed coat over a thick woollen dress, and a tasselled shawl covering her head and shoulders. Wisps of curly, dark blonde hair framed her round face and grey eyes looked straight into Alice's own. Under other circumstances, if Alice had met her perhaps at church or in a local shop, she would have liked Thomas Barton's sister on sight.

There were no polite greetings, nothing said before the young woman launched into the reason for their meeting. "We need you to go along to Denge, to give a message to Ed Brooks: tell him his wife has been ill but we've kept her alive and when he's had a little longer to miss her we'll be ready to talk."

"You're Mr Barton's sister?" Alice wanted to be sure.

"I'm Lucie Barton." She gave nothing else away.

"And why me? Why am I being sent with this message, rather than someone who understands the reason for you to hold Emily Brooks?" Alice's heart was pounding, but those first days spent in Dungeness had already made her stronger and she was determined not to follow their orders without questioning the purpose.

"For that very reason: you carry the message but are of no use to them. You know nothing."

So many questions, but clearly no point in asking them; the less she knew, the less she could tell. But she did know; Alice knew more than Lucie Barton suspected. Alice knew where Emily was being held and if she told Ed Brooks then maybe he could free her. Or would letting him know of her whereabouts put his wife's life in danger? Perhaps Emily was safer in Dungeness than she was with her husband who had shown himself to have a temper. Alice had already failed her once and she had to make the right choices this time. The Reverend Tibbs often advised that if you are not sure what to do then do nothing and wait until God sends you a direction. It was a time to wait.

"How will I find Mr Brooks?" Alice asked.

"I'll walk with you past the lighthouse to the coast and then you'll go on alone, around the point into West Bay and the first settlement you come to is Denge; there is no mistaking it."

"Is it far?" Alice asked. She recalled a group of huts seen on her first day when she had walked to the beach.

"Not far," Lucie replied.

Lucie led the way and they walked in silence for several minutes. Had it been a clear day when they reached the point, Alice could have seen across East Bay to Hythe and Folkestone, then across the west to Rye. However, she could barely make out the fishermen's cottages at Dungeness village and their boats on the beach. To the west, there was the indistinguishable shapes of shacks and small boats.

"That's Denge. You'll find Ed Brooks easy enough, there's only two or three families living there."

"And if I run into trouble?"

"We'll come and get you," Lucie said with confidence. "There's not enough of them to stop us."

"Very well." Alice pictured herself bound by old rope taken from their boat and being left in the corner of some damp outbuilding. *Why am I doing this?* she asked herself, *I don't have to do it. At least I don't think I have to.* Yet deep down she felt obligated to do something – if only to allay some of the guilt she felt at not helping in the first place. In another world, in her former life, she would have turned her back and set off to find the local constable.

"You remember the message?" Lucie asked, before Alice turned to leave.

"Yes. Emily has been ill but is alive. She is being kept safe and when he has had longer to miss her, you'll be ready to talk." Alice took her first steps in the direction of Denge.

"Stay along the coast," Lucie called out. "You don't want to get lost in the mist, and it will probably get worse later."

Without giving a response, Alice turned and began the trudge along to Denge. There was nothing to see with the clouds closing in all around; the rhythmic blast of the fog trumpet was her only companion. The sea came close, crashing on the beach and dragging pebbles back in its wake. Ten minutes or so passed and the grey forms of wooden shacks started to take shape.

In that time, Alice thought about Emily: first as a body on the shingle and later as the mysterious woman staying at the isolated cottage on the shingle. She wondered how the young woman usually spent

108

her days and what brought her to be lying on the stones, seemingly having come from the sea. As she neared the settlement, Alice wondered about who else lived there and if Emily had family, other than her husband.

Denge was no great distance from Dungeness point; yet it seemed to have even less to offer. There were no more than six low, wooden buildings with an assortment of wood stores, animal shelters and sheds. One building was a little larger than the others and displayed a crooked sign on its plank wall: *The Hope and Anchor*. A public house. Of course, the men would need a place to gather and relax in the evenings. *Please God in heaven, may I not have to enter a pub in order to seek out Ed Brooks.*

The first form of life came to her notice when a mournful sound was carried to Alice on the strands of mist. And then she was confronted by a group of goats tethered to strong stakes. The short ropes allowed them little freedom to forage and their pitiful bleats told of a lack of fresh greenery. But even after her few days living at Dungeness, Alice recognised the need for fresh milk and clearly this land could not sustain cattle.

Contemplating the buildings, Alice couldn't help noticing that every shack had smoke curling up from a chimney. Although it was still early afternoon, curtains were closed tight, and some windows were hidden behind roughly hewn shuttering. It was as if the people of Denge had decided to hibernate over the coming months. There was no way of telling which one Ed Brooks lived in, so Alice rapped on the door of the nearest shack. After a moment it was opened, just an inch or two, and a woman spoke, her tone full of suspicion:

"What do you want?"

"I am looking for Mr Brooks," Alice replied to the door.

109

"Well, I don't know what you'd be wantin', comin' out all this way." The door opened a little more and dark eyes in an olive-skinned, shrivelled face looked out. "He lives out the back of us, just step around the back an' his place has a boarded-up window." Alice nodded her thanks. "You'll not be welcome, girl. I'll tell you that much," the old woman called out before closing the door and giving no time for a response.

It really was no better than a garden shed: the one window to the front, not shuttered but boarded up. The shiplap walls were their natural colour. There was no door knocker, so Alice thumped on the bare wood with her fist.

The door opened and Ed Brooks' black eyes stared out. The fiery temper had passed, and he looked to be a shadow of the man she had met before. Dark rings surrounded his eyes, and it was clear Ed had barely slept for some time. As he stepped back to allow Alice into his home, she saw his body had visibly slumped. If, for some reason, this man had a lesson to be learned then Alice felt it had been accomplished. There was no doubt he was suffering for the loss of his wife.

Once inside the hovel, it took Alice's eyes a moment to adjust as the only light was emitted from the fire set on a brick hearth, by the end wall to her left. A kettle was slung over a metal hook above the grate and a couple of pans hung on the wall. This fire was clearly meant for both cooking and heat. To one side of the chimney breast there was a pile of driftwood and logs, to the other a solid pine cupboard filled the whole space from floor to the low ceiling.

The one window to the front had been boarded up inside and out, and leaning against it, to the left of Alice as she stood on the threshold, was a selection of tools. A huge fishing net was folded several times and hung from hooks in the ceiling, draping across the window.

Two smaller windows to the rear of the shack were adorned with tatty curtains of an unrecognisable colour and pattern.

A tired wooden table and three mismatched chairs stood on the wooden floor in the centre of the room. To the right was a large unmade box bed and a cupboard. Hooks on the rear wall displayed thick coats and a shawl. It was a miserable home, showing few signs that anyone had ever cared to make it a more attractive place to live in. To Alice, it certainly gave the appearance of a single man's place and not one to be shared with a woman.

But worse than any visual assault was the over-riding stench of raw fish and seaweed, coupled with burning wood. Undertones of rotten milk and body odour mingled in all of this. Alice longed to leave the door open and fling open the rear windows.

"You're the teacher. The new one." His eyes met hers, and she saw no hope left in his.

"I am. They sent me to speak to you."

"Why you? What d'you know?" He turned and sat on a chair; his upper body supported by the table.

"I know Emily is alive; she has been very ill, but she is alive." Alice remained standing by the doorway; she hadn't been invited to sit and wasn't inclined to.

"I told you she was alive. Tell me something new."

"They are keeping her until you are ready to talk. I'm sorry, that's the message and maybe you know what it means, but I don't."

"I asked why they sent you." Ed reminded Alice.

"You did. I think because I am a stranger. Because I don't know anything, there is nothing I can tell you. I asked them about Emily, but they would not tell me. I know nothing about her, only what they told me."

"You've not seen her then?"

"I've not seen her," Alice lied.

"I'm ready to talk; I just need her back."

111

"I'll tell them. But I think they want you to wait longer, maybe to make you suffer more – for whatever it is you are supposed to have done."

Ed stood up quickly, causing his chair to fall back onto the floor and for Alice to see a glimpse of the man whom she had first met at the schoolhouse.

"Who was it? Who gave you the message?"

"It was a woman; I'd not met her before."

"One of the fishermen's wives?" he barked.

"It could have been." Outwardly, Alice kept calm. It wasn't the time to show her how nervous she felt.

Ed said no more but turned to right the chair and Alice took the opportunity to leave, closing the door behind her and saying nothing as she departed. She scurried away, anxious to put some distance between herself and Denge, yet every step was hindered by the uneven surface. Certain he would come after her, she listened for his heavy steps on the shingle. Alice knew there would be no stopping Ed if he chose to vent his fury upon her. The door remained closed – for some reason the desperate man chose to allow her to leave. *He knows where I am though,* Alice reminded herself. *It would be nothing to him to come to the schoolhouse at night where he believes I am alone. Thankfully, Hazel is with me now.*

Alice paused to put on her backstays and continued. Within a few minutes, Denge was disappearing into the thickening mist. With the beam from the lighthouse acting as her guide, she made good progress, and it seemed as if Alice had escaped from Ed Brooks unscathed. However, on nearing the Dungeness point, she became aware of someone following her. A scattering of stones and the rustle of movement through the rough grass or kale, led her to fear this was not caused by an animal loose on the headland.

Chapter Thirteen

Heart pounding with trepidation, Alice looked back to see a small, hunched figure and not the tall, dark threat of Ed Brooks. Whoever it was, Alice had no desire to meet them and concentrated on her route over the stones. Eager to be free of the mist and at home with a cup of tea, she tried to increase her speed. But Alice was inexperienced at moving over the shingle and by the time she reached the point, the figure was almost upon her.

"Ain't you going t' stop then?" The voice was rough and breathing ragged. Alice looked back to recognise the old hag whose door she had first knocked on when she had arrived at Denge.

"I didn't realise you wanted me..."

"My niece, she's a good hard-working girl." The old woman reached out a spindly arm and showed an unexpected strength as she gripped onto Alice's arm. Looking down at her face, Alice could see broken teeth and black eyes. "She does what she has t' do t' survive, like we all does. We need her home."

"I know you do," Alice replied, her tone gentle; there was no need to distress this woman. "I don't know where she is or why they have her. I'm merely a messenger. Go to the constable in Lydd if you need to."

"Paahh, you're right, you really don't know nothin' if you think them lot in Lydd would bother wi' Denge business."

113

"Them lot in Lydd?" Alice was confused.

"The constable, in his smart suit. He won't leave his fancy desk and come out here for no good reason."

"Your niece is missing," Alice reminded her. "So, if you are worried..."

"I told you, that's no concern of the constable." The old hag tightened her grip.

"I'm sorry, you must be desperately worried. Perhaps if you told me why they have her then it would be easier for me to help."

"All you need t' know is our Emily is a good woman and needs t' come home t' her rightful place beside her husband. The poor man is in a miserable way and how will we survive the winter if a strong man like him don't have the will t' go out fishin'?"

"I understand," said Alice, "Truly I do." She was beginning to think she did understand, having seen Ed Brooks in his home – a broken man who was unable or unwilling to bother to care for himself or to go out fishing for the community.

"Denge ain't like Dungeness, wi' strong men and decent boats. We've had bad luck wi' storms an' had our boats smashed up so they are only good for the fire. You know what bad luck breeds? More bad luck 'til most of us are gone to the grave or inland t' a new life. The rest of us cling on, doin' what we does to survive."

"What of the children?" Alice asked.

"What of the poor lil' blighters? Most of 'em don't live beyond a year and who can blame 'em? Who'd want t' live this life?"

Alice pondered on this, coming up with no satisfactory answer, so finally replied, "I don't know." She wondered how many children there were at Denge, not many she presumed. "Where do they go to school?"

"School?" the old woman cackled. "Do you think

114

we can waste time on school? Sometimes they have to walk miles t' collect enough wood for the fire or go inland t' steal a nice chicken for dinner. Denge people don't have the need for fancy learning, waste of time, tha's what it is."

"You never know what help it could be to read and write..." Alice began tentatively.

"So, they turn out fancy an' go off leaving me to fend for meself? No, you leave your teachin' for them the other side of the point." She took her gnarled hand from Alice's arm and stepped back. "You're no use to me, we'll find her though; we look after our own at Denge."

Alice took her chance to move on and soon the old hag was a wisp in the mist and then no longer visible. The familiar form of the lighthouse stood high, its top generating a weak light through the heavy skies, guiding her in the direction of home. From the lighthouse the curve of the nearby station roof was her next beacon and from there the train tracks led her back.

"You've left the door unlocked." Tom Barton stepped out as Alice rounded the corner of the building. "Anyone could have walked in."

Alice gave no reaction. Already she had become accustomed to the unexpected. "Perhaps a caller would have some manners and think to knock first," she snapped at him. "Besides, Hazel was here when I left." In the rectory, at home in Ashford, that place where life followed an orderly pattern, her Albert only ever came knocking by prior arrangement.

"She has gone to spend the afternoon with her family," Tom reminded her.

Alice looked towards the village homes, all completely hidden by the mist, and hoped Hazel would return before darkness settled over the headland. She had become accustomed to the company, and very much liked sharing her home with Hazel. As an only child, Alice wondered if this is what it was like to have a sister, or even a favourite cousin. Her gaze returned to Tom, and she said: "I assume you are coming in."

"I can knock first if you prefer," he retorted.

Alice heard the humour in his voice and smiled to herself as she pushed the door open. "I thought you might have brought your sister with you. It would have been the right thing to do." She removed her damp layers of shawl and coat, and placed them on the drying rack, then suggested that Tom do the same.

In the rectory, and indeed all homes where proper manners were in place, a young woman would never entertain a gentleman friend on her own. Even in the poorer families, the young couples went courting under the watchful eye of a sibling, or a maiden aunt. There was no chaperone in the schoolhouse, and Tom Barton understood Hazel was not at home. *He really should have brought his sister with him,* Alice thought, as she pushed the kettle onto the hotplate. *But there is no point in insisting that he leave as I'm sure he would refuse. Besides, he is here now, and I am in need of tea with some of Mrs Webb's fruit cake.*

Thoughts returned to her routines in Ashford and Alice wondered how she would feel if Albert were to surprise her as Tom had done. Perhaps to step out from behind the privet hedge and tell her he was taking her out for tea, or a walk by the River Stour. But they usually met for afternoon tea, under the watchful eye of her mother, who fussed over Albert, giving him the crispiest pastry or the softest piece of cake. Even her dear father, the gentle Reverend Tibbs, was relegated to second in favour when Albert came calling.

"I'm terribly hungry, it was quite a walk," Alice said. "Would you like some tea and cake?" Even as she said the words, regret crept in. It would have taken a matter

116

of minutes to retell the conversation she had taken with Ed Brooks. Now they would be forced to remain in each other's company for at least twenty minutes.

"Thank you, but why don't you sit down? You look tired," Tom replied. "I'll do it. Is the cake in the larder?"

"There's a tin..." Alice replied, as he opened the door. Frowning, she moved towards the teapot.

"I'll do it all," he said. "It's a hell of a trek over to Denge when the mist is like it is."

Confused, Alice sank into the chair. Albert had never made her a cup of tea, nor shown any concern over her well-being. In his home she had been served tea by his mother, and in her own home he had sipped from the china teacups provided by Mrs Tibbs, Alice or Mabel, the home help. *But Albert never sent you out in the mist to the home of a man who could well have been dangerous,* Alice scolded herself. *Albert had no need to fuss over you, for he never thought to treat your life with such disregard.* Nonetheless it would have been pleasant to think that occasionally, Albert would want to nurture her. His time to prove himself would come when they were married; there would be a home to decorate and furnish. Alice saw herself sewing curtains and Albert hanging wallpaper with a floral pattern. It would all be very pleasant.

With these thoughts running through her mind, Alice studied Tom and she couldn't help feeling rather perturbed whilst watching him warm the pot, slice the cake, and pour milk into a jug. She was so determined to despise him, and until now there had been no reason to feel otherwise.

"How was Ed Brooks?" Tom asked, when he sat at the kitchen table, although Alice remained in the armchair.

"He is destroyed," Alice told him. "He looks as if he has no more fight in him. And his home... it's like nothing I have ever seen before. It is both fishing hut

117

and a place to live, all in one room."

"The man has to be at his lowest," Tom replied. "Only then will he be prepared to do what is needed in order to take his wife home."

"What does he have to do?" Alice asked.

Tom took a bite of cake and appeared to ponder on the question before answering. "I can't tell you that. For your own safety. If he believes you know nothing, then you are safe."

"I hope so."

"It won't be long now. Emily is weak; she is not ready to go home, but at least her husband knows she is alive and safe."

The mist hung low over Dungeness for the next five days; a thick, damp, mass that rolled and twirled in the breeze. Unable to go to sea, fishermen were forced to leave their boats on the shingle beach and to stay bound to the land, making good use of their time by attending to necessary repairs to their nets, boats or cottages. As always, when there was bad fishing, there seemed to be a united melancholy which drew them to either the Britannia or Pilot, where they could down a few pints and lament on the lack of fresh fish at their tables and that they had nothing to trade with. Then by the Thursday, they sat beside their fires at home, no cash left in their pockets for the public houses.

Arriving at the school, children appeared like sprites through the mist. At the end of the day's lessons, they disappeared as they had arrived, into an eerie darkness. It was mid-November, and the days were becoming shorter. In the schoolhouse, neither Alice nor Hazel ventured out in the afternoons or evenings, instead they made small repairs to clothes, read books, and wrote letters. Alice was grateful for Hazel's company and although it irritated her to acknowledge it, also grateful to Tom Barton for making

118

the arrangement.

Whether they were teaching or relaxing in the schoolhouse, or whenever there was a quiet moment, the rhythmic sound of the fog trumpet carried across to them. It was the first thing Alice heard when she woke in the morning and the last thing she heard at night.

One evening, Alice wrote to Albert, certain this was the first of her three letters that he would receive.

"We could go to Lydd on Saturday," Hazel suggested. "We'll go on the train together, post your letter and go to a teashop if you fancy."

"That would be wonderful," replied Alice.

It may not be Ashford, and she knew Lydd to be a small town. However, it would have a church, shops and pavements, so that was good enough for Alice!

Dear Albert,

When this letter reaches you, I am sure you will be pleased to know, I am quite settled here at Dungeness, having been here two weeks. I do miss you, Mother and Father very much and hope this letter finds you all well.

The school is a good, sound building, with one class of mixed ages: boys and girls. I am very much enjoying the teaching and it is not so different from my own schooldays. I live in the schoolhouse, which is attached, and I have a teachers' assistant, named Hazel, who shares the accommodation with me. She really is a pleasant person and has become a very good friend to me. The headteacher is a Mrs Stubbs. She used to live here at the schoolhouse until she married a policeman from the nearby town of Lydd, where she now shares the police house with her new sister-in-law. Mrs Stubbs travels here daily by the local train which makes an unscheduled stop for her right outside the schoolhouse.

It is an unusual place, here at Dungeness, and not at all like the seaside towns we know, such as Hythe and Broadstairs. It is a shingle headland and the whole area is pebbles. There are no trees or flower gardens. I long for our country views and pretty walks through the water meadows. The people are mainly fishermen and their families, or those living and working at the lighthouse.

Next weekend, Hazel and I are going by train to Lydd, and I'll post this letter then. It's not a grand town like Ashford, but I shall enjoy the outing. In four weeks' time, I shall be home for the Christmas holiday break, which I am looking forward to very much. In the meantime, I will impatiently wait to receive letters from you all.

With my fondest thoughts, your Alice.

Dear Mother and Father,

I hope this letter finds you both in good health. I have met your friend, the vicar here at Dungeness, several times. His parish is quite different from your own, Father. He lives in a wooden single storey home, which is very snug with the range to heat it. The church is like nothing I have come across because it is not a building in its own right. During the week it is the school where I teach, and only on a Sunday, or for a funeral, is the curtain pulled back to reveal an altar and the room is rearranged for worship.

The school is also my home as there is teachers' accommodation attached. We have a living area, and two good-sized bedrooms. This is very fortunate and a blessing as a week ago my teaching assistant, Hazel, moved in. Her company is a comfort during the long evenings. The privy is outside, but I have become used to it. We have a daily help, Mrs Webb, who cooks a meal for the teachers, except for the weekends –

120

which is a good thing really as I do like to fend for myself some of the time.

The children are a cheerful lot. A little cheeky at times, but willing to learn. The lessons are like those from my own schooldays. The piano needs tuning and you would shudder to hear me play it! I am reading one of my favourites, Black Beauty, to the children.

At the weekend, I am going by train to Lydd, the closest town. This letter will be posted there and next time I'll be able to tell you about my visit.

With fondest love from your daughter,
Alice

Chapter Fourteen

Alice woke on Saturday morning feeling light-hearted at the prospect of an outing to Lydd. She had been living at Dungeness for two weeks, but it felt like two months, and she still had the long winter ahead of her. But of course, it was not just that she had been away from home for two weeks; it was as if she had been trapped here on the wastelands, so detached from everything she was used to. Was she being fanciful? Had she relished *Jane Eyre* so many times that she saw mystery where there was none? No, the horror of the body on the shingle and the letters home unsent were very real. Alice was living her own mystery story and she longed to escape it. A trip out was just what she needed and would raise her spirits for the coming week.

With an extra service running on a Saturday morning, they could leave on the quarter-past ten train, then return on the quarter-past two from Lydd. Four whole hours away, Alice's mind was full of the possible opportunities to be found in the town. But first there was washing to be done. With Hazel's help, she heated water, pummelled their clothes, and pulled them through the mangle in the outside shed. Finally, they pegged them on the line to dry in the brisk wind.

Alice decided to wear her smart boots when they set out for the railway station. Hazel laughed at her vanity, but then decided to follow suit! For Alice it was also a chance to wear her warm tweed skirt, a blouse with a lace collar and a cardigan rather than the severe black dress of a teacher. She added a seed pearl brooch and felt ready to explore the town.

"It's only Lydd," Hazel said, "Not somewhere fancy like Folkestone or Canterbury."

"I don't mind," Alice said, brushing her hair until it shone. "I'm just thrilled to be going out after being entombed in all this mist."

"Maybe we'll get a fringe cut for you," suggested Hazel. "Make your hair pretty, like that young woman we saw. You remember the one with the red hair?"

Alice did remember, of course. She had little else to think of whilst the mist hung heavy in the air. A plan was forming to contact Emily, but that was for another time. Today was a time for having fun, exploring a new place, and allowing the tension to ease from her body.

The little tank engine came backwards into the station. It pulled one coach and only one person alighted. For the people of Dungeness this ten-fifteen departure was an ideal time to visit the shops, friends or family in Lydd, New Romney or further afield. There were several people waiting to step into the coach; Alice and Hazel found themselves sitting with an old woman who clutched a sturdy shopping basket.

The whistle blew and almost simultaneously the engine gave the first turns of its huge heavy wheels; the coach lurched forward, and they were on their way, being pushed rather than pulled by the robust engine. By the time they passed the school, the train was picking up speed. Alice was curious to see everything she had missed on the day she arrived. This time the sky was clear and windows free from condensation.

The train clattered along with the familiar bump and click as it passed over the joins in the track, Alice noticed that the vegetation increased but the ground was clearly still shingle. She first noticed brown fields

123

in the distance to her left and then, as the engine progressed, the freshly turned furrows of farmland reached the trackside. Finally, when the chimneys on the buildings and the pinnacles on the church tower were clear for her to see, the railway track itself was flanked by fields on both sides. The train slowed as the orange brick station buildings came into view, finally grinding to a halt before most of the passengers alighted, pausing for a moment to reacquaint themselves with their surroundings.

For Alice this was her first view of Lydd; she could hardly include the distorted images seen through the misted window on the day of her arrival. It was a pleasant enough station, just as one would expect for a small rural town. The station staff were smart, and the area looked to be well cared for.

"I'll show you the town," Hazel said, as she led the way out and onto the main road. "It's no distance at all."

Keeping the tall church tower to their right, Hazel led Alice first to a green known as The Rype. It was an odd sort of place, rather vast for a village or town green with a sparse covering of grass and some stunted pine trees. Houses surrounded the area: terraces and individual homes, including a few attractive properties which looked to be quite old. They walked part way along The Rype and then crossed it by using one of many tracks. Children played in groups with balls and hoops, and Alice conceded that it made a wonderful playground for them.

When they sat down for lunch at The George Hotel two hours later, Alice was self-consciously displaying soft curls framing her face, and tickling her forehead.

"You can twist your hair in rags at night and you'll have lovely curls in the morning," Hazel advised.

"I've never had it like this before," Alice's fingers

explored the curls. "It will take a little getting used to, but I can still put grips in to hold it back when I'm teaching."

"That pretty hair grip you bought will do nicely."

Alice opened her handbag and took out the silver clip with a flower head enamelled in blue and cream. "It is lovely; I'll wear it tomorrow."

They decided to treat themselves to a roast dinner. "Look at this!" Hazel exclaimed as the waitress approached with steaming plates. "Mutton!" So much of her diet consisted of fish, and she lifted her cutlery immediately.

Used to the routines of the Tibbs household, Alice silently thanked the Lord for the meal in front of her, and for the opportunity to be sitting in this fine room with its high ceiling, elegant sash windows and roaring fire.

They ate in silence, so engrossed in the rare treat that had been served. After their plates had been cleared of the very last morsel, Hazel asked, "Are you going to have another cider?" as she drained her half-pint glass.

"Oh no, I never... I mean I wouldn't usually have even the one. A cup of tea would be perfect."

"A pot of tea and fruit pie for two," Hazel said as the waitress approached.

"Very well, madam," the young woman replied.

"Listen to that," Hazel whispered as the waitress moved away. "She called me madam and she must be a year older than me!"

Alice smiled. It was good to be somewhere new and having fun. They had already seen the church, which was large and boasted an interesting piece of wall dating back to Roman times. It was the longest church in Kent, Hazel had explained before pointing out the tall tower. From the church to its grounds, a search for the grave of the unknown woman found on the beach, gave the young women a chance to contemplate her fate. Then they had explored the shops, spending time looking through the ribbons, jewellery and other fineries, before Alice bought her hairclip and Hazel treated herself to a brooch. For Alice, the highlight of the day was finally to be able to post letters to her parents and Albert from the town's post office. The roast dinner made a fine ending to a wonderful time in the town.

"Lydd, Lydd. All alight for Lydd. Next stop Dungeness," the station master called out as the train eased to a stop alongside the platform. Doors were flung open and passengers alighted, many of them in their best clothes, having been on a rare trip to Ashford. Porters stood to attention by their trolleys.

Alice and Hazel stepped into the coach. They were joined by another five or six women, all with shopping baskets bursting with the luxuries to be found in the town, making it a bit of a tight squeeze on the bench type seats. One of the passengers was Peggy Webb.

"I got a nice bit o' beef," a woman called across the aisle.

"Did you now, my Bert he asked for bacon, he did; I've got a joint to roast for tomorrow, we'll have it cold on Monday and the rest in a soup with split peas." This was one of the lighthouse keepers' wives; they lived in one of the houses circling the base of the tall building.

"I've got mutton, a big ol' bit as it's got to do the teachers as well," Peggy Webb nodded towards Alice and Hazel. "I'm cookin' for three of 'em now. I'll cook it at my place tomorrow then mince it for Monday, then a bit o' smoked bacon on Tuesday, after that it's fish for the week."

"That sounds lovely, Mrs Webb," Alice said. She had decided to revert to addressing the daily help in a formal manner.

"You've had your hair done different," Mrs Webb

126

suddenly announced, causing everyone to turn in their seats to stare at the young teacher.

"Yes… well, yes, just a little different." Alice looked down at her hands in her lap and twisted her engagement ring.

A few minutes later and they were passing the school. Alice reflected on how close she had been to her new home and place of work, just two weeks before, and not even noticed it through the driving rain.

"Are you liking teaching here, in our school?" asked a middle-aged woman, the landlady of The Britannia public house.

"Yes, very much." Alice replied, as they approached Dungeness Station. "I like it very much indeed."

Quite a crowd of them got off the train, pausing to slip on their backstays, with baskets and bags at their feet. It was Peggy Webb with those sharp eyes of hers who first noticed the people collected beyond the lighthouse.

"There's a fair gathering over there." She paused waiting for the others to look up. "I don't see no reason why anyone would be wanting to get together over there on the point unless…"

"You're right, Peg. We'd best go an' see what's been going on while we've been out enjoyin' ourselves." The landlady from the Britannia stepped down from the station platform, "If there's been trouble then you can be sure I'll be busy behind the bar tonight."

"You're right there." Peggy was at her heels. "We'll want to meet and talk it through."

The two young women followed in the wake of the older women. They didn't speak to one another, but the feeling of apprehension in the pit of Alice's stomach foretold another tragedy. By the time they reached the point, it was clear to see there was a circle of people around something... or someone. Peggy and the landlady had managed to push their way in amongst the crowd; Alice and Hazel could only stand at the perimeter. Their view was compromised: a patch of dark grey cloth, a glimpse of tweed, the tassel fringe of a shawl.

"Do you think it's another...?" Hazel whispered to Alice.

"I really don't know." Alice didn't want to assume. How could it be possible that there was now a third body in a matter of two weeks? She moved a little, but there was no more to be seen.

"Well, who is it then?" Peggy Webb asked, her voice carried through the crowd.

Who is it? The words echoed in Alice's head. *Who is it? Surely not another...*

"We don't know," Bess Stevens replied. "But it looks like she has been here for a while and she's not been swept up from the sea, not all the way up here on the bank.

"Unless she was alive and climbed up here, looking for help," someone else suggested.

"I've been walking straight past here these last few days," Mr Stevens said. "But the mist was heavy, and I only walked from lighthouse to fog trumpet. She's in a dip you see, so even on a good day, if I wasn't looking in that direction..."

"Has someone gone for the vicar?" Alice asked, finding her voice from somewhere.

It was at that point the tight circle shifted as they turned towards Alice, giving her a clearer view of the body.

"Yes, I sent my Victoria and Bill." Bess moved towards Alice, and placed a hand on her arm, sensing this was a shock for the young woman.

"But I think..." Alice took a step forward. "I think I

128

know who she is."

Incredulous that the new teacher could possibly identify the body laid sprawled upon the shingle, they stepped aside allowing her to move forward.

"It's a woman from Denge." Alice looked down at the bundle of ragged skirt and tatty shawl. There was something about the way she lay... something about her leg... yes, that was it, she must have fallen and broken her leg or hip because her body was twisted at an odd angle. The gnarled, brown-skinned hand was still clutching at her shawl, the wizened face and the tiny body with the hunched back – yes, this was the old hag who had followed Alice from Denge when the sea mist blanketed the land.

Alice could feel her head spinning and the words forming could no longer be expressed. She was encircled by a blur and everything went into slow motion. Bess Stevens had been watching her closely and was there to break her fall. And then others were holding her too and lowering her to the ground.

"Can someone cover the body?" Mr Stevens ordered, his voice breaking into Alice's consciousness. His tone commanded action.

The next thing Alice became aware of was Bess and Hazel on either side of her, supporting her as she sat on the shingle ridge.

"I'm sorry," Alice said.

"Don't say another word, dear." Bess was rubbing Alice's hands, presumably concerned she would become chilled after the shock.

So, Alice sat, huddled up, looking at the figure covered with the old woman's own shawl. Within a few minutes there was movement to her left and she turned to see the vicar, who was almost with them. He was escorted by young Victoria and Bill Stevens. Also joining the party was Tom Barton and another man, whom Alice recognised but didn't know his name. They

129

were carrying a ladder.

The vicar knelt beside the lifeless form of the old woman and said a short prayer. The heads of the onlookers were bowed, and they fell silent. Then, with help from Tom Barton, he rose to his feet and said: "Oh dear, this is unexpected, what a shame, what a sad day indeed it is."

"Miss Tibbs knows who she is," someone announced.

Again, all eyes were on Alice, who really felt she should be standing, but couldn't quite manage.

"I… yes… she is from Denge. I met her just a few days before."

"Well Miss Tibbs, then you must help me tell her family as you are acquainted." The vicar smiled with relief. "The men will carry her back home and we'll have to break the sad news."

"I don't even know her name," Alice replied, as she visualised the woman clawing at her arm, having pursued her from Denge. "I met her, that's all… I met her briefly in Denge and then later out here on the point. She is the aunt of the young woman who is missing. Emily Brooks. Her husband was looking for her last week."

There were murmurs of acknowledgement. Did they know, Alice wondered, did they know it was because they held Emily that the woman was dead? She had followed the young teacher back through the mist to try to learn where her niece might be and must have fallen after they parted. Perhaps Alice had still been a short distance away, but the mist muffled sounds and walking on the shingle was noisy. It may well have been that she had called out for help and not been heard.

"She was here looking for her niece and that is why she is dead." Alice's voice rang out loud and clear. Now they were all silent and she knew every one of

130

them, possibly excepting the vicar, realised the woman was dead because they had taken her niece. They were aware that they were to blame for the old woman's death. But as to the reason why they held Emily – this remained a mystery to Alice.

Tom Barton was the first to speak, "We'll get on with carrying her back to Denge then."

"And Miss Tibbs will come back to the cottage with me," Bess said. "She's just fainted and not fit to be walking out there and back again. A cup of tea by my fire and then these young women can walk back to the schoolhouse."

"Quite right, Mrs Stevens. Poor Miss Tibbs, we must look after you." The vicar nodded frantically.

As the onlookers turned their back on the dip within the shingle ridges, the frail body was placed upon the ladder. It was lifted with ease and so the small procession made its way towards Denge: two men with the make-shift stretcher, and the vicar in their wake.

Chapter Fifteen

All talk of how Alice had met the old woman of Denge was thoroughly exhausted between the three women – Alice, Bess and Hazel – while drinking tea at Bess Stevens' home. Alice told her friends how she had been walking on the point when the woman had appeared through the mist and begged her to help find her niece. She recounted the conversation, and how she had insisted there was nothing to tell of the missing woman's whereabouts and, as that was all that could be said, they parted. What had happened next was pure speculation, and no doubt would be the talk of the village for days.

"I can't bear to think about it, or speak of it anymore," Alice said, as she and Hazel walked back to the schoolhouse, exhausted and subdued. "There's the ironing to be done, and then I shall read a book and doze by the range, with a blanket over my knees."

If Hazel was amused by such an image, then she said nothing, knowing her friend to be in need of time to rest after the shock of that afternoon's discovery.

The young women absorbed themselves with the work of bringing in the dry washing and started on the laborious business of ironing the mound of clothes. The curtains were closed tight, and they were cocooned in the peaceful atmosphere of their own world for the evening. Bread toasted with cheese followed the ironing, and it was while they were washing up that there came a loud knock on the door, shattering the tranquillity. Alice was half expecting it; she knew matters would not rest since she had seen the body of Emily on the shingle and others would be compelled to draw her into their plot. The new body added a further twist to the tale.

"There's to be a meeting at the vicar's house and my brother says you are to come." Lucie Barton blurted out as soon as the door was opened. "The vicar says so too. You were the last to see her."

Lucie Barton didn't ask; there was an expectation on Alice to do whatever Tom Barton ordered. It was as if she were nothing but a pawn in a game where the fishermen, lighthouse keepers, and their wives were the all-powerful playing pieces. If that were so, then Tom was the king on the chess board.

"I'll get my coat." Alice turned to Hazel, "The vicar is wanting to see me as I was the last person to see the woman. I'll go over now and be back within the hour I hope."

It was midnight-black, with a million tiny diamonds shining brightly in the sky. The air was biting cold with a strong smell of ozone snapping at Alice's nostrils. She felt a great deal of antipathy towards Tom Barton's sister, and this irritated her as there was no real reason. Lucie Barton was merely a messenger, just as Alice had been last week when she went to Denge. Alice wasn't inclined to speak, and Lucie made no attempt either, so they moved across the stones in silence.

They neared the Britannia and could hear voices raised as the topics of the day were discussed. Unlike the cottages, the windows were neither curtained nor shuttered, leaving a warm glow passing through the discoloured panes of glass. Alice could see the shapes of figures within. Then, stopping at the vicarage, they propped their backstays against the shiplap wall, where they joined another three pairs of the flat

133

wooden boards.

Lucie raised the latch and opened the door. They stepped into a stifling heat scented with the pungent smell of burning wood, enriched with overtones of ale, sweet sherry and tobacco smoke. Alice tried to welcome the heat but longed to leave the door thrown open and breathe fresh, cool air. Four pairs of eyes turned towards the newcomers, but it was only the elderly vicar who raised himself from his armchair to welcome the young women.

"Ah, Miss Barton and Miss Tibbs, come to discuss this poor woman from Denge," he said. "How kind, how very kind indeed. We have two chairs ready for you, and a sherry... you'll have a sweet sherry?"

They nodded, although Alice would have preferred a cup of tea. She knew she must take small sips if she were to stay in control. As they sat in the spare upright chairs, the six of them formed a circle with the book-laden side tables between them. *What do they know*, she wondered? *Do they all have the full story, or do they each know a part of it? And what do they want with me now, because I'm certain this has little to do with the dead woman – the most recently dead woman – and more about Emily Brooks.*

"Miss Tibbs, Connie and Ben Webb." Tom Barton made the introductions.

Alice smiled weakly and clutched at the stem of her sherry glass. "You're related to Mrs Webb, my daily help?"

"She's my aunt by marriage," Ben Webb replied. He was a man in his mid-thirties, with light brown hair already greying, and a muscular frame. His face was pleasant enough and it didn't appear that he was here to make life uncomfortable for Alice. His wife, Connie, appeared tired; there were fine lines around her eyes and mouth. She yawned and pulled her shawl tight around her, although the heat from the range was stifling.

"You said, Miss Tibbs, that the poor woman, God rest her soul, was looking for her niece. So sad she was worried about her when I have just learned that Mr and Mrs Webb here have been looking after poor Mrs Brooks who has been very sick." The vicar summed up what he knew.

He didn't know about Emily before, Alice concluded. *Of course, he couldn't be trusted. He is so forgetful. Yet now he has become a part of this drama.*

"How very kind of them to care for her." Alice played her part as expected. "I do hope she is fully recovered."

No one replied to this and it was Tom Barton who spoke next: "It's time to return Emily Brooks to Denge but not before we've had a little chat with her husband and got him to see the error of his ways."

"May I ask what he has done?" Alice enquired. "He lives in a one-room shack with an open fire and boarded up windows. What crime has he committed to lead to his wife being kept from him for two weeks?"

"Murder." Tom Barton's reply came with no embellishment.

"Murder?" Alice repeated, her throat tightening and mouth dry. She took a sip of the sherry, "He has a temper, but murder? Who?"

"Not so much going out and killing with a knife or a musket," Ben Webb informed. "But it's murder nonetheless when you go out in an attempt to stop the lifeboat men from doing their jobs and that causes lives to be lost, which could have been saved."

"It's murder if you push a captain or one of the crew overboard when they try to stop you getting at their cargo." Tom Barton looked straight at Alice as if challenging her to disagree.

Alice felt horror ripping through her body and shivered despite the stifling heat in the vicarage. "What

135

is he then, this Ed Brooks? A wrecker or a smuggler?"

"Now, don't go getting smuggling confused with wrecking. For all your education you maybe don't understand that smuggling isn't theft and there's no need for anyone to get hurt. No, a smuggler is an honest man who takes nothing but a bit o' tax from those that have more than enough money in their silk-lined purses. No, we are not talkin' about smuggling and not wrecking either..." Ben Webb paused for effect, "We're talkin' about landing on boats in trouble, boats who have sent a signal for help, and going along and helping themselves to a little of what the captain and his crew can't take care of whilst they are fighting for their lives."

"Piracy?" Alice whispered.

"Not them pirates from your story books, but similar, yes. Just sitting around, watching and waiting, then out they go on their little boats and heave to alongside."

"Ed Brooks does this on his own?" Alice asked.

"Him and his no-good cousin, Jake Brooks." Tom replied, "They are all at it though, watching and waiting and now it looks like they take the women too, if they are fit enough. Why else was that wife of his washed up on the beach?"

"I've been to Denge," Alice said, "and it's a desperate place. They live in one room hovels; the children don't go to school but spend their days scavenging for firewood and food."

"There's no excuse for murder," Tom snapped.

"No, I just... I just mean to say that they have been pushed to take desperate measures to feed their families."

"They know the tides and the currents, especially round the point. Where one ship may be floundering, it's nothing to them to put out a little boat and pull up alongside. There's no one tougher hereabouts than those Brooks cousins." Ben told it so Alice could see it all: the floundering ships and the ruthless pirates circling, waiting to go in for their loot.

"What do they get from a ship in trouble, two men and a small boat?" Alice was curious, thinking of their hovels and realising that whatever they did scavenge, it was not leading to any great comfort in their lives.

"A sack of grain, a thick coat or a blanket is enough for them to push a sailor overboard. They are not expecting money or jewels; those rats will settle for anything." Ben Webb paused for a slug of ale, "A life for a cask of ale or a bale of wool, it's not right."

"They make it harder for the lifeboat crews," the bitterness in Tom's voice was clear. "The boat in danger might think they are coming to save them, or we've had them blocking our path, trying to get away as we arrive. Ed and Jake only go for a boat that they can get to, before we or the Rye crew reach it."

"She's not a bad lass, that Emily," Connie Webb added. "She just got caught up with a nasty lot."

"Emily was out there, the night when I arrived and the lifeboat had been called," Alice reflected. "What was she doing? Helping them? She went overboard, I presume, and nearly drowned. Then ended up here at Dungeness… half-dead she was, and you cared for her, but why? Why not take her back for them to look after? Why care if she lived or died?"

"She were left to control the boat that night," Connie said. "They needed all the help they could get and, with her on board, that gave Ed and Jake the chance to take over the troubled ship. They can't go leaving their boat all alone. Stands to reason they needed more help."

"There's one good thing about Ed Brooks – he loves that woman with a passion," Tom Barton said. "She may be the one to set him straight."

"Or if she's kept from him for long enough, he may

137

well agree to anything to get her back," Alice concluded.

All this time the vicar had been dozing in his chair. Alice wondered what went on in his confused mind. As a man of the cloth, did he condone the kidnapping? For that was what it was, whatever the circumstances. She suspected, from what was said earlier, that he liked to believe they were doing no more than helping the half-drowned woman.

The small group had fallen silent for a moment, reflecting on the words said and opinions raised. It was then that the vicar spoke with unusual clarity:

"Young Mr Barton, it seems as if you are the one to go to that pitiful place and see this Mr Brooks. I fear that our Mr Webb is a little too angry to resolve this. Of course, Miss Tibbs must go too. Her presence will keep Mr Brooks calm, I am sure."

"I really don't see…" Alice began.

"Of course, you don't my dear." The old man looked over the top of his glasses at her. "But you are doing splendidly and are fast becoming one of us."

"Very well, I'll go to Denge with Mr Barton." Alice was becoming resigned to life becoming unpredictable.

Tom rose to his feet. "We'll be off to see this Ed Brooks then, and if he sees sense and pledges to stop robbing innocent people, then I'll bring him back to see his wife." He was fastening his overcoat and then pulling a hat on snug over his ears.

"We'll be seeing you shortly," Ben Webb said. "But it will be Emily who decides if she's fit to travel back to Denge, and only when he agrees to mend his ways."

"Fair enough," Tom replied.

With those parting words, Tom and Alice stepped out into the sharp evening air, pushed boots into backstays and started the short journey to the west of the point. They didn't speak for a while, other than for

Tom to point out an obstacle in the path or to check Alice was comfortable with the pace. As the air was clear, there was no need to follow the coast, so they passed the inland side of the lighthouse and then on to Denge.

"You got your letter posted?" Tom asked as the hovels of Denge came into focus.

"At the post office in Lydd," Alice confirmed. She didn't feel inclined to speak any further about the matter; she believed it was due to him or others like him that the first letters had not been sent.

Then they were nearly there. Alice could see the first building she had knocked at on her previous visit, that of the dead woman. It now stood empty, without light or smoke from a fire. Behind it was the small home belonging to Ed and Emily Brooks; at first it too seemed deserted but then Alice's attention was drawn to a grey trail of smoke coming from the chimney.

"It's this one," Alice said.

Tom rapped hard on the door. The scrape of a chair being pushed back, and a shuffling noise could be heard and then Ed Brooks was at the door. Through the half-open doorway, the stench of the fishing net, wood-smoke and unwashed body wafted out – a sharp contrast to the frosty fresh air. It was Ed who spoke first:

"Oh, it's you, Tom Barton, and that teacher who should know better than to get mixed up in Denge business. Haven't we had enough grief for one day, with Aunt Ida lying stiff in her home?"

"We have. Miss Tibbs and I are here to put an end to it. There's been enough death hereabouts recently and we've come to see if you are ready to talk sense."

"And Emily?"

"She can come back so long as you are ready to put an end to your thieving ways."

"So, you're here to barter, are you?" Ed snarled. "You'd best come in an' say your piece."

They stepped into the hovel. There was no welcoming warmth from the weak fire and again it was the only light in the room. The nets were dry, Alice noticed. Of course, with all the recent mist the fishing boats had been grounded for days. The Dungeness fleet would have been out as soon as the mist lifted, she was sure of that. Whereas it seemed that Mr Brooks had not bothered to stir himself.

"I've been talking to my cousin, Jake, and we'll not stand for Emily bein' kept any longer." Ed Brooks remained standing and didn't invite his guests to sit at the table which had a coating of crumbs and spilled ale or tea.

"Your wife is much stronger now, maybe fit enough to travel home," Tom informed him.

"I'll come an' get her then." He took a step towards the door.

"Ready to come home *when* you've agreed to stop your pirating, you and your cousin."

Ed shook his mop of greasy black hair and eyes showed disgust. "Pirating? You and your tales, Tom Barton, where's me pile of gold an' casks o' brandy?"

"It doesn't have to be gold," Alice spoke quietly, but both men turned to take notice. "If you go out and steal from ships who are in danger, if you pull up alongside them and take what you can while they fight for their lives, then it's stealing and stealing in a most horrible and heartless way."

"I have to feed my family an' the old folk here," Ed Brooks replied with a little less fight than before.

"So, you'll push a sailor overboard or sail past someone floundering in the sea, for a few coins, an overcoat or pair of boots. Maybe just for the food from their table?" Tom replied. He stood as tall as Ed Brooks, but his manner was a little milder. "Around the

140

point we have two boats for going out and saving lives, and there's another at Rye Harbour. Here at Denge you and your cousin have a boat for robbing."

"I do it for the family. It's not much but it makes a difference. I've got a boat that I share with Jake and the two of us can't provide for everyone here. Sometimes we can't go fishing for days, or weeks. You know how it is. The others are getting too old and their boats are rotting as we speak." Ed kicked at the floor. "This isn't bringing my Emily home. You've said your piece, now I want my wife."

"You'll stop this robbing and your cousin Jake too," Tom said. "Then Emily can come home, although I suggest you tidy the place up first."

"I thought there'd be a deal to be done and I'll do anything for my Emily, but it will mean telling her that we'll have to leave the coast and head inland for work."

"Very well, Mr Brooks," Alice said. "You may come and collect your wife, but I suggest you have a good wash and change into some cleaner clothes. Shall we expect to see you in the morning?"

"I'll be there within the hour," came the snarl of a reply.

"We'll be at Ben Webb's house," Tom said, as they left.

Chapter Sixteen

Emily Brooks was just as Alice had imagined her. She had seen her before, of course, but only as the fleeting beam of light had shone on her bedraggled body. Lying there, as if she were dead, Alice had barely registered Emily's existence before someone, presumably Ben Webb, had scooped her up from her bed of stones and tangled rope. A week later she had seen the glow of auburn hair in the distance and was sure it was the same woman.

Now, here she was, Emily Brooks, sitting in the corner of the living room in the Webb's cottage. Her beautiful hair was tied back in a thick plait and coiled at the base of her slender neck. Grey eyes were in shadowed sockets and her face was pale; she looked haunted and weary. Her hands cradled a cup of tea and she sat with a thick shawl around her shoulders, despite the warmth from the range.

Alice smiled when they were introduced, but guilt settled uneasily in her stomach. Did Emily recognise her as the person who could have rescued her, but instead hid and allowed her to be taken? Alice wanted to explain, to say that she was new here herself, and scared... too scared to help. It was not the time for explanations, or excuses. How many times had she wished that she had stayed to see if the young woman was dead or alive?

"Your husband will be here within the hour, he says," Connie bent low to hear the whispered reply for it seemed she was the only person Emily trusted enough to speak with. "He wanted to tidy himself up first, you know what men are like, they let things slip if we are not about to care for them."

"He has missed you terribly," Alice volunteered.

The large grey eyes just looked at Alice and then down at the tea. The two men: Ben and Tom, sat together at the plain dark wooden table; they spoke quietly and supped at tankards of ale. The women sat in the armchairs.

Connie spoke to Alice about her teaching, the weather, and the visit to Lydd earlier that day. It hardly seemed possible that only six hours before, Alice and Hazel had been eating roast mutton at The George Inn and life had seemed a little more carefree. They tried to include Emily in their conversation, asking if she had been to Lydd recently or what her own memories were of the little school amongst the shingle. Emily nodded or whispered the occasional comment which could only be heard by Connie. She held her shawl tight as if to cocoon herself.

All the time they sat and talked, the foremost thought in everyone's mind was that Ed Brooks would soon be with them. Finally, within the hour, there was a knock on the door and Ben Webb answered it.

"You'd better come in."

He only had eyes for his Emily, that big angry man whose eyebrows were permanently knotted in a frown. In a couple of steps, he was kneeling at her feet, his hands in hers, gazing up into her face. Then he wrapped his big bear arms around her slender body, and she began to cry. Finally, Ed sat on a stool beside his wife, still holding her hand, while she dried her tears on her shawl.

"She's been weak, with a temperature and a chill all at once," Connie began to speak gently. "She was battered and bruised, but it's fading now. It's her spirits

I worry about though: she's lost the baby and is all shaken up..."

"The baby? I didn't know." Ed looked at his wife's face, but her eyelids were lowered.

"I couldn't tell... I couldn't. How were we to manage?" Her voice was soft, and she forced her gaze to meet his. They sat in silence for a moment.

"I'd never have let you take the boat, had I known," Ed began. "I'm sorry, I hadn't realised. I didn't know."

"She's been sitting out the back on good days," Connie said. "Well wrapped up but a bit of sunshine does the power of good."

"There's to be no more robbing," Ed told his wife. "I don't know how we'll manage, but maybe I'll look for work in Lydd. We'll put all that other stuff behind us, Jake too. We'll move away and I'll get us a nice house and I'll find a job..."

"I can't stop thinking about it, Ed, that boat over Rye way last summer. It had grounded itself on a sandbank, and then you boarded it – you an' Jake – and the captain, he put up a fight, an' then he was overboard and swimming towards me. I had to turn about, I could have saved him, but then it might have been me overboard. I watched him die, Ed."

"I know, love. I know, but I did it for us and the others at Denge."

"What did you get for a man's life?" Ben Webb called across the room.

"Come on, Ben, we've got to move on from this," Tom said. "Let Emily say her piece and we'll leave it at that."

Emily's eyes filled with tears again. Her husband looked at a loss as to how to comfort her. He sat on the stool at her side, looking at his good black boots – the captain's boots – and didn't have the words to tell her how he'd provide for her and keep her safe.

"Tom's right, love." Connie spoke gently, "We need

to get you well and back home with your husband."

"I love him, but he's not my husband," Emily blurted out. "How could we afford to get married? It's a blessing that the baby wasn't to be born illegitimate, God rest its soul. He's a good man." She looked now at Ben Webb, "He's a good man really, Mr Webb, but I don't want to go back there, not back to Denge."

Silence fell upon the room; Ed Brooks sat with his head in his hands and Emily had pulled the protective shawl tighter around her body. Alice could only think of the double box-bed that ran along one side of the Brooks' hovel and she could not imagine what sinful intimacies might have taken place there. The two men at the table looked uncomfortable after the outburst; this was women's business and it was getting complicated. Everyone waited for Connie to deal with the latest revelation.

"It's getting late and Emily needs her rest." She stood and bent down to take Emily's arm. "Come on now, this isn't helping you get better. We can talk about it tomorrow or whenever you feel ready."

Emily pulled herself up and looking at Ed she said, "Thank you for coming, I'm sorry I can't go home yet."

The big man with the shock of dark hair just looked at his love and, as she left the room, he stood too, walked across the room, opened the door and was gone into the night.

Alice didn't pause to ask the others what should be done. She felt the man's grief and had no doubt of his love for Emily. He had shown he had a temper but when it came to the woman he called his wife, there was nothing but tenderness. Alice was out of the door and before he had taken many long strides, she was calling after him.

"Mr Brooks, Ed, wait a moment… please."

He turned and waited for her to catch up.

"It is late, and Emily is tired. Remember how ill she

has been, she looks tired and weak. I've not met her before, but I imagine she was strong and plucky before."

"She was, but I'd nurse her back to health if only she'd let me."

"She loves you," Alice persisted. "Give her time and show her that a life in Denge is worth coming back to. You can visit her now you know where she is. But in the meantime, go out early tomorrow and catch some fish for the others that need you at Denge. In the late afternoon, I'll call on you and together we can make plans to bring Emily home."

"You're right," Ed replied, "I've not thought of anyone, my head has been so filled with my own worries. Now I've seen her, I'll clean myself up and get the home good and tidy. and show her that I mean well by her."

"You could do with a friend to help. I'll be with you Sunday afternoon."

"I never thought I'd be needing a teacher for a friend!" A smile broke through, he turned and was gone.

Alice turned back to the Webb's cottage. Inwardly, she felt pleased that she had made a positive connection with Ed and knew her parents would be proud to know she had gone out of her way to help a fellow human being, especially one so desperately in need of help. And then the moment of pleasant reflection changed to one of melancholy. Alice felt weary and overcome by the urgent desire to be back in the comfort of the schoolhouse. She hoped Hazel had put a warmed brick in her bed.

But first, she would be expected to report back. Opening the door of the cottage, she closed it behind her, but remained standing in the doorway. It was just Tom and Ben there, still sitting at the table.

"I said to him that he needs to get out on his boat

146

before low tide in the morning. He needs to make an effort, so she'll want to come home. I'll go over to see him later and see what can be done to make the place more respectable for Emily."

"That was good of you," Tom replied.

"I'm going now," Alice told them. "I'm tired."

She couldn't simply cut across the shingle, like the school children did; she wasn't familiar enough with the terrain to negotiate it at night. It was back to the lighthouse and then the railway station before finding the tracks leading her home.

"Friends and neighbours. As we gather here today, we give thanks for our own health and the good harvest of fish that has blessed our fishermen in the last few days, but we must also pray for one that is less fortunate." The vicar leant upon the side of the pulpit and closed his eyes before beginning the prayer. "Dear Lord, we pray for our neighbour, Ida Thomson, that she may have a smooth journey to the afterlife and bask in the light of your care. May her family and friends turn to you in their grief and find comfort from their faith. Amen."

The small congregation muttered their response. Then without further announcement the vicar launched into *Abide with Me*, surprising the old fisherman at the piano, who struggled to keep pace.

Sunday morning had come too quickly for Alice, after a restless night pondering the fate of Ed and Emily Brooks. She was relieved when the church service was over and quickly moved through the connecting door rather than make conversation with the curious locals. It would all be about the body of Ida Thomson and how Alice had been the last to see her. She wasn't going to go through it all again, a cup of tea and a couple of chapters of *Northanger Abbey* would suit her far better. Hazel had gone to spend the rest

147

of the day with her family and so Alice settled down to read.

After her midday meal, Alice gathered a basket and filled it with soap, a scrubbing brush and various cloths. She wrapped half a fruit cake, added a few of the apples from Mrs Stubbs' garden and a jar of jam. A large apron was taken from a hook on the wall and placed on the top of the basket. She set off across the shingle at a fair pace.

On reaching the point, Alice could see some activity at Denge. It seemed that the people who lived there had come out of their winter hibernation. Although the only fair-sized fishing boat was now up on the beach, it was clear it had been out on the early morning tide. A small group of three children and a couple of elderly women were sorting through the catch, tossing some aside and keeping others. The men, Ed and presumably Jake, were pulling out the huge net and placing it over the shingle. A young woman and a toddler picked off bits of seaweed.

Ed looked up and on seeing Alice he moved away from the others. "Good day, Miss Tibbs. We've got some cod an' a bit o' pollock. Enough to feed us lot for a few days an' some to be smoked. If we do as well tomorrow there'll be enough spare to take into Lydd."

"Wonderful. Was it dreadfully cold out there?"

"It usually is!" Ed grinned at her. "Our Helen, that's Jake's wife over there, she said we should put the net in with Ida, it's not like she'll be minding."

"In with Ida?" Alice was confused.

"We'll set up some hooks an' use her place as a net store. We don't need it for anything else."

Alice could see this was an excellent plan, to remove the nets from hanging in his home would make a big difference, reducing the fishy smell and giving much-needed space. There was something different about Ed too, his beard had been trimmed, not

148

professionally but it was shorter and smarter.

Ed saw her looking and said, "Helen did it, gave me hair a tidy up." He removed his woollen hat and showed a shorter, if not neater, head of black curls.

"We had better get on then," Alice indicated towards her basket. Then she looked towards the industry on the beach. "Shall I make a start if you are needed here?"

"No," he replied firmly. "When you go back, I want you to tell Emily that I helped tidy up and that I'm doing my best to make this place the home she deserves."

Two hours later, the iron hooks had been removed from the ceiling beam and all traces of seaweed and debris fallen from the nets had been swept and scrubbed from the floor, ceiling and boards across the window. The whole floor had been washed and the rag rug had been taken outside and vigorously beaten.

There was a fair collection of driftwood logs in a small shed and Alice found a basket, in need of repair but useful to put beside the hearth for the logs. The food cupboards were almost bare, but all food was taken out, checked for insect life and returned to a clean shelf.

When Alice left, she took with her two blankets, which she was determined to wash and dry, despite the short days and frequent mist. She told Ed she would wash two a week, at the same time suggesting that he made the same effort with his own clothes. He meekly agreed to all her demands.

Dear Mother,

I hope this letter finds you and Father in good health. I trust all is well in the parish. These are trying times for the needy as winter sets in.

I have become involved with a family from the next hamlet, just a short way from Dungeness, and have been helping spruce up their simple home. They are

149

poor, relying on two men and one fishing boat to feed and support both their extended families. The wife of one, her name is Emily, has been ill and is being cared for by people in Dungeness. In order to bring her back, I have been busy helping to make improvements to her home, which is little more than a shack, and can only pray my endeavours will raise her spirits.

I was thinking of the blue curtains we had hanging in our dining room. They were very faded from the sun but could be taken apart and re-stitched to fit the much smaller windows. Would you be so kind as to ask Martha to pack them up for me? If you had any spare sheets, they would also be very welcome.

I will sign off now and look forward to seeing you within a couple of weeks when I return for Christmas.

Much love, Alice.

Chapter Seventeen

"I saw you on the shingle that night. I thought… I thought you were dead. Did you see me? Did you know it was me?" Alice had rehearsed the words over and over but when she finally saw Emily on her own, they came no more easily for all her practice. "I didn't know… I was going to help."

"I don't recollect," Emily's frown was deep. "Maybe you can tell me? Help me to remember."

Another week had passed. It was the most uneventful since Alice's arrival. There was nothing to be done to help Ed Brooks in the evenings, as darkness was already falling by the time the pupils left school; it was not sensible to walk around the point and there was little to be achieved from it. The old blankets had been washed on the morning after she had brought them back to the schoolhouse and had dried in the strong winds. Alice had plucked them off the gorse bushes where they had landed having escaped the restraints of the clothes pegs and placing them on the rack above the range had ensured there was no dampness remaining.

Now, on Saturday morning, Alice had the clean blankets folded and secured with string. Before setting off for Denge, she decided to visit Emily. On nearing Ben and Connie Webb's cottage she had recognised her seated outside, huddled up with the plank wall as her windbreak, and approached with the words of apology running through her mind. Alice sat down beside her and received a weak smile.

"I'm sorry, I had to tell you how sorry I am, even though you don't remember. There is no excuse for walking away."

"Perhaps you were frightened?" Emily looked calmer today, a little less tired and anxious.

"I was," Alice admitted. "I'd just arrived, I didn't know what to expect. It was so different. I came from Ashford."

"You're the new teacher. Connie told me about you. You were there on the beach that night; can you tell me about it?"

"I had been to see the vicar and he said I needed to go to the schoolhouse," Alice began. "I didn't know the way, and it was dark. The rain had stopped but the sky was overcast, then there was the light from the lighthouse, blinding me every few seconds." Her words were stilted, but Alice tried her best, frowning as she recalled that evening: "I was struggling with the shingle. We have paths in Ashford, you know. I tripped and there you were."

"I was lying there, by the vicar's home?"

"Do you know how you got there?"

"I got swept into the sea and the boat came back, smashin' against me, sending me down... I kicked my way up and I knew I couldn't get back to Denge," Emily's head was in her hands as if heavy with the burden of remembering. "I know these currents though and I let them carry me to Dungeness beach. I remember pullin' myself up the bank, out of the way of the tideline."

"But your husband... Ed, he said that you went missing on a Friday night and I saw you late Saturday afternoon," Alice paused to reflect. "No wonder you were close to death. You had been there half the night and all the following day."

"Connie didn't think I'd make it." Emily pulled her

152

shawl closer. "I must have woken and pulled myself up towards the cottages, I don't remember." She began to stand, and continued, "I'm getting cold. It's time to go in… would you…?"

"No. I'll be on my way. I'm going to see Ed; he's tidying your home. Making it nicer for you."

"That's kind of you to help," Emily said, "but you don't need to make amends, I know what it's like to be afraid and lost."

It took about thirty minutes to reach Denge from the Webbs' cottage. Alice's heart was pounding from the exertion; she would be grateful to sit for a moment with Ed Brooks. For all that he had a temper and was the tallest, broadest man she knew, Alice felt no fear of him. She hadn't really thought he would harm her the night they first met when he was searching for his wife, or when she was sent to give him the message about Emily. Alice believed his love for Emily softened him and, when he was with her or thinking of her, it made him think before he allowed his temper to take hold. She was looking forward to seeing him, hoping that he was still positive about the future.

There was no smoke coming from the chimney of Ed's shack and no activity on the beach. The boat belonging to the Brooks' cousins was pulled up on the beach beyond high tide mark. Alice rapped on the door of the shack, but she already sensed no one was home. Lifting the latch, she tentatively opened the door and peeped in.

It was with relief Alice saw that the place was in good order, with the table and sink area clear of food debris and unwashed implements. The smell from the open fire could not be avoided, but the stench of seaweed and rotting fish had gone. She placed the freshly laundered and folded blankets on the table and took a reel of tape from the basket. Reaching up to take the measurements of the two windows, Alice jotted the figures down in her notepad.

Next Alice stripped the two blankets from the bed, holding them away from her and dropped them, unfolded, into her basket. Then she reached over the bed to straighten the sheets before replacing the blankets. She longed to plunge the sheets into a copper of soapy water, but that was for when her mother had sent replacements.

She was so occupied with her endeavours that Alice didn't hear the creak of the door as it opened or the scrape as it scuffed against the uneven floor. She was leaning across the bed, in a way that would not have been appropriate had Ed Brooks been present: her slender ankles and stocking clad calves were on display. When the door slammed shut, she turned quickly, expecting Ed, but found herself sitting on the box bed looking up into the scornful black eyes of Jake Brooks. He stood over her, so close that his legs almost touched her own, now hanging over the side of the bed.

"What have we here? The teacher in my cousin's bed whilst his wife is sick." He leered at her showing broken teeth. "Miss Tibbs, not so prim and proper now. I wondered what you were up to comin' around here with yer fruit cake and yer scrubbin' brush. Makin' the place cosy, were you? And for what? So you could get Edward into bed with you?"

She said nothing, but stared back at him, cornered like a wild animal in a trap. Sickened by his insinuations, although barely understanding the meaning of them, Alice could think of no way of escape. Her eyes darted to the door.

"You think he'll come an' save you? He's gone off to Lydd. Be away for hours." Then seeing the fear mount in her eyes, Jake continued, "No need to fret, if you're wanting a Brooks then one cousin is as good as another." Slowly he looked her up and down from her newly cut fringe and neat mouth, to her flushed neck and the pin-tucked blouse, then on to the glimpse of her stockings still on display. The predator eased his knee between hers, stopping Alice from covering herself and causing her to lean away from him.

"No need to be so eager!" He laughed briefly and she blushed furiously, her mouth so dry she was unable to speak and knowing that to scream was pointless. "I've not decided if you're to my taste… I like my women with a bit more flesh on them, but, then again, they say a change does yer good now and again."

Alice turned her face away, so she couldn't see into his eyes as he leered at her or smell his rank breath. As he leaned closer, placing a hand on her waist, Alice found her voice:

"I'm not here for your cousin; he is as good as married so keep your foul thoughts to yourself. I'm engaged to be married in the summer."

"Engaged to be married, are you? Your man will thank me for teaching you a thing or two." He took her chin and turned her face, so their eyes met. "He'll thank me very much indeed."

Jake moved back slightly, leaving Alice lying defenceless on the bed. As he straightened, he began to shrug off his braces and his breeches fell to his feet. She lay there, unable to move, and compelled to watch the repulsive features of her attacker. Then, out of the corner of her eye, Alice noticed the cottage door open behind him. Her first thoughts were that she was to be saved, but that her reputation would be tarnished forever when this depraved scene was witnessed.

Previously, while she pushed the sheets into the corner of the bed, Alice had been unaware of Jake entering the hovel. In turn, he had not heard the two men arrive. She saw his eyes widen with horror as a hand – Ben Webb's, she thought – clamped down on his shoulder. There was a brief howl of protest when Jake was pulled back, a crack as his head hit the tabletop and a thud as his body hit the floor.

Alice drew her legs up to her stomach and crouched on the bed, her face on her knees, unable to look at her rescuers. The shame at what they had seen burned within her.

"Get up and home to your poor wife," Ben Webb snarled at the fallen man. "Get up and explain why you've got yourself one hell of a headache."

"I don't think he can." It was Tom Barton who spoke next.

Alice sat, hunched up with her eyes tightly closed. To open them would make the scene become real.

"He's not… he's tougher than that… he's…." That was Ben. His voice was lower than Tom's. Alice didn't want to hear his words though; she wanted to be shut away from them all.

"Look at his eyes; they're the eyes of a dead man." There was silence between the men, while Tom moved to the body on the floor. "He's not breathing."

"You think he's…"

"I don't doubt it," Tom muttered. "He always was a bloody piece of filth, but this was an accident. By God, we won't hang for ridding the world of Jake Brooks. I'll not have it. We've got to move him before the blood stains through the rug. There's no time to stand around discussing it. We'll roll him up in it."

"And what about her?" Alice knew they were looking at her.

"She's all right. She won't see us in trouble for this." Tom spoke with confidence.

Alice still hadn't looked, and they hadn't spoken to her. She heard the table moving and a rhythmic thud as the body was rolled up.

"I've got a better rug at home," Tom said. "We'll

156

bring it along as a gift for Ed." Then Alice felt the bed give as he sat on the edge beside her, and asked gently, "Did he hurt you?"

She shook her head, but her voice was not strong enough to be heard.

"He's gone and there's no time to waste; we've got to get him out of here. There's no one about but that could change, and we'll not be caught for this."

"But we can't... we've got to tell someone... the constable," Alice began.

"It was an accident; we never meant it to happen," Tom spoke slowly but clearly. "Do you want to tell the law, tell them what happened?"

Alice was stronger than she looked. After a lifetime of protection from her parents and conforming to people's expectations, she had known nothing but love and support before coming to Dungeness. She had helped her mother with the poorer families in their community and gained an inner confidence and strength not always obvious under her prim exterior. Since coming to Dungeness, she had experienced a more savage way of life and rather than crush her, it had strengthened her further. Alice knew if she stayed curled up in a ball of despair, she would put the lives of these good men at risk. So she stood up and turned to straighten the bed, then looked at the men and said, "I've got to take these blankets back to wash," and set about folding them into a bundle which could be carried.

Aware that the men were waiting, Alice concentrated on her own task. When she was ready, she opened the door, and scanned the area around the cluster of houses and beach.

"Do you see anyone?" Ben Webb asked.

"No." Alice stepped out onto the shingle.

Tom Barton and Ben Webb were both fishermen and lifeboat men, strong and broad, still young enough

157

to cope with the rigours of their lives. But Jake Brooks, fisherman and pirate, was a tall man and it took all their strength to hoist him over their shoulders, before carrying him away from Denge. Alice hadn't heard them discuss what they would do with the body; it seemed to be by unspoken agreement that they set off inland, avoiding the coast or going too close to the settlement at Dungeness. Every so often they paused for a moment while their load stayed on their shoulders. Then they moved on, and Alice trailed behind, her body weary and mind unable to form any rational thoughts, or to put the events of the day in order.

After ten minutes, they came to a dip in the shingle and wordlessly the body was laid down. The three of them knelt and pushed away the stones to make a hollow pit deep enough to hold a man and a foot of shingle above him.

"Take the rug away, then if he's found there will be no evidence." As Alice said the words, she knew they made her as guilty as the others for the crime. Aiding and abetting it was called.

"I'll burn it back at home," Tom said. "And bring over the new one within the hour."

Three pairs of hands pulled at the piles of stones allowing them to pour over the body. It was soon covered, and a relief for them to see no more trace of black hair, tatty cloth or the toe of a boot. Alice knelt at the graveside and prayed for the dead man's soul, whilst the men stood in silence, their heads bowed. Then they moved away, without looking back. They didn't speak at all until they reached the railway tracks, the point where the men would go back towards the coast and Alice to the school.

"This stays between the three of us. We never tell, not our wives nor sweethearts." Ben looked straight at Alice.

"Of course," she answered, a hint of defiance returning. She was determined to never speak of what happened.

With no further words, the three of them separated. Alice moved on... one foot after the other... sliding over the shingle. Looking ahead but only seeing the slight hump in the shingle pit behind her.

For the following week, the rain flung itself down upon the shingle headland, finding its way through gaps in window frames and under doors. Half-drowned children scurried into the school, their coats were then spread over drying racks by the fire, creating a humid, stale atmosphere in the schoolroom. Skies were darkening by early afternoon, and it was as black as midnight by the time they came to the end of the school day.

Alice, burdened by headaches, struggled through the days and dreaded the nights when she was plagued by visions of Jake Brooks forcing himself upon her. She frequently woke with a jump, as the loud crack of his head hitting the table ricocheted around in her mind. She felt Peggy Webb's beady eyes upon her, wondering what was wrong. But for once Alice knew that Mrs Webb had no idea what went on in her troubled mind.

In the evenings, Alice and Hazel cut the thick dark blue velvet which had arrived from the rectory and reshaped it into two smaller sets of curtains. It was tiresome work under the weak, fluttering light of the oil lamps. Alice was grateful for Hazel's company and support; she used her headache as an excuse for being quieter than usual.

Then on the Saturday morning, four weeks after her arrival, Alice woke and decided that she would no longer live her life in the shadow of guilt and shame. She had not encouraged him to assault her and she had no doubt that decent men should not hang for manslaughter. She was nineteen years old and was going to do her best to be a good teacher and, following that, a good wife. *If the tiniest memory of what happened begins to taunt me,* she thought, *then I will push it from my mind and think only of pleasant things, like apple trees in blossom and spring flowers. That is exactly what I will do.*

She was the first to be out of bed and busied herself tending the stove – opening the damper, topping it up with logs and placing the kettle on top. Hazel came through to the smell of frying bacon and tomatoes.

"You're feeling better then?" Hazel asked.

"Thankfully, my headache has passed, and I need to take these curtains to Denge. Will you come with me? The rain has stopped; it will be cold though as we have a frost. Can you believe it after all the rain? But see how pretty it is on the stones."

Chapter Eighteen

Dearest Albert,

At last I am coming home for Christmas! I can't wait to see you, and of course dear Mother and Father. My train leaves at quarter-past ten on Saturday 22nd, and should be in Ashford by half-past eleven. If you are able to meet me at the railway station, then I will be pleased to see you. If you cannot, then I am sure my parents will collect me. I shall return on Saturday 5th January.

I am very much looking forward to spending time with you all.

With love from your Alice.

Alice was hoping that her parents or Albert would be waiting for her on the station platform as the great iron wheels came to a rest. She was standing steady, poised at the doorway, as the buffers bumped against each other, giving each coach a light jolt. Peering through the grubby window, she searched for a familiar face amongst those in dark winter coats, with their hats pulled low over foreheads. One hand was on the brass handle and the other on her suitcase, and Alice was twisting the handle at the first opportunity. She opened the door before the porter reached it and stepped out onto the platform.

The air was thick with smoke from the numerous filthy great beasts who had belched fumes into the station throughout the morning. *I'd never really noticed it before,* Alice reflected, screwing up her dainty nose, as she tasted the bitter soot on her tongue. *At least, I knew the railway to be a dirty place, as Mother always complained of it, but it never bothered me before as it seemed full of promise for a day out. I've become used to the fresh sea air, I suppose, and a brisk wind, such as those we experience at Dungeness, would soon blow away all this stale air.*

The fine, ornamental station buildings and decorative ironwork all had a coating of grime in varying degrees. The platform was buzzing with the voices of passengers stepping on and off the trains, people meeting friends and family or wishing them a safe journey. Station staff were carrying bags, pushing trolleys, answering queries and checking tickets. Alice felt momentarily stunned by the busy surroundings, although pleased, at least she thought she was pleased, to be home for Christmas. She stood still, not pushing herself through the crowds.

"Alice dear, Alice, over here."

She turned, and there were her mother and father. Then she was in her mother's arms and her father was patting her arm with one hand, while taking her suitcase with the other.

"I'm home," Alice said; her words sounded unnecessary.

"How wonderful to see you." Mrs Tibbs placed her hand on Alice's forearm and began to guide her to the bridge spanning the tracks.

Alice's ticket was checked at the gate, and they stepped out of the station, leaving much of the soot-laden air behind them. A boy was standing with the horse and trap, borrowed by Reverend Tibbs; he took his penny and scampered off, darting between the horse-bus and narrowly avoiding a smart gelding trotting along at a good pace with a gentleman astride him. Alice and her mother stepped into the trap and her father seated himself at the front with the reins in his hand.

On turning into Marsh Road, they slowed for the boys who were shovelling horse droppings from the road into a handcart. "A treat for someone's vegetables!" the rector said. His wife raised her eyebrows and said nothing, but Alice smiled at the familiar remark.

For Alice, now acclimatised to the salty air, and having ventured no further than Lydd for many weeks, it was the fumes from the Lion Brewery which next assaulted her senses. To their right, and set back from the road behind some houses, the Brewery was a prominent landmark: substantial red-brick offices and factory buildings rose high above the roofline of the surrounding buildings. The tallest of the structures were adorned with fine cupolas, and higher still were the chimneys from which the offending odour came. From the direction of the town centre, there came two covered wagons returning to the brewery, which was a hive of industry for five and a half days a week. Pulling her shawl over her face a little, Alice tried to ignore the stench in the air, knowing they would soon pass it. She turned her attention to the view ahead: the rows of houses, dating from different eras, lining the road and gradually becoming denser until they reached the town centre with its shops, banks and offices. Rising above them all was the parish church, with its turreted tower, and rooftops stretching out.

The pony slowed as it pulled the trap up the rise towards the town centre and, with no prompting from the rector, it turned off the main road and into the more genteel surroundings of East Hill. Alice looked behind her to the High Street. "I've no Christmas gifts," she said to her mother. "I'll take the horse-bus to the town next week."

"Alice, you've left it a little late," her mother

163

admonished. "Surely your evenings are your own time in which you could have turned your attention to sewing or crochet. It takes no effort at all to plan ahead."

"I could have bought some thread in Lydd," Alice admitted. "But there will be a better selection here in Ashford. The light is so very poor by the time my teaching is over. Here, I can sew in the parlour when the sun shines through the window." She considered this for a moment and pacified her mother further with: "My stitches will be all the neater for my using the best of the daylight."

East Hill came to an end and now the River Stour came into view. Again, there was industry – this time in the form of corn mills. They crossed the bridge and left Ashford town behind, although they were reminded of its railway heritage when crossing the tracks on the Canterbury and Ramsgate line. "It's seems a long time since summer and our day-trip to Ramsgate," Alice reflected. Albert and she had been for the day with both her parents and his mother.

"Such a selfless plan," Mrs Tibbs replied. "Albert thought of everything we could need for the day. What pleasure he must bring to his mother."

"I'm sure he does," Alice replied, wondering if she brought any pleasure to her mother, who always appeared to be fretting over one thing or the other. *If nothing else, she is pleased about my engagement,* Alice told herself.

It was no distance at all before they reached the village of Willesborough, an area spreading out from the main thoroughfare which would eventually lead to Hythe, some twelve miles away. Cottages and terraced houses fronted the road, with numerous small shops tucked amongst them, displaying everything from fruit and vegetables, to tools and household goods. Eager to see it all, and to search for any

164

changes, Alice leaned forward in her seat. Crowning them all, was the windmill, its sails turning slowly and giving a gentle creak every now and then.

On turning into Church Road, Alice eagerly anticipated her first glimpse of the distinctive spire of her father's church, St Mary the Virgin. There it was: the tiled spire and the church with its triple roofs covering the nave and aisles. But before they reached it, the horse instinctively turned into the driveway of the substantial Georgian rectory, and the family home was before them.

"Albert couldn't leave work earlier, I assume," Alice said to her mother. "I knew half-past eleven was a little early, but I wondered..."

"He is working hard and saving for your future," her mother reproached her. "He will be going home to make himself respectable and will be with us for afternoon tea."

Now it was half-past two and Alice was sure Albert would be at the door any moment. Impatient to see him, she went to the landing window and looked across the front garden, past the privet hedge and along Church Road. *What will it be like, seeing him after seven long weeks? Will it feel more romantic than it did before; we have never been separated before, never been a week without seeing each other.* She looked at her engagement ring and smiled to herself. *It will be wonderful, of course it will.*

During the past few hours, Alice had put away her clothes, having ironed the creases out of her skirts and blouses. She had answered questions with caution and suffered the disappointment in her mother's voice due to there being such a delay in the first letter reaching them. *Oh Mother, I wrote two beforehand, but they were never sent. How can you think I would have*

165

not bothered? Alice was tempted to snap at her, and then she would silently rebuke herself: *I can hardly be cross with Mother; she doesn't know what it's like there and if she did then I would never be allowed to return.* Dinner had been served by Mabel at one o'clock, and Alice squashed the disappointment that Albert had not broken with routine and found a way to be there.

It was not until Mabel was putting the teapot on the table at three o'clock that the doorbell rang, and the maid was scuttling from the dining room to the hallway and the front door.

"No, Mabel, let me go..." Alice stood up from the table and called after her.

She opened the front door and there he was: Albert. Stepping in, he removed his hat to reveal a neat centre parting and slicked brown hair; he looked to be freshly shaved, with sideburns neatly shaped. "Alice!" he exclaimed, almost seeming to be surprised to see her. Then his overcoat was placed on the coat rack, as if it was something he did every week, which of course he did. He wore a mid-brown two piece: trousers and a waistcoat; his white shirt was freshly laundered, and a tie gave the appearance of respectability. "Alice – at last!" Albert took her hands and gently pressed them to his own. Then, standing back, he studied her and frowned, "You look different."

"Oh? It must be my hair," she touched the loose curls gently. "I had a fringe cut."

"I dare say I shall get used to it."

Alice took his hand and gazed up into his face. He really did look very smart, and she appreciated the effort he had made, knowing that working as a fitter in the engineering works was a dirty job. "It is lovely to see you, Albert."

"And you, Alice, and you."

"Mother and Father are waiting; the tea is in the pot." Alice led the way into the dining room.

166

Albert shook Reverend Tibbs' hand with enthusiasm and kissed her mother's slender hand, then seated himself in his usual chair. He had been taking afternoon tea here for the past six months. Mrs Tibbs poured his tea, passed him dainty sandwiches and scones, and fussed over whether he had enough jam for the scones and sugar in his tea. While buttering her own scone, Alice felt that her mother had taken over her own role in caring for Albert.

"Some apple cake, Albert?" Alice tried to fulfil her role as future wife.

"No, thank you Alice, I have eaten plenty."

It all seemed rather formal. So very polite. But of course, these were the ways of well-mannered people; how unreasonable to think of and long for the less-polished ways she had become used to. *No, this was just as it should be,* Alice reprimanded herself. *But if only Mother would allow me to pour Albert's tea and not take over so. He is so very handsome and polite as always, but it doesn't quite feel as if he is mine.*

"One of my colleagues is due for retirement and will be returning to be near family in Devon," Albert announced as he drained his second cup of tea. "He has a company house on the green at New Town and thinks I've got a good chance of securing it when he leaves. I have been working there for eleven years now since I was fourteen." He paused and smiled at Alice, "...And now I am getting married in the summer. There is every chance we'll have a new home for when we begin married life. What do you think of that, Alice?"

"It will be very convenient for work," Alice commented, trying to visualise the small development of terraced cottages and flats for the workers.

"A house, you say?" Reverend Tibbs looked up from his cake, "There are several blocks of flats I believe: decent, solid buildings."

"Yes sir, it is definitely a house. Two bedrooms and

167

its own back yard. They may be forty years old, but the railway took a pride in those houses when they built them; they are highly regarded as being quality homes. They are known as Dutch Gable houses, due to the Dutch influence in their style. Imagine that, Alice, our own house!"

It will be small, Alice reflected. *Small compared to the vicarage, and even smaller than the schoolhouse which has generous rooms... and lacking the open space surrounding both these places I call my home. A yard, he said. A garden would be lovely with a flowering apple tree and a small vegetable plot. But a home of our own, that would be very fine indeed. Better than living with his mother, which is what I feared.*

"It sounds lovely, Albert. Perhaps we could take a walk around the area and see where the house is. Do you know which one it is?"

"I don't know exactly but I believe most of the homes face a green and the one on offer is an inner terrace; the end of terrace have three bedrooms." Albert replied. "A walk around the area is a splendid idea; shall we say tomorrow afternoon? Mother would love to see you, so perhaps we will take a walk and then back home for afternoon tea?"

"That's a wonderful idea, Albert. How is your mother?"

Over the next hour, Alice became used to the routines of the rectory, which had once been so familiar. With the picture of a new home in her mind, and the promise of time alone with her future husband on the following afternoon, she began to relax. Her mother still tended Albert's every need, worrying over his comfort: the temperature of his tea, the blemish on his napkin and whether he was weary after a morning at work. Alice would have liked to catch his eye and exchanged a moment of understanding. Perhaps to have a hint that he too found her mother's administrations a little much. But he seemed to be so very comfortable at the tea table and it was only her father who raised his eyebrows occasionally and suggested to his wife that Albert were able to reach for his own sugar or ask if he was in need of more sustenance. Any comments such as this were ignored by Mrs Tibbs. *In the summer I'll have my own home and many years of caring for my husband,* Alice reflected. *I can only hope that my mother has not spoiled him with her attentions as I am sure I will not fuss over him half so much.*

Chapter Nineteen

The following afternoon found Albert punctual at the rectory for half-past one. When Alice opened the door, she found him gazing at the sky and a frown on his face.

"It's terribly overcast," were his opening words.

"Good afternoon, Albert." Alice looked up. "Yes, it is a little grey," she conceded, "It is to be expected in December."

"No doubt rain is due."

Alice stepped onto the gravelled area in front of the house. "Perhaps a little, but the wind is blowing the clouds away from the direction we are to walk."

"I was thinking of postponing." Albert stepped forward and placed a careless kiss on Alice's cheek. "You know how easy it is to catch a chill and I'd hate to be careless with you, my love."

"How kind of you to think of me but I have no intention of allowing the weather to put a stop to our outing," Alice told him. "If we waited for a fine day, we should never go anywhere or do anything at Dungeness. It's right on the coast, as you know, and there is rarely a day without a strong wind. The misty rain is miserable, it looks like nothing much but soaks through my clothes in no time at all. It can be quite depressing, but we just have to get on with things."

"Very well, but we must take an umbrella and make haste to get there, in case it does rain." Albert looked towards the furls of black material and shapely handles in the hallway stand. "You seem to enjoy making it sound dreadful, but I am sure you stay quite dry under an umbrella at Dungeness."

"I can't imagine ever being able to use one," said Alice, who was feeling quite invigorated by the memories of the windswept point. "I am sure it would be blown apart in seconds!" She took an umbrella and fastened her coat, then they stepped out into the dull December day.

Albert offered Alice his arm as they set off down the path. "You do seem to be a little livelier than I remember!" he remarked, "It must be all those children you have to keep in order."

"Oh, I hadn't thought… but of course they can be a little unruly." Alice resolved to be a little less forthright, as the couple walked along the lane towards the railway tracks. They passed her father's church, and she placed her hand on Albert's arm, while wondering if he might pause for a moment and place his lips on hers. Their pace slowed by the hedgerow, where they were quite alone, but he merely looked down at her and carried on. *I suppose it isn't the proper thing: to be kissing in the lane,* Alice admitted to herself. There would be time later, when they sat on his mother's couch while tea was being prepared. That was the time for a kiss and some sweet whispers.

"If it does rain, we'll have muddy boots to clean this evening." Albert eyed the clods of earth on the road as the village was left behind and the lane narrowed.

"That's another thing different about life in Dungeness," Alice remarked. "Can you imagine not having to clean mud from boots? It is all stones for as far as one can see."

"You mustn't let standards slip," Albert replied. "There must be a little earth to brush off after a walk."

"Damp boots are always in need of a polish," Alice offered.

171

They came to a break in the hedgerow and paused to look over the water-meadows, a favourite place of theirs to walk the previous summer. The river appeared to be swollen; the fields were damp, and the grass bedraggled. "When you are here again in the spring, we can hope for dry weather and pleasant walks," Albert said. He turned to face her, "You're looking very pretty today, Alice. Teaching must suit you."

"I think it does!" She smiled and felt her heart wobble a little as she looked into his blue eyes. He was standing close to her. Her lips parted a little, and Albert leaned forward to place the lightest of kisses on them.

"I think you were right, my dear..." The moment of intimacy was lost. "... I wouldn't have wanted to wait another week to see our future home, and the sky does appear to be clearing, although I can't be sure the rain will hold off. We must hasten as Mother will have tea brewing at three o'clock on the dot."

At the crossing, they paused for the keeper to shuffle out from his cottage, check there were no trains approaching, and allow them to pass over the tracks. Then Albert loosened his arm from her grip. It seemed as if he thought nothing of romance and more of the practicalities of a terraced home near the Railway Works. But Alice was eager to see New Town and their pace was brisker when unhindered by her clinging to his arm. The umbrella remained furled and swung to and fro at Albert's side as they walked. To his satisfaction, the rain clouds decided not to linger over Ashford and revealed a clear blue sky. It was a lovely day for a walk on a winter's afternoon.

In no time at all they reached the outskirts of New Town. To their right, the brown brick buildings of the South Eastern Railway Company workshops dominated the scene. Today they stood silent but six days a week the noise of the machinery filled the air,

172

along with the smells of heated metal and smoke from the workshops. The clock tower at the entrance stood proud. But it was the development before the Railway Works, attracting the couple's attention: houses, shops and flats surrounding a large triangular green,

"Ah, look at this, Alice." Albert put his hands on his hips, as if to show his satisfaction with the scene. "It has a feel of a village, don't you think?"

Alice considered this: with the houses facing the green, it looked as if it had been styled on a traditional village but lacked the variety in age of properties; New Town had been created over the past forty years, to suit the demands of railway workers needing homes. It was an area for families: young boys kicked a football about on the grass while other children played with hoops nearby. *Where were their parents,* Alice wondered? *Perhaps their fathers are reading the Sunday newspaper, or tending their allotments, and the mothers must be preparing for Sunday tea. What will Albert and I do on a Sunday? No doubt we'll call on my parents one week, and his mother the next. Between them Albert and my mother will have it all planned.*

An elegant, brown brick building with six pillars rising high above the first-floor windows stood facing the green. Tall, ornate windows with curved tops gave decoration to the first floor and a row of shorter second floor windows, matched those below. The building boasted an Italianate style, used by the South Eastern Railway Company and now reflected in its buildings for the workers.

"The public baths," announced Albert. "Eleven baths in there. Open Thursday, Friday and Saturday. Ladies in the morning, gents in the afternoons. I've taken to going there myself on a Saturday afternoon!"

"It's a beautiful building," Alice said with appreciation. "But I've never been... never had the

173

need to use a public bath." She looked at Albert, but he didn't appear to be listening, and so Alice turned her attention to the building on the right of the baths. "Look Albert, a shop. Small but useful, I am sure. What a shame it is a Sunday, and we can't look inside. Perhaps Mother and I will take a stroll this way during the week."

"Splendid, and if you were to walk towards the railway works, there is a library, reading rooms and mechanics' institute. I imagine you would like the library; you should look in there with your mother."

"I'd like that, thank you, Albert."

"There's the pub, The Alfred Arms," Albert pointed to the left of the baths. "Closed today of course, but many of the workers go there for a pint after work or in the evening. In fact, it even opens before six in the morning for the workers to start the day with an ale or porter." He reflected on this for a moment before adding, "But, of course, I won't get into that type of habit."

Alice nodded, unable to picture the scene, as she had never been in a public house before.

On either side of the baths, shop and pub, making up one part of the triangular development were the rows of plain, flat-fronted, two storey flats. They were set back from the path with a small area of grass and shrubs in front of them. Again, they were in the brown brick that seemed to be the theme for the area.

"Decent flats," commented Albert, "But as an engineer I can hope for a house. My wages will easily cover the extra rent and the company pay both the rates and taxes."

With the bath house and flats dominating one side of the triangular green, the other two sides proudly displayed terraces. Each consisted of six homes with those at each end clearly being larger. Their ornate gable ends faced the road, highlighting an additional room in the loft space. Tall chimneys in sets of eight graced the roofs.

"Oh Albert, what pretty houses. Look how trees have been planted amongst the terraces. I wonder which will be ours." Alice began to stroll across the green.

"I'll ask Mr Baldwin on Monday, then you can picture where it will be."

Alice was now looking at the details, wondering what was behind the wooden doors with decorative glass inserts. What would her life be like living here with Albert?

"A parlour at the front, then the kitchen and a small lean-to scullery, I imagine." Albert stood, hands behind his back, looking up at the houses. "I wonder if there are flushing lavatories upstairs!"

"Wonderful," Alice said with enthusiasm, thinking of the miserable earth closet at Dungeness.

"I hear they have gas, they don't always you know, not workers' cottages," Albert continued. "Although I would say these are houses not cottages, wouldn't you agree?"

"Definitely," Alice happily confirmed.

"Do you see the gas street lamps?" Albert pointed to one. "A lamp-lighter comes around every evening and I hear the engine drivers appreciate them when they have to get up so early in the morning."

They were nearing the houses now and Alice noticed an unusual feature. "Look Albert, do you see that some of the gateposts are painted white? I wonder why."

"Now Alice, I can tell you about them. You can always tell an engine driver's home by its white posts. It's so the call-boy knows which to knock at to wake them early!" Albert led them back to the corner of the green they had first come in from. "Now if we go around here, we can see the allotments."

They walked behind the terraced houses, noting the small yards. "I don't mind at all that there are only yards, not when we have this green and these trees," Alice said. "It doesn't matter, does it?" She looked past the allotments, where several men were working, to the water meadows and beyond them to the railway tracks. "Imagine, Albert, if we lived here, we would have the fields at the back and the green at the front. Both views are equally pleasant."

"Yes, as you say, it really is very pleasant. With both our savings, we'll be able to buy all the furniture we need, but I imagine the range and some of the fixtures will be ready waiting for us. We could redecorate if necessary."

"Perhaps when I return at Easter, we could take a walk into town and look at the furniture shops? Imagine choosing all our own curtains and wallpapers and not having those that someone else has used before." Alice reached out and gave Albert's hand a squeeze. He turned and smiled at her.

"We'll do that on a Saturday afternoon and have tea in the corner shop. That will be a treat! By then we'll know exactly which house it is, and we can have another stroll around here."

"It sounds perfect, Albert. See how quickly we walked here from the rectory and your mother is only another five minutes away." Alice was beginning to picture it all and the future seemed attractive. "How long would you say it will take to walk into the town? Perhaps twenty-five minutes?"

"Twenty-five minutes or perhaps half-an-hour. That sounds fair enough," Albert replied.

They had walked around the back of the houses which faced the green and Alice's attention was now drawn to another building, one which stood out from its brown-brick neighbours. This was a Gothic style construction of ragstone, which initially looked like a

176

church with tall lancet windows and a high gabled bell-cote. Low boundary walls were topped with iron railings. It must be the school and so it drew her attention; she wanted to compare its size and grandeur to the one at Dungeness.

"Look Albert, the school. It's larger than our one at Dungeness, for we only have the one classroom. It does look rather grand though, don't you think? I imagine there are so many more pupils in the area it will, of course, be bigger, but mine at Dungeness is a fine building too."

"Yes, it caters for the railway workers' children, and I am sure it is excellent."

As they neared the building Alice could read its name on a sign: "New Town Railway School. And look, Albert, see the school motto here on a sign: 'Let cheerfulness abound with industry'. How suitable!"

"Very apt," Albert approved.

Alice thought of being in that little house all day, waiting for Albert to come home from the engineering works. Then she thought of her school and how lively the days were with the children, bright and eager to learn.

"Albert do you think … how would it be if I were to, if I were to seek a teaching job? Perhaps for the mornings?"

Albert turned and looked down at her for a few seconds, "Alice, how kind you are to consider those children and how you might be able to nurture those young minds, but we cannot have people thinking that I am unable to support my own wife. That wouldn't do at all."

They turned, all interest in the school crushed, and walked back towards Albert's home for afternoon tea. Christmas was over; the new year came with bright blue skies and clear starlit nights. The ground was hard with crisp white frosts every morning. Alice's parents took her in the trap to Ashford station on Saturday 5th January; the train was to leave at half-past twelve and they expected Albert to be there to see her off. He was already at the entrance as they arrived and, as Alice stepped down, he took her hands.

"I shall look forward to your letters and when you come again it will be spring. We'll walk along to see where our home is to be."

"And to the town to look in the furniture shops," Alice added.

"Of course. I will be due a few days off work, so how does a day out in Hythe or Canterbury sound to you?"

"Wonderful," Alice smiled up at him. Until this moment she had accepted her return to Dungeness, but now she felt there was so much to miss here in Ashford, but also so much to look forward to on her return at Easter.

Chapter Twenty
1895

The train slowed down and eased itself into Lydd Station. Alice looked out, eager to see if she recognised anyone on the platform. She was pleased to spot the auburn hair and slim figure of Emily Brooks alongside the sturdier Connie Webb. Both women were well wrapped up and clutching at their shawls; the wind was so strong that Alice could feel the force of it pushing on the coach and thrusting its way through the window frames.

"Lydd, Lydd, all alight for Lydd. This train goes through to Dungeness." The station master held onto his hat and did his absolute best to uphold his important position, but his words were whipped away on the wind and Alice only saw his lips moving from her relative comfort of being in the coach.

As Connie opened the door it was pulled from her hand, smashing against the side of the coach and back again towards the women. A young porter ran over and held it steady whilst the two women stepped into the coach. They both smiled when they saw Alice and sat opposite her.

"We were just saying maybe you'd be back on this train after your Christmas holidays," Connie said.

"It's marvellous to see you." A warm feeling of belonging settled in Alice's stomach. "Mrs Brooks... Emily, you look so much better, despite the cold."

Emily's skin and eyes glowed, having lost the

shadows around her eyes and the haunted look within them. There was colour in her cheeks, and her red hair was glossy. When she spoke, it was with a confidence Alice had not heard before: "I've moved back round to Denge, back with Ed and we got married on the 29th December, last Saturday, just the two of us with Ben and Connie, and Tom Barton, he came too. He's been good to Ed, really helpful."

"That's wonderful. Congratulations. I'm so pleased for you." Alice felt herself relaxing; 'Dungeness Alice' was back. A young woman who could like Emily and Ed for who they were and not judge them for living in sin the past year or more.

"Their Jake has gone," Connie informed. "Just went one day with not a word to his wife and family. His Helen was that upset, being left with three young children. They packed up before Christmas and left with just what they could carry."

"Where did they go?" Alice asked, trying to mask her horror.

"Over Camber way, she's got her family there." Connie leant forward to share her opinions, "A nasty man if ever there was. I'm sorry Emily, what with him being family, but you know what I mean; your Edward is better off without that cousin of his."

"You're right Connie, I never liked him much, but family is family and we didn't have much of that. Ed's aunt passed away, as you know, so it's just us and his parents now. Ed wonders if Jake had another woman somewhere and his Helen said as much." Emily looked at Alice and coloured a little. "Oh Miss Tibbs, I'm sorry… what with you being a vicar's daughter. I let my tongue run away with itself, I…"

"Don't you worry about that, Emily," Connie patted her arm gently. "Miss Tibbs sees all types here at Dungeness, she's used to our ways."

"I see all types in Ashford too," Alice reminded her.

"We have to help people in the parish, Mother and I."

Alice was thinking about the situation the Brooks family were now in with fishing to be done and only the one man left who was fit enough to handle the boat. *Only one man,* Alice reflected, *but boys grow up fast and I am sure there is someone there to help him.* Yet Alice knew that not to be true as it had been made clear how tough life was for Ed when his cousin was there alongside him. She had managed to push aside all thoughts of the accident while in Ashford and filled her mind with houses and Christmas festivities. Now the sound of Jake Brooks' skull cracking on the edge of the table filled her mind. *I mustn't think of it,* she told herself. *I must not. It was an accident and he was about to… no, I will not. I will not think of what he might have done. My teaching will keep me busy and that is my reason for being here.*

"How is Ed managing?" Alice asked tentatively. "With the boat?"

"He's got his father," Emily replied. "He always helps a bit, but Ed doesn't like to push him too much, not at his age. But it's been wonderful, really it has. Listen to this: Mr Barton, Tom I call him now, and Ben, well they have arranged some help for Ed. We've got Bert. You know Mrs Stevens from the lighthouse, he's her brother-in-law. And there's Will too, he's a young lad, but he's another pair of hands and Ed says he'll be all right once he's learnt the ropes."

So that was how the two young men had eased their guilt over the death of Jake Brooks. Not that it had been any more than an unfortunate accident, but they had seen the problems it would cause to his cousin. Ed Brooks couldn't cope without another strong man to assist him and the Dungeness neighbours had managed to help without looking as if charity were being given. Alice was pleased that they were still doing their best to give support to the Brooks family.

181

"So, Jake going hasn't caused any real problems for Ed and Emily, not now they've got more people looking out for them," Connie summed it up. "And good news for Emily today, you tell her Em."

Emily coloured a little, "I've been and got myself a job; that's what Connie and I were doing in Lydd. Just three days a week helping in the bakery. I leave on the early train and they say it's fine if I come back on the twelve minutes past two, so even in the winter I'll be back before nightfall."

"That's good news, Emily. Life is certainly getting better for you and Ed."

"I'm going to save up for a range. We've decided, Ed an' me, that it will make life much more comfortable."

"It will make your home far more pleasant," Alice agreed. "You'll have no need to worry if you step out for a bit as the fire will be perfectly safe and always ready for you when you need it."

The train slowed and the three women gathered up their belongings. Connie held the door as Alice struggled with her suitcase. Stepping down onto the platform, Alice was greeted by the full force of the wind coming from the west. It took her aback for an instant, and she felt that it was only the heavy suitcase keeping her weighted to the ground. She stepped into the station building, a temporary reprieve while she made sure her shawl was gathered tight around her shoulders, before setting off to the schoolhouse.

The sea mists stayed clear of the headland for the next few weeks, but the wind did not, and with it came a chill that had surely come straight from the Arctic Circle. The sky was generally clear, and any clouds scurried along way up high. With no trees or substantial buildings to soften the impact of the icy winds, the residents of Dungeness moved from place to place with their long coats wrapped tight around them, hats pulled low, then swathes of shawls and scarves. At night, the stars shone bright; by morning a hard frost lay over the beach and low-lying scrubland.

Pupils arrived with pink cheeks and glowing eyes, exhilarated by their race across the shingle. Once in school their frozen fingers stung as they thawed in front of the fire. Coal was delivered regularly to the school, having come by train, and the two fires now burned in the classroom, but the airy space remained chilly.

From four o'clock in the afternoon until the arrival of Mrs Stubbs in the early morning, Hazel and Alice sat close to the range in their chairs, or under piles of blankets in their beds, with only each other for company. They felt like a pair of hermits as neither was inclined to set off in the darkness to visit family and friends in the village, and in return no one visited them in the evenings. Most Saturdays the young women set off on the morning train to Lydd, sometimes with Ruth or other local women.

The sparse trees and solid buildings in the town gave limited protection from the wind. As it forced its way through the streets, there was little reprieve from the icy weather. However, it was a change of scene and they all enjoyed looking in the shops and spending a shilling or two on something to give them pleasure, such as a book or piece of jewellery, as well as the essential goods.

It was early February when Ruth arrived one morning having walked in from her home. As daughter of a lighthouse keeper, she lived in one of the houses circling the base of the lighthouse. She joined Mrs Stubbs, Alice and Hazel for a cup of tea before the day's work began.

"Your Ma came with a message last night," Ruth told Hazel. "She was hoping you would join them for your sister's birthday this Wednesday evening. You too Miss Tibbs."

"Thank you, Ruth." Hazel replied as she poured the tea. "I can't miss Annie's birthday, even if it does mean stepping out in the cold."

"How kind of them to think of me." Alice was thrilled to have an excuse to break the monotonous routine imposed on them by the weather. "I don't mind a bit how cold it is; it will do us good to have some company of an evening."

"It can't stay like this for much longer and the days are becoming longer," Mrs Stubbs commented.

"Then we'll have the mists back and will be sorry!" Ruth laughed. "If it's not one thing then it's the other."

Wednesday came and after school Alice and Hazel changed from their plain black dresses into less formal clothes of softer shades. For Hazel it was her favourite mid-grey dress with a tiny floral repeat pattern and a white crocheted collar. Alice wore her brown tweed skirt with a neat cream blouse, its pin-tucks had been ironed thoroughly the evening before.

Hazel insisted that Alice's new fringe was to be twisted around rags for an hour, so her face would be framed by curls for the evening. Her own fair hair was plaited before being coiled at the nape of her neck. Together they chose favourite brooches and hairclips.

At half-past five, the friends pushed their boots into backstays and set off over the stones. They followed a wide track leading from the school in a north-easterly direction towards the Pilot. Just before the pub, they veered off and headed towards the cluster of cottages on the coast and entered Hazel's family home without knocking.

Back in the Willesborough rectory, the dining table had extra leaves that could be inserted, and chairs were taken from the corners of the room. Visiting children were seated separately, in the kitchen, to eat.

No adult would be invited to dine if there were not a seat and table space for them; dining with or without guests was a formal occasion and good manners were paramount. So, when Alice entered the cottage of Mr and Mrs Tanner and family, she was both shocked at the informal arrangements, and appreciative of the warm and friendly atmosphere that enveloped her.

The comfy chairs had been pushed to the edges of the room and a couple of older relatives had claimed them. Two small children played alongside a baby on a rug, with the feet of the old couple sharing the space together with the younger generation.

The centre of the room was a hive of activity: the usual dining table had been turned and another, presumably borrowed, was being manoeuvred into position next to it. At the same time, chairs were being moved and Mrs Tanner was giving orders from her place at the range.

"This way a bit, Ben… no… yes, that's it. All lined up good and proper." Mr Tanner was at one end of the additional table and Ben Webb the other. "That will do us nicely, put your chairs up that end."

"A couple more chairs?" Ben asked.

"If you wouldn't mind," Mr Tanner replied. "Now Hazel, my darling, lovely to see you. And you Miss Tibbs. Tablecloths are on the side. Ma wants it all looking nice."

Again, Alice was transported back to the rectory, as she imagined the horror on her mother's face if guests were to arrive before the table was set. *But this is marvellous,* she thought. *So much friendlier, and to think of people bringing their own chairs!*

Mrs Tanner was busy at the stove. "Good to see you both; nasty weather out there but our Annie will be pleased you came along. Now Miss Tibbs, that's my mother and my husband's father sitting over there. The three little ones are my Annie's; her and Stan have just gone along to the Pilot for a couple of jugs of ale."

"The food smells delicious," Alice commented, as she helped Hazel straighten the tablecloth and then add an overlay of lace.

"You can't go wrong with a nice bit of rabbit this time of year," Mrs Tanner replied. With rabbits running loose over the area, it was a free source of meat. They couldn't burrow into the ground but had adapted to living amongst the roots of the hardy plants.

As the cutlery and plates were arranged on the table, Mr Tanner and Ben returned accompanied by Hazel's brother, Wilf.

"Connie is just on her way," Ben said. "She was wrapping up the pound cake and I put the jelly on the bench outside; Connie says it will melt if we have it here in the warm."

"She's a good help," Mrs Tanner spoke with affection.

The room was full of chatter, so no one heard running footsteps on the shingle. No one sensed the party was to be over before it had even started. Unbeknown to them, a ship was in danger on the icy sea and had just sent up a flare. It was while Stan and Annie were returning from the pub that they spotted it and alerted the others.

"Pa, Ben, there's a flare out to sea, out to the east. Get your gear on." Stan hurriedly put the jugs of ale on the dresser. "Annie's gone to knock for the others."

The words were barely spoken before Ben was gone, letting the door slam behind him. Mr Tanner and his son were pushing past the extra table and chairs, going through to the front porch to get into their weatherproof jackets and boots.

Then to Alice's surprise the rabbit stew was taken off the range. Mrs Tanner was fastening her long coat and pulling on her woollen hat. "Hazel, get the blankets warming by the range, will you, love?" And with that

186

she had also fled into the starlit night.

"Your mother, where's she gone?" Alice was unnerved by the reaction to the news of the flare.

"Out to launch the boat," Hazel replied before leaving the room, presumably for the blankets.

"Launch the boat?" Alice repeated as Hazel returned.

"Come on, I'll show you." Hazel put down the blankets and spoke to her grandparents, "I'm taking Alice out to see the boat; you'll be fine with the little ones, won't you? Annie will be back in a moment."

"Of course, we will," her grandmother replied. "Stay safe out there. Miss Tibbs, stay close to Hazel."

Coats and shawls were hastily put back on and the friends left through the back door. Their skirts were pulled away from their ankles to enable them to race freely over the ridge and down to the beach. As they ran, figures came from all directions to gather at the boathouse. That night it was the R.A.O.B lifeboat being sent to the rescue. Having just arrived in October, it was her first call out.

Alice and Hazel held back from going in the boathouse. To get in the way would be unforgivable while the men fastened their life jackets in place and pulled on woollen hats. But it was what was happening on the shingle bank leading down to the icy sea that interested Alice: heavy planks of oak with ropes fixed to each end were being hauled into place by pairs of women.

"Those are the skids, the planks, I mean," Hazel informed. "We can't just leave them there, not with the shingle moving all the time, so it's up to the lady launchers to get them in place. We can't spare the men you see."

They watched in silence for a few minutes, and it wasn't long before the R.A.O.B was being pushed out of the shed on its cart. It gathered speed, moving down the bank. As it launched into the sea, it was the lady launchers who took the brunt of the bitterly cold water spraying out either side of the boat. For their men, this was going to be challenging enough without heading off into the night already wet through. The launchers hauled the cart out of the water and returned to their homes to dry themselves, before going back to the beach when the call came to say they were needed again.

Standing there on the shingle bank, Alice couldn't imagine how the lifeboat men could bear to be out with the bitterly cold wind that would find a way to sneak through the multiple layers of clothes and pierce a man's skin with its vicious energy. As the tide receded, ice was forming on the beach, yet for her and the lady launchers, a warm fire was only minutes away. The lifeboat could be out for hours. Alice felt her respect for these brave lifeboat men growing.

Supper was a subdued occasion. The rich rabbit stew spooned on crisp jacket potatoes was followed by a choice of pound cake or jelly. Conversation was polite and muted as all thoughts were on their men, Mr Tanner, Stan and Ben, who were out in this perishing cold weather. Alice wondered about the boat that was in danger, where was it heading? What was its cargo? Did it have passengers? Quietly, they prayed for both the lifeboat crew as well as the passengers and crew of the unknown vessel. Only the chatter of the toddlers kept the birthday meal from being eaten in silence.

Then the call came: the lifeboat had been sighted and the land crew was needed. Lady launchers and blanket bearers pulled on coats and hats before racing back to the beach. Alice followed in the wake of Hazel's family, eager for news from the lifeboat. They were still at the top of the steep pebble beach when a call came from someone by the water:

"Man overboard, to the west. Man overboard."

188

Chapter Twenty-One

Shouts carried on the wind to the watchers on the shore. But to Alice, standing on the bank with blankets in her arms, the voices were disjointed. Although the women were ready to catch a rope from the boat, then attach it to the capstan, the lifeboat crew were doing their best to hold the R.A.O.B steady just out from the shore. Ten pairs of oars fought to control it against the rolling waves whilst someone attempted to throw a rope to the man in the water. All the shore crew could do was wait and try not to panic. Whoever had fallen into the water was a son to one of them, a husband to another and a brother or cousin to several.

The pools of water left behind by the tide were frozen and it was clear that no one could last in the water for long. Their heavy clothes would be sodden, and the men would be exhausted after a couple of hours at sea. A lifeboat jacket would keep them afloat, but the tide was retreating, and the Dungeness currents were strong.

Within a few minutes those on land were horrified to see the lifeboat had given the signal that it was to be brought in and the rope now hung loose at its side. The land crew occupied themselves with the recovery of the vessel, moving the skids up the bank as the boat came in. They had to concentrate on the task at hand, to not let their fears affect their work. Shards of ice fell from the boat, glistened in the moonlight and smashed upon the beach.

Then, as the bow came clear of the water, a man jumped into the shallows and waded into the sea. Now there was both hope for the first man who had gone overboard, and the fear that another could be lost. The moonlight revealed nothing – clouds scurried past it, dimming its light. *He wouldn't have returned to the sea if there was no point,* the thoughts ran through Alice's mind. *Please God, let them both be saved. Let me see them returning to the shore.* Her wishes, and those of every man and woman at the scene, were granted as a great cheer came from those on the R.A.O.B and the launching crew, as two men emerged from the icy waters, one being carried by the other who had saved his life. A second man jumped from the lifeboat and ran to relieve his crewmate of the heavy burden and, with the stones rolling under his feet, he staggered clear of the lapping waves.

Several of the watching women ran to the water's edge and it was Annie who first screamed out:

"It's Stan, it's Stan. Please God, don't let him be..."

"He's breathing," announced the exhausted crew mate as he laid him down on the stones. "Annie, stop fussing and get him out of this wet jacket; we've got to get him warm."

The other women backed away; they had a duty to all the crew members and whoever had been saved from the stricken ship. Annie tended to her husband, with the help of Hazel. Alice, still holding a dry blanket, turned to the man sitting hunched on the beach. One of the crew was with him, pulling at the life jacket.

It was then that Alice saw the man who had launched himself into the freezing sea to rescue Stan was Tom Barton. She knelt beside him and, without asking for approval, began to peel his ice-encrusted gloves from stiff fingers. Then, with her companion, she tackled his coat, undoing the fastenings and pulling him free of it. As it moved, more ice fell on the

190

shingle and the sea-drenched layer was removed with no help from its owner who was now shaking violently.

Alice draped a blanket around Tom's shoulders and rubbed his cold hands, but he began to shudder despite her efforts. The other crew member was cold and wet too; they both needed to be moved off the beach and to have their wet clothes replaced with dry ones.

"Mr Barton, Tom, you've got to stand up, to get into the warm." Alice pulled at his sleeve and spoke to the other man. "And you too, you both need to get out of this wind."

Tom stood, still shivering, and wordlessly he began to put one foot in front of another while being guided up the bank. A man came running towards them and took the burden from Alice.

"Come on, son. Come back home. Your Ma has got it nice and warm, and we'll have you fit in no time." Then turning to Alice, he said, "Miss Tibbs, isn't it? I hardly recognised you out there on the beach. You've helped keep him warm. Thank you."

"Did everyone else get back safely?" Alice asked the elder Mr Barton.

"Our men are all accounted for," he replied. "We've four men rescued, but I can't say if we got them all. We'll find out soon enough."

They were at the top of the bank now, and a stretcher passed carrying Stan under a blanket, with Annie running alongside him. "He's conscious," Hazel called out. "Just so cold he can't do a thing for himself. He needs warming, but not too fast."

Alice was now concerned about the crew member who had come to take Stan from Tom's arms. He had waded into the sea and was already wet from being on the boat. He had done his bit and needed to take care of himself now. She turned to him and said, "Let me help with Mr Barton, you're soaked and frozen right through, please go and get warmed yourself." The man nodded his thanks and turned towards the lifeboat house.

By now the lifeboat was slowly being winched up the beach. Alice learned later that the process could take a couple of hours. Local coastguards and young men not yet part of the active crew took charge of proceedings once the crew and rescued had alighted.

The winch, or windlass as they called it, was a wooden drum some three feet in diameter with four handles extending from the uppermost surface. It was these which were manhandled around and around, winding the thick towing rope and pulling the boat up the steep bank.

Alice knew there was plenty of help for the crew and the rescued. The best she could do was to help Tom to get to the warmth of his parents' home. She wasn't strong enough to support him physically, but she could encourage him to keep walking and raise his spirits. It wasn't far and, as the three of them paused by a wooden cottage, and the elder Mr Barton opened the door, Alice held back, unsure of herself.

"Some help with his boots would be good," Tom's father said, and so Alice stepped in with them.

Tom slumped in an armchair with the blanket wrapped tight around him. Alice's fingers, stiff with cold, fumbled with one set of laces and, as they began to thaw, the stinging sensation became unbearable. Despite the discomfort, Alice had to remove the boot as quickly as possible – she had read about frostbite in a National Geographic magazine at home. Finally, the first lace came loose, and she was able to pull off a boot, together with the thick knitted sock.

While Alice worked in silence, Tom's father spoke quiet words of reassurance as his stubby fingers laboured on the next lace. "There we are. We can get those feet dry in no time. Miss Tibbs here, she's doing a great job." Then to Alice, "I'll get his top off, and you carry on rubbing his feet."

As the warmth gradually returned, Alice wondered about how many other women were doing this very same thing in the neighbouring cottages. There was the crew and those they had rescued, all of whom would need slowly warming. She concentrated on drying Tom's feet and lower legs, keeping her eyes firmly away from the muscular upper body gradually being revealed as wet layers were peeled away. When the blanket was again wrapped around him, the door opened, and his mother entered.

"I came as soon as I could, but I saw Tom was safe, and it's so cold out there… So many are in a bad way and needed help."

"He's doing all right," her husband replied. "He was shivering something chronic but it's easing now."

"Need to get those trousers off now; I've not done that in a long while," Mrs Barton smiled down at Alice who was still sitting at Tom's feet.

"I'll go now you're back, Mrs Barton," Alice said. "I'm sure Tom will be fine now."

Mrs Barton saw her obvious discomfort and had another suggestion: "The kettle's on the range. I'm sure a cup of tea would help warm him through."

"Of course," Alice replied and moved out of the way so Tom's mother could take her place. "Do you have any news of the others?"

"It's the cold that's got them tonight. I'm sure the others will be fine, but I can't say for Stan, he was in the water for five minutes longer than Tom was. He's a strong lad though, hopefully he'll pull through."

Alice poured three cups of strong tea, stirred in sugar and set them on the table.

"You'll stay for a cup, won't you?" Mrs Barton asked.

"I think I had better check on Stan and Mr Tanner and then… I don't want to get in the way… so I'll go back to the schoolhouse." Alice was unsure of what was best. "That is unless I am needed elsewhere."

"I can see you are worried about your friends, so how about you pop in, then come back here and tell us how they are. Tom won't rest without news of Stan." Mrs Barton got up from her son's side. "I'll top up the pot and have a cup ready for you."

Alice wrapped her coat around her and again braved the chill night air. It took a moment for her to get her bearings and then she turned towards the Tanner cottage. On reaching the back door, Alice paused to knock, but then opened the door and walked in.

The scene within the cottage was like the one she had just left but three times as busy. Mr Tanner and Ben Webb sat side by side on the sofa, both wrapped in blankets over clean, dry clothes. On their laps were bowls of steaming rabbit stew. Hazel was pouring tea and Connie was stirring sugar in. Annie sat beside her husband who appeared to be dozing.

"There you are. We were wondering where you had got to, but Hazel thought she had seen you helping with Tom," Mrs Tanner spoke, as she washed up the supper dishes. "Is he all right? He saved our Stan's life and risked his own; he's a brave man."

"I know; I saw him carrying Stan out of the sea. We didn't know it was Stan of course. They all looked the same until they got closer." Alice looked towards Stan and frowned a little, "Has he warmed through?"

"He seems to be fine," Annie replied. "He stopped shivering and managed to eat a little stew, then I gave him a brandy and he fell asleep. Exhausted and no wonder."

"That's good to hear." Alice knew Stan couldn't have survived much longer in the icy water. She turned

194

back to Mr Tanner and Ben, "Are you all warmed through?"

"We're fine," Mr Tanner replied while Ben nodded between mouthfuls of stew. "It was bad out there though; one of the worst."

"Cup of tea, Alice?" Hazel was about to pour.

"Oh no, I don't want to get in the way. Mrs Barton is making me a cup as I said I would let them know how Stan is, then I'll go back to the school. Thank you for the supper, Mrs Tanner, and I'm sorry your birthday got spoiled, Annie. I'm just thankful the crew are safe." Alice moved towards the door, saying her goodbyes.

"I'll walk back with you," Hazel called. "Knock for me when you are ready."

Back out in the cold again, Alice sighed to feel it nipping at her skin. She suddenly realised how exhausted she was and would be thankful when she was finally opening her own front door. It wasn't to be though, and a few steps led her back to the Bartons' home where she knocked before entering.

Tom was sitting up, a cup cradled between his hands. He turned as Alice stepped into the room and gave a weak smile. His sister, Lucie, had now joined the family group and was sitting beside him.

"How's Stan?" Tom asked.

"He's fine. Sleeping in the chair, but he's eaten a little and had a brandy."

"That's probably what sent him to sleep," Tom grinned.

"Sit down, Miss Tibbs." Mrs Barton was pouring the tea. "You know my daughter, Lucie, don't you? Tom was just telling us they saved the four crew but not the captain."

"Not the captain, how very sad." Alice's thoughts were back in that wild, grey sea.

"He wouldn't leave. Went down with the ship," Mrs Barton reported. "Men can be like that over their ship, some sort of pride."

"He wouldn't leave?" Alice repeated, frowning in disbelief.

"That's right," Tom confirmed, "and it's not that unusual. I've known it happen before. The captain thinks it's his place to stay with the ship."

"Did he believe he could save it?" Alice asked.

"No chance of that." Tom shifted a little in the chair to straighten his body. "No, it's just the way it is. Perhaps he didn't want the humiliation of losing his vessel."

"So, he lost his life," Alice reflected. "How very sad."

They talked for a few more minutes in a desultory way; Alice felt her limbs relaxing and her eyes beginning to close. She stifled a yawn.

"Time to get back," she said. The walk would be a long one tonight and the schoolhouse would feel especially remote.

By the time they got back to the schoolhouse, Alice and Hazel were exhausted. The kettle was pushed onto the hotplate and stoneware hot water bottles collected for filling. "I couldn't drink another cup of tea," Hazel said as she flopped in an armchair.

"It's been quite a night." Alice lit their oil lamps for the bedrooms. "I'll never complain of being stuck in with the bad weather again. It's bed for me now."

Within half an hour the two friends were in their beds. Before she fell asleep, Alice thought of the letters she would write home, and she wondered what Albert would think of her involvement with the lifeboat and the lady launchers.

*

196

My dear Alice,

I had to put pen to paper to express my distress when I read about the lifeboat rescue. How very brave those men are but I can hardly credit that one was so careless as to fall overboard. What imagination you have in describing the 'lady launchers'. I could almost believe it to be true, and marvellous of them to support the good men who launch the boats.

My love, I feel I must express my concerns. It wouldn't do to be repeating these tales back home in Ashford. I am sure Mother would be most worried about you forming friendships with the women of the fishing families. Less said, as they say.

Here, I am waiting in anticipation for news that I have secured a home for us. My application is being reviewed and I can see no reason why we will not be successful.

I saw your parents last night but did not discuss the lifeboat incident, not wanting to distress them unduly.

I look forward to the spring and with it your return to Ashford in the school holidays.

With my fondest thoughts, Albert.

Alice put the letter in the soft leather pouch with her writing paper and stamps. Her spirits had been dampened and as much as she told herself that Albert had never been to Dungeness and couldn't understand what it was like, Alice couldn't shift the feeling that he was being unreasonable. Then she felt cross with herself for being unfair to Albert.

The freezing weather had passed, thankfully. February turned into March and with it came a return of the sea-mists, often lingering all day. Then, just as it seemed that spring would never arrive in this desolate corner of Kent, the mists became less frequent and there seemed to be a definite increase in the temperature. At times Alice even felt a gentle warmth on her back and it gave her a feeling of contentment. But this was the Dungeness point on the Kent coast and the next gale was never far away.

Chapter Twenty-Two

Alice woke in confusion. An almighty crash had descended into her idyllic dream where she and Tom, no Albert... of course it was Albert... were walking along the canal or was it a river? It had all been very pleasant and sunny and they – they being her and Albert – had been holding hands and.... That was the trouble with dreams, so real for a moment and then they faded away and she was left trying to pick up the pieces and getting back to sleep with confused thoughts in her head.

It was lovely and warm in the soft bed, but a distant creaking sound was niggling Alice. Not loud enough to be clear what it was, but enough to alert her that something was amiss. All the time she was bothered by the persistent creak, she would never settle back to sleep. Whatever could the time be? It was still pitch black, but then it was still only March. Another crash, or more of a thud, came. "Oh, I'll have to go and see what it is," Alice muttered. "I'll never be able to settle."

She swung her legs out of the bed and felt for her slippers, then wrapped her woollen shawl tight around her shoulders. On opening her bedroom door, Alice jumped, and her heart crashed about beneath her ribs; Hazel was standing there in her long white night-gown.

"You heard it too then," Hazel said. "Please God it wasn't one of the chimneys coming down. That happened to our nan a couple of years back and it made a terrible mess."

"Oh, no," Alice considered it. "Just think of all the slates here on the schoolhouse, they would be all smashed and falling down to the ground in little pieces. It wouldn't be the one big crash and then nothing. I'm sure the front gate is open and swinging; we must have forgotten to tie it, but the crash... maybe out the back?"

"The hen-coop? We'd best look, although there's nothing to be done if the poor things have lost their home. Not now, not in the dead of night."

Alice had been living in Dungeness for nearly five months now and thought she had experienced all the types of bad weather that could possibly happen here. But on opening the back door, it was clear it was only the shelter of the solid schoolhouse stopping the wind from picking up the two young women and depositing them in Lydd or beyond. They stood at the corner of the building listening to the howl of the gale and the noise of debris scurrying along in the wind. Pieces of slate, wood and branches of ragged broom knocked against the side of the building or were deposited on the shingle, often to be picked up again in the next squall. The moon was full, casting patchy light on the area, as clouds raced across its face. While they stood to take in the scene a slate fell, missing Hazel by inches, causing her to clutch at Alice. They pressed themselves against the rough wall of the schoolhouse, partially protected by the overhanging eves.

"It's not safe to be out here." Alice, as teacher and with three years more experience of life, pulled Hazel back in through the doorway. "Did you see the privy, and how lopsided it was? Nothing we can do about it now though. We'll just have to take our chamber pots as far as we think right and empty them out in the morning."

"We'll go over to see Peggy's husband. He does the odd jobs out here on the school."

"Very well," Alice replied. "We can check with Mrs

Stubbs and one of us can go to see him in the morning. Gosh, I'm cold, not surprising out there in our nightdresses. There's nothing more we can do until the gale eases. Let's try and get some more sleep."

They slept in fits and starts, bothered by the erratic creaking of the front gate and tense with the anticipation of hearing another crash. When the very first weak light from the rising sun crept around their curtains, the young women were pleased to have an excuse to rise from their beds. They huddled in armchairs, bleary eyed, in front of the range and with mugs of hot chocolate in their hands. When the first sounds of the steam train could be heard, crocheted blankets were discarded from their knees and the young women raced to get dressed before Mrs Stubbs arrived.

"I think we should be thankful if we have escaped with just a few slates lost and the privy cast askew," Mrs Stubbs concluded. "Not that I am belittling the loss of a privy. Most inconvenient. Of course, we must see if Mr Webb is available to make repairs and I am not inclined to wait for Peggy to take the message to him after dinner time. The wind has dropped so I suggest the pair of you hasten over to the village and call on Mr Webb. Check on your family, Hazel. Ruth and I can manage for an hour."

The wind had eased, although it remained a brisk south-easterly. Still low in the sky, the sun was deceptive, giving promise of a pleasant day, which could never be fulfilled. Alice and Hazel set off towards Dungeness village, heads bowed towards the wind but grateful its pace had slackened overnight. The landscape had always looked wild, but today it had an unkempt look about it. Severed branches of gorse and broom lay wilting, their pale flesh torn at the point where they had been ripped off their parent plant by the force of the gale. Wooden shingle roof tiles were strewn randomly on the ground; shards of smashed slate lay in grey pools. Lone pieces of netting and tarpaulin moved listlessly in the wind.

All over the headland men and women could be seen alone or in pairs. Alice presumed the salvage work had begun. To see so many figures scattered over the area in this way was unusual; they usually kept to the village and beach. There they were, hauling bits of wood or a reluctant goat back towards their cottages. The children were busy too, caught up in the excitement of chasing after a chicken that had found its freedom or passing a tile to a father on a roof. A storm such as this came with an unwritten rule: A full day at school took second place to family duties.

"There's a few who have lost their goats and chickens overnight," Hazel commented. "It's always the way after a bad storm. We've got to gather them up as soon as we can."

They neared Mr and Mrs Webb's cottage to find Peggy putting a chicken back in its newly repaired pen.

"We'll not be gettin' any eggs from this lot for a while," was Peggy's comment as Alice and Hazel drew closer. "Now what brings you two here when you should be up over there at the school. Summat wrong?"

"Nothing much, Mrs Webb. It's just that the privy fell down in the night," Alice began, "and Mrs Stubbs asked if Mr Webb could..."

"Come an' fix it? He's just out checkin' on the boat an' then he'll be along shortly. Been up since the crack of dawn, he has, fixin' the coop and now off to the boat."

"Wonderful, thank you."

"We'll see you later then, Peggy," Hazel said as they turned away.

"Smoked dabs for yer dinner." Peggy called after them.

The children knew to leave their disagreements behind them as they arrived at school in the morning and afternoon. Mrs Stubbs had no interest in childish tittle-tattle. However, they sometimes found a sympathetic ear from Hazel or Ruth once the headteacher had left for the day. It was rare that an argument from the playground found its way to the schoolroom but that day they began to bicker as the lines of children entered the building.

"It's not fair, it's always him that does the tellin' an' it's my story. It were my pa that told his, so we knew first, not him." Young Dora's eyes brimmed with tears and her cheeks were flushed.

"Well, jus' get on and tell then, Dora, or he will. You know he will. Boys are like that, always wantin' to make trouble." Em, the youngest of five, spoke from experience.

"Me Pa says there's a body, another body found out over Denge way." Fred raised his voice as he announced with glee: "It were a man this time, just lying there an' he ain't newly dead neither."

"He did it, he told," squealed Dora and the tears flowed, whilst her girl friends gathered around, scowling at Fred.

Fred's face had the kind of superior smile you see on a child who has bettered another. He stood half a head taller than the little girl and was two years older than her. That was two years more life experience than Dora, and, to top it off, Fred had two big brothers who had excelled in their duty to train him to be annoying. He looked across at the little girl and said:

"'You know I tell it better, Dora. It needs a man to tell about things like bodies and dyin', don't it?"

"I don't see no man here, Frederick Brown," laughed Victoria Stevens. "Jus' a silly little show-off."

Fred scowled at Victoria, his eyebrows knitted together. "Well, I still told it first," were his final words.

203

"Enough," snapped Mrs Stubbs. "Frederick Brown, you know better than to come in here shouting your news. This is a school room not a street market. Dora, stop wiping your eyes with your apron, find a handkerchief and use it. All of you, back outside, line up sensibly and in silence. Now." Mrs Stubbs drew a deep breath and turned to Alice, "Miss Tibbs, call them in, if you please."

How she walked across the room to the doorway and called the children in, Alice never knew. She moved like some form of machine, following Mrs Stubbs' directions. It was clear whose body had been found and strangely there was some relief in hearing this. For three months Jake Brooks had lain in his shallow grave, inland from his home at Denge. A whole quarter of a year with no proper funeral service and without being laid to rest in the correct way. In all that time his wife and family assumed he had run off and abandoned them; they deserved to know the truth. Well, not the truth... but to know that he had not just gone without a care for them.

This man needed to have a proper burial service and perhaps then he could answer to God in heaven for his sins. It wasn't up to her... to her, Tom and Ben... to lay him to rest in unconsecrated ground, perhaps leaving his spirit to dwell forever in an in-between place between life and death. Alice hadn't really considered it before, she had refused to think of it, pushing him away from her thoughts if he ever threatened to prey upon them. Now she saw it very clearly; Jake Brooks must have a funeral service and be laid to rest in the decent way.

In the time that had passed, Thomas Barton and Ben Webb had gone out fishing, manned the lifeboats, made repairs to their homes and whatever else the men did. Alice had taught at the school, written her letters home and kept herself busy with daily chores.

The three of them never mentioned the accident, for that was what it was. But how could they ever truly live their lives without guilt whilst a body lay covered beneath a thin layer of shingle just a short distance away? Even when she returned to Ashford her memories of Dungeness would be tarnished by the one terrible event.

"You've not got one of your headaches coming?" Hazel asked Alice as the school day ended. The children had left for the day, and it was just the teacher and her assistants left to tidy up.

"A headache... I... well, just a slight one," Alice tried to pull herself into the present. "Nothing to worry about."

"It's just that you do look awfully pale, doesn't she, Ruth?"

"I expect Miss Tibbs is just tired after the storm last night," replied Ruth. "I know I am, and you were both up in the night."

"Yes, that will be it." Alice snatched at the excuse. "I'll be fine in the morning."

"So, we'll have a cup of tea and a currant bun then the three of us can go out and find out who it is. If it's even true, because there's no one gone missing from hereabouts and it don't... doesn't... sound like he's come from the sea, not if he was found all the way inland." Hazel led the way through to the schoolhouse.

"I hadn't thought," Alice began. "I hadn't thought we would be going out to find out who... who he is or was. Isn't it a family matter?"

"But we won't know whose family he is unless we go and find out, will we?" Hazel put tea leaves in the pot. "There's buns in the larder, if you don't mind, Ruth. I think Alice must have one of her headaches coming on; we'll sort out the tea, shall we?"

Alice found herself caught up in it all, trudging up and

205

down the shingle banks to satisfy the curiosity of her companions. There was a disjointed ribbon of people between the body and the Dungeness homes, some, like them, still on their way to view to body, and others returning to their homes. Alice watched them meet, exchange a few words and continue their paths.

Is this what they do every time a body is found? Alice wondered. *Do they set off, every one of them in order to view it? Every time a body is found...* She repeated the words in her mind. *What am I thinking of, what is it with this place that makes me accept that finding a body is commonplace?* Her thoughts moved to the actual body, whom she knew to be Jake Brooks and she wondered if he had been identified yet. *Will I have to face him again?* A wave of sickness rose through her body and caught in her throat. *Will I have to see his face?*

By now they were at the midway point, and Alice forced her thoughts away from that moment when Jake Brooks had come across her in Ed's shack. She never wanted to see his black eyes, or the dark stubble on his chin, or his filthy hands pulling at his braces as he lowered his trousers. *He won't be like that now,* she reminded herself. *He will be changed. But whatever he is, I don't have to face it. And it's hardly proper that I should.*

Hazel and Ruth were a few steps ahead of Alice, so she had to raise her voice in order to get their attention. "I really shouldn't be here," she called to them. "What will people think of me coming out to look at a body when it will be no one I know, not a family member or even a friend."

"You can come along with us," Ruth replied. "We are almost there now."

"We couldn't leave you on your own," Hazel paused to allow Alice to catch up.

"I don't know that Mrs Stubbs would be at all happy

about it..." Alice tried to reason with them.

"Oh, she knows how it is..." Ruth said. "We have to know, don't we? The children will be talking about it tomorrow, so best we've seen for ourselves."

Alice continued, resigned that she must yet again face Jake Brooks.

Their destination was marked by a couple of old men, sat hunched up together, as sentinels for the body. The body itself appeared to be covered with a blanket. The last of the spectators were now some distance away and the area had almost returned to its previous state of being quite desolate, having no properties nearby and nothing to offer either farmer or fisherman. It had been a good location to conceal a body, but not good enough.

The men looked up as they neared and one spoke: "Come to pay yer respects have yer?"

"That's right, Bert," Hazel replied. "We thought we should as soon as school ended. You're keeping an eye on him, are you?"

"Tha's what the vicar said was right and proper. He's gone on the train to Lydd and most likely he'll bring the constable back wi' him. This being not a normal sort of death, if you see what I mean."

"A normal type of death?" Alice asked, her voice high and unnatural.

"Like a drowning or illness..." He paused to ponder on it, "or even a normal type of accident. No, when a body is just lyin' around and that body is a young man then it's not a normal type of death whatever way you see it."

"I see," Alice replied. Her body stiffened and her throat constricted.

"We've come over to see who he is," Hazel informed. "I can't think, none of us can, that it could be anyone from Dungeness."

"Ah, no it ain't no one from Dungeness but he's

207

from hereabouts," Bert turned and nodded towards the figure. "It's that bad un from Denge, that Jake Brooks, him what was up t' no good."

"Oh gosh," replied Hazel. "They said he'd gone off and no one knew where."

"Well they do now," Bert replied, his companion nodding in agreement.

"His wife left for Camber," Ruth said. "She'll have to be told."

"Of course she will, lass, an' no doubt the constable is on his way already." Bert paused to ponder on it for a moment and continued, "They'll bring a cart no doubt."

"A cart?" Alice repeated.

"I'm thinking of the body. Stands to reason that the vicar don't want no body rottin' away at his place. Now newly dead is a different matter, they waits at the vicarage until the funeral. No, this one will be going straight to Lydd on a cart and no need for you girls to worry about it."

All the time they spoke, Alice could barely take her eyes off the blanketed body. She took a step closer and eyed its contours; the rough blue blanket had settled in nicely around him and at the corner it rose and fell gently with the breeze, revealing the heel of a black boot. Alongside the body and head, stones had been placed to keep the cover in place.

"You don't want t' see no dead body," said Bert, following her gaze.

"Oh no... no... I just. It's all very sad," Alice finished lamely.

"It's been that cold, it's kept him nice and shipshape," Bert informed. "Not that a damned sinner like him deserves to lie peaceful in a grave, but tha's up to the vicar and God to say."

"Of course, it is," Hazel replied briskly. "No doubt the cart will be here soon and that will be the end of it.

We'll be getting back now. We just had to see who it is, to be sure it wasn't anyone we knew, anyone from Dungeness."

"It will only be that Ed Brooks to shed a tear over 'im, and he's been a changed man since that Tom Barton set him up with some decent men to work alongside him on the boat. He'll not waste much time worrying over that no-good cousin of his, not if he has much sense about 'im. No, he might just say good riddance like the rest of us."

"I'm not sure about that, Bert," Hazel replied as the three of them turned away. "But I've no doubt Ed knows he's better off without his cousin."

With that, the three young women retraced their steps over the undulating shingle and back towards the railway tracks. They didn't talk, two of them wondering why the body of no-good Jake Brooks had been buried in a shallow shingle grave a little inland of his Denge home. They hoped that it had nothing to do with any of the Dungeness villagers or his cousin Ed, who was fast becoming one of their own. Hazel and Ruth could never have imagined, as they glanced at Alice, that her thoughts were so much more turbulent than their own. Behind her calm gaze there was both fear of what might happen next and relief that the body had at last been revealed. At the railway tracks, they parted with a few brief words. Ruth turned towards the coast and her home at the lighthouse keeper's cottage.

Alice and Hazel walked on in silence, soon reaching the picket fence surrounding the schoolhouse. As they paused at the fence, they saw in the distance, on the track that led directly from Lydd, a cart and three dark figures. They waited and watched, in silent agreement, the progress of the figures who soon revealed themselves as being the constable and the vicar, as well as a labourer who pushed the cart which would, on its return journey, carry the body.

209

Chapter Twenty-Three

"Not going up to Lydd today then?" Peggy's sharp eyes were on Alice as she bustled in and placed her basket on the table.

"No, I had a few chores to do," Alice looked up from her darning. Was it that time already? She hadn't wanted to face Peggy's scrutiny. She began to gather her repaired stockings. "It's a lovely day; I thought I would walk to the beach. Who would have thought that having just suffered that dreadful storm, it is calmer than ever?" Alice was talking too much, and she knew it. She resolved not to give away any of her inner thoughts to Mrs Webb, who already seemed to know and see too much.

"A lovely day for some," Peggy repeated darkly. She unwrapped skinned rabbit and slapped it down on the wooden table. "Not so nice for that wife of Jake Brooks. Poor woman has turned up here already. Must have been walking since before dawn. Gone to see Ed and then the vicar, no doubt."

"Poor woman," Alice reflected on what it must be like to believe your husband had run off with another woman, only to learn that he'd not even made it as far as Lydd. She fastened her walking boots and gathered her shawl. "Thank you for preparing our dinner, Mrs Webb. I'll see you at church tomorrow."

Alice didn't follow the railway tracks towards the coast but took the path that led towards the Pilot and the fishermen's cottages. It wasn't a path in the sense that it was much different from the ground around it, but the stones were a little firmer from the years of being pressed down upon by foot and carts. Some of the younger children were out playing bat and ball games; she gave a wave but was determined not to linger. The older ones would be busy with chores; a mother needn't work the water pump if there was a strong child to do the job for her.

It took at least twenty minutes to reach the cottages standing just back from the beach bank. Alice walked between the fishermen's homes and stood on the ridge looking out to sea. The steely grey water, having lost much of its recent spirit, had slunk back as low as Alice had ever seen it. Waves rolled in, with a marked lack of enthusiasm, deposited little in the way of debris and backed away pulling a little of the brown sand with them.

The narrow band of sand was clean but being so flat it remained too waterlogged to tempt Alice to stroll along it. Instead, she carefully side-stepped down the steep bank and walked along the base of it. There was no hurry and she often paused to bend down and inspect an unusual shell or remains of a sea creature. Twice she pocketed a stone with a hole right through it. Hag-stones they were called by the locals, who believed they had magic powers. For Alice they made an attractive decoration strung up by the back door of the schoolhouse. Maybe something to take home with her and remind her of her time in Dungeness.

From her position at the bottom of the shingle bank, Alice couldn't see the cottages or even the fishing boats perched on top of it. When she began her ascent, the bows appeared. The boats were all on the ridge, it being a Saturday: a day for relaxation and repairs. Several of the fishermen were there and nodded a greeting, but they left her to her walk. Alice spotted Tom Barton and, as she passed, he called out a casual greeting:

"Good day, Miss Tibbs. A fine morning for a walk."

"It is. How thankful we all must be that the wind has eased." Polite words, covering a multitude of questions and thoughts that stormed around in her head. "Did you suffer any storm damage?"

"Just my net shed, it's taken a battering, but I've been able to right it." He stepped closer and spoke quietly, "They found him then."

"He can be laid to rest now," Alice replied.

"His wife's over at Denge, with Ed and Emily. She'll stay for the funeral and then go back to Camber."

"The funeral... of course." Not in the school, please not in the school.

"It'll be in Lydd, Monday afternoon. Some of us are walking up and coming back on the train. Ben and I, we've got to go, to support Ed and Emily. Not that it will be easy of course."

"No, no it won't be." To go to the funeral of the man you've killed and already buried, to go there and give your last respects. Alice's stomach recoiled at the very thought of it; she wouldn't go. No, there was no need for that at all. "And has anyone been asking? The constable I mean... has he... has he spoken to anyone?"

"He's been along to see Ed and of course someone spoke to the wife last night. There's nothing to tell. Emily was over here with Connie, and Ed was in Lydd that day. He'll go over to Denge and see the old people, but they saw nothing. The constable will do his job, up to a point. Ask a few questions and go back to Lydd. He'll not be hanging around here longer than he has to."

"I see." But Alice didn't see how a body could be recovered from a shallow shingle grave and once found, that it could be dealt with in such a casual manner. It wasn't the way it would be in Ashford;

212

certainly, there would be a proper enquiry and paperwork. Yes, there would be papers to write and forms to fill in. But Alice didn't know, not really, exactly how it would be dealt with in Ashford because this was beyond the realms of her experience.

"I'll be seeing you then." Tom turned back to his work. It wasn't the place to be discussing the matter any further and both were satisfied the secret was safe between the three of them and the shingle grave.

Jake Brooks was buried at the expense of Lydd Parish on the Monday. Those who attended the funeral walked along the tracks, passing the school, and on to Lydd. From the high windows of the schoolroom, Alice didn't see them pass but her mind was on them, as they made their pilgrimage to pay their last respects, not to the dead man but to his wife and family. He had no one left at Denge now and even his cousin was working with the men from around the point at Dungeness.

Alice didn't want to hear of the funeral. Who had been there. What had been said. Whether it was mentioned or not, the thoughts of the dead man filled her mind. Mrs Stubbs had no cause to discuss the service and wasn't one to gossip. Eventually, it was Peggy Webb who felt the need to raise the subject, as the teachers and assistants ate salted cod from Peggy's own stores.

"He'll be in the earth by now," the old woman commented, while she washed up large pans at the Belfast sink. "Jus' earth, no nice brick sides, not on the parish."

"No one here will shed a tear," Ruth replied.

"Denge or not, he brings shame on his family to be in a common grave," Peggy persisted.

"A penny a week for funeral insurance isn't always easy to come by," Mrs Stubbs replied calmly. "I'm sure

213

his wife tried her best, but she has children to feed and clothe. She put her children first and I commend her for it. There's many a family who go without food or heat to pay for a respectable grave."

"She'll be returning to Camber tonight and not looking back," Peggy snatched the plates away as soon as the last morsels were eaten.

"Lovely cod, Mrs Webb. Delicious." Mrs Stubbs closed the subject.

Later that afternoon, as Mrs Stubbs prepared to leave for the day, the unmistakable sound of the train rattling by reminded Alice that those who attended the funeral would now be returning home by the twelve minutes past two from Lydd. It was over.

The following Saturday, Alice departed with the fish on the early morning train to Lydd. She had left Hazel a note, saying that she would meet her as the mid-morning train came into Lydd. There was a chore to be done and that was the reason for leaving early. Before her friend had risen, Alice was very quietly raising the latch and creeping off across the shingle. How she would explain herself more fully when she saw Hazel later, Alice had no idea, as sneaking off to Lydd at this early hour would seem most out of character.

The fish was being loaded as Alice reached the small station. Wooden crates were being passed into the luggage van and stacked, most likely ready for a journey to London. The south-westerly wind was brisk, so the fishermen had their hoods up while keeping their eyes on the job. After a night at sea, they were intent on the task in hand and if any of them noticed the young teacher stepping into the coach, they were not inclined to comment on it.

In the early hours of the Saturday morning, Alice was the only passenger, for which she was thankful. With her shawl pulled tight around her shoulders, she huddled in her seat and gazed unseeing across the shingle ridges, as they blended into flat farmland before eventually reaching the distant hills. Within ten minutes, the scalloped canopies of the station buildings were clear to see and a couple of staff emerged. They stared at her, not expecting a passenger at this time, but Alice's serious face discouraged idle comments, so she went on her way without any bother.

The station was a short walk from the town centre, and once out of the yard, Alice walked briskly along Station Road. She gazed at the weather-boarded smock mill to her left and then with disinterest at the houses on the roadside as she neared her destination. Nodding politely at people who passed her on the street, she could not have said if they were man or woman, young or old. It wasn't a day to be paying attention to the details.

Station Road, now flanked by terraced cottages, swung to the right then straightened again. Past the slumbering Star Pub and the ornate red brick Mission Hall, Alice walked on. Then, as the main road again bore to the right, she chose to ignore the deviation and continued straight ahead into Church Road. Only now that her goal was in sight did Alice's pace falter and she wondered about the wisdom of her outing. She slowed to admire the pretty cottages on either side, their low roofs of weathered red tiles, and plants creeping up rendered walls, giving promise of floral beauty in the coming months. For now, primroses and bluebells sat in clusters within the narrow band of earth between cottages and road. Then she studied the cottages with their upper storeys clad in black weatherboarding and pondered whether she preferred the distinctive black or more traditional white boarding. Finally, before entering the churchyard, Alice paused to appreciate the substantial old house, set back a little from the road. She wondered what lay behind the fine square windows and smiled at the tiny dormers peeping from the red tile, hipped roof.

The road came to an end and there was nowhere else to go but to step through the gateway into the churchyard. She gazed up at the eastern end of the medieval church, liking the form of the traditional window with detailed stonework. Then looking to the tower on the far end, Alice wondered if, at some point during the day, the eight bells would ring with joy for all to hear in the small town.

It was to Alice's right, where the churchyard was bordered by a low brick wall, she noticed the recently prepared grave of freshly dug earth lying dark and moist in a gentle mound. She picked up her skirts, to prevent the hems being soaked by the dew-laden grass and walked steadily towards the grave. There was no marker, as befitted a pauper's grave. The only signs of the recent ceremony being some bundles of evergreen leaves and wilted spring blossom.

Alice stood beside the grave in silence for a minute or two, her head bowed, and eyes fixed on the soft bare earth. Then she spoke, very quietly, without faltering:

"May God forgive you for your sins: he knows there were many. May he forgive me for allowing you to lie in a shingle grave. I will take the blame for nothing else. I leave you now, knowing that you have been buried as you should be and with the hope that you will repent in heaven. Dear God, I pray for this man's family. May they find peace and comfort in this harsh world and may his children live to be better men than their father." At this point Alice took a step from the grave and, before turning her back on Jake Brooks forever, she recited the Lord's prayer in the same level tone: "Our Father, which art in heaven, hallowed be thy name...."

In those few minutes Alice had stood at the

216

graveside, it was as if only herself and the dead man existed. She had lost all sense of her surroundings and had no awareness of any other person being nearby. So, when she turned and saw someone standing just a few yards behind her she was momentarily stunned. It felt that all her inner thoughts and fears were laid bare for this stranger to read. She stood frozen, for a moment, her brown eyes fixed upon the grey ones of this other young woman.

The stranger's hair was pale, bleached, as if life had drained all colour from it. It was pulled back in a small bun, flat behind small ears that protruded a little. Her cheekbones were prominent, and her skin had no colour to it, nor any distinguishing marks. The large grey eyes were the only sign that in another time, another life, this woman could be beautiful. As she stood, her long black skirt hung awkwardly as if it was meant for a larger woman, having been gathered in at the back. Thin, blue veined hands clutched at a ragged black shawl, pulling it tighter in a vain attempt to keep the slim body warm.

"Did you know 'im?"

"I... no. No, I didn't, not at all."

"Jus' passin' by?"

"Just passing by," Alice confirmed. "I stopped and just spent a moment. Giving my respects."

"He don't deserve yer respects. He was a bad un, our Jake. I weren't sorry, not when he went off and not when they found 'im dead."

"Oh...I."

"I shouldn't say that, should I? Not to a lady like you." She paused and frowned a little. "Have I seen you hereabouts before?"

"I've been staying at Dungeness, at the school."

"You're that new teacher. The one that helped Ed." She nodded as her dulled brain pieced together the memories. "That were good of you. He's all right, Ed

217

is. I hope he gets a chance now with Jake gone."

"That's right, I helped Ed tidy up their home."

"So, now you're here. Jus' passing by and you stopped off to say a little prayer, even though you knew nothing of 'im"

"It seemed like the right thing to do," Alice confirmed.

"Yes, I can see it would, what with you bein' a vicar's daughter or so I hear."

Alice took a step back from the widow. "I'll leave you to have a moment alone. I've some errands to do in town."

"Thank you. I'll have a word and then I'll be off meself. I stayed overnight with me cousin; the constable wanted to see me, but it's done now, and I'll set off to Camber shortly. Maybe get a lift if I'm lucky."

"Goodbye then," Alice took a few steps back towards the church. Then feeling deep in her pocket, she took a handful of coins and turning back she thrust them awkwardly at the stranger. "Here, take them. For the children."

"Ta. I don't like to take charity, but I can't say that the children don't need it."

Alice walked away neither looking back at the grave nor the young widow. Hot buttered toast and a pot of tea at one of the local tearooms beckoned.

Chapter Twenty-Four

"Look Miss, a rainbow." Young Dora tugged at Alice's sleeve. "Look Miss, it's going right over my house an' all the others."

Alice looked up and saw to the south-east a glowing arc, radiating from near the lighthouse. It shone vividly from red through to violet within a steel-blue sky, then faded a little as it brushed over low lying clouds above the sea, before reaching its destination. Alice didn't long for a pot of gold at the end of the rainbow; no that was for the likes of her namesake who visited Wonderland. Where this rainbow ended would suit her very nicely. She was sure, if only it were possible to reach it, that the rainbow completed its journey in Hythe. Once in Hythe she would sit in a toast-rack tram carriage with Albert beside her, just like last summer, and be transported to the seafront. The sun would be warm on her skin and the sky a cerulean blue. They would stroll along the promenade and maybe have tea and cake at The Imperial. Then a walk along the Military Canal, pausing to admire the well-kept flower beds and standing on a bridge to look down on graceful swans. That would be her pot of gold at the end of the rainbow.

"Children, come here," Alice beckoned them, and they stood in a semi-circle around her. "Let us make our own rainbow, in our own colours from the stones we have here. It can go from charcoal and brown, through to pale grey, beige and white. Will we be able to find enough white stones do you think?"

She started organising them all into groups and the children soon caught her enthusiasm, eager to go searching beyond the boundaries of the school playground.

"Who's that walking under the rainbow?" Eliza asked her friend, Dora.

Dora squinted into the distance, "I think it's Mr Barton. My ma thinks he's ever so handsome, but he's old, maybe even thirty."

"What do you think, Miss Tibbs?" asked Dora.

"Don't be silly, girls," Hazel interrupted, "Miss Tibbs has a special man friend back home in Ashford. Now come along, you're meant to be looking for whites, I'll help you."

It was Tom Barton striding out towards the school. By the time he reached the perimeter fence, the rainbow had been completed and the children were lining up to go inside.

"'Ere Mr Barton," called Fred. "Did you know you walked under a rainbow? Have you come to see ours?"

The orderly line was broken as the younger pupils vied to be the ones to show their bit of the pebble picture. Alice allowed them a minute or so and then called out: "Now then, back in your lines, boys behind Ruth, girls with Hazel. Quickly now." Then she looked at Tom, and asked, "Was there something I could help you with? Or do you have a message for someone?"

"It was you I came to see," he looked down at her, grey eyes softly creased around the edges, dark blond hair curling wildly in the wind. "I've some news, but I'll wait while you see the children off." Then he sat himself down on the edge of a ridge, which served as a seat for the children at playtime. It was as if he had all the time in the world to wait and clearly wasn't going to say any more yet.

220

She turned back to the school and helped Ruth tidy up whilst Hazel read the class a chapter of Alice in Wonderland. Then, as the children raced home or walked along in small groups, according to their age, Alice went back to the playground.

"You've something to tell me?" Alice asked.

"It's about my uncle." Tom continued to sit on the shingle bank, looking up at her. "He's not been managing too well since my aunt died and he's going to move in with his daughter, my cousin Mary. So, there's a spare cottage and in fair condition with a living room, two bedrooms and a big attic for the nets to dry in."

"Are you wanting it for yourself?" Alice asked, unsure of where he lived.

"No, I'm happy enough in my grandfather's old place. I've got plans for it. I was thinking of Ed and Emily and how they could move around the point to Dungeness, now they are married."

"Tom... Mr Barton, that's a wonderful idea! Emily will be thrilled; I don't think she's ever settled back in Denge. I believe she's forever visiting Connie Webb."

"So perhaps you'll come and let them know. We've two hours until sunset; plenty of time to be there and back."

"I'd love to," Alice replied. "I'll be with you in a few minutes, if you don't mind waiting."

She rushed through the school, full of apologies to Hazel and Ruth, asking them to tidy up and saying she would be out for a while. Then into her bedroom, anxious to be rid of the formal black dress, Alice pulled on a soft tweed skirt then a pretty blouse and cardigan. The dress was thrown on her bed, with no regard to possible creases. Back through to the kitchen, Alice wrapped chunks of fruit cake; she was hungry after a day's teaching. Snatching a coat from a hook, she ran back through the school, ignoring the surprised

221

glances from her young assistants.

"Tell me about the house. Whereabouts is it?" Alice began, having offered Tom a piece of cake.

"It's just past mine, towards the Pilot," Tom replied. "It could do with a few repairs on the seaward side, but that's to be expected. It's a nice place though. Comes with most of the furniture and I know he got a decent range a few years back."

"A range. Emily will be thrilled!" Alice could see the open fire in the Denge shack and whatever had been done to make the home better, a smoking fire spoiled everything. "She was saving for one; did you know?"

They walked on in silence for a while after that, taking a route straight across the ridges, keeping the lighthouse to their left. Alice struggled at times and often carried her backstays, preferring to trudge over the shingle in her walking boots. Tom slowed his pace or let her take the lead.

The sea sparkled a deep blue and a couple of ships could be seen in the distance. A light breeze encouraged cotton wool clouds to scurry across the sky forming and reforming shapes as they went. The air was fresh and slightly salty.

Alice had been deep in thought about Ed and Emily Brooks and the changes in their lives; finally, she voiced some of her thoughts: "Will Ed move, do you think? He is a proud man and loves his home."

"For all his mistakes and a bit of a temper, he'll see sense over this, I'm sure," Tom replied. "I've plans to get him on the lifeboat crew."

"A chance to make amends," Alice reflected.

"There's only Ed's parents left at Denge, and a cousin who goes to work in Lydd." Tom paused and offered a hand to help Alice up a shingle ridge. She paused, uncertain, then accepted it for a moment, letting go as soon as she was steady.

Silence hung between them as they both knew

222

why the population of Denge had halved overnight. With Jake Brooks gone, his widow had no choice but to move further along the coast to Camber, knowing that she could neither support herself and her three children at Denge nor expect Ed to bear the burden.

"They'll still be close enough that Emily can check on them daily." Tom was now thinking of the family left behind, "They could all move in together, but I was hoping to improve their home, not make it more crowded. I imagine the old folk will want to stay at Denge, I just hope they won't stand in the way of this move."

"I'm sure Ed and Emily will do what's right and there are others here who can help out," Alice replied.

As they neared Denge, Alice could see there had been some changes. Something was different but at first she couldn't quite place what had changed. Ed appeared from behind his home and gave them a wave.

"I've been making repairs to my parents' place," he said, "It got the worst of the storm last week."

Then Alice realised, "One of the cottages has gone."

"It was in a bad way, so my Pa, he's been taking it down all week and we can make repairs to the others."

Emily appeared, having heard voices and her face was all smiles on seeing Tom and Alice.

"I'm glad to have found you both; we've got some news." Tom began. "I'll get straight to it – there's an empty property round the point and I thought it might suit you."

"What for us, really?" Emily turned to look at Ed, "Can we? Can we move round the point?"

"Just hold back a minute," Ed replied. "Come on in and we'll have a cup of tea and a chat about it. I'm not saying no, Em, I'm just saying that we need to hear more about it."

"Of course, you do," Tom said, "and a cup of tea would be welcome, thank you."

The kettle was boiling in no time and Emily had a tin of drop scones full of plump sultanas which she placed on the table. Alice noticed the shack was a lot fresher now the nets had been moved, although the smell of woodsmoke was still strong. A small settee sat below the window where the nets had been, giving a more homely look to the room.

They all sat at the table, which now had four matching chairs. "We got these chairs from Ida's," Emily informed them.

"It's certainly looking smarter in here," Tom said.

"Thanks to Miss Tibbs," Ed replied.

Alice glanced at Tom and they both knew that the other was remembering, although they never spoke of it. She wondered if the two men ever mentioned Jake's death amongst themselves. Their secret lay buried in a shallow shingle grave. Ed and Emily's tidier new home had come at a higher price than they could ever have imagined: the life of his cousin. But that wasn't fair, Alice reminded herself. He (she couldn't even think his name) had done wrong and what followed was an accident, a terrible accident and he had paid the price of attempting to assault her.

Alice brushed the thoughts away; she would not be plagued by them. "Tell them about the cottage, Mr Barton. I don't think Emily can wait until the tea is brewed."

"It's a smart little place. My uncle lives there but he's getting no younger so he's moving in with my cousin, Mary. It could do with a few repairs, they always do, being on the coast, but nothing you can't fix during the summer. It's along by the Pilot, not far from my place and only five minutes or so from the Webbs' cottage.

"And it's all right is it? All right with your uncle?" Ed

asked.

"I've had a word and there's no one else that needs it. I've got my Granddad's place. My cousin, Mary, is happy where she is, and her sister moved to Lydd. It's yours if you want it. If you'd like the furniture and the range, you can come to an agreement: pay him a bit every month until it's settled."

"What do you think, Ed?" Emily's eyes shone as she looked up at him, sitting beside her.

"It sounds like a great plan. We could do with a bit more space and to move the boat around the point would mean the lads who help me wouldn't have to walk here every day."

"How many rooms does it have?" Emily asked.

There's the kitchen-cum-living room, about the same size as this and then two bedrooms, both a good size. Out the back, there's the water closet and a shed. My cousin, Mary, she has a copper and wash-house by hers and they all share it, the four houses." Tom paused, "And the loft is a fair size with a ladder going up the outside, you know what I mean. Plenty of space for your nets."

"Thank you very much, we appreciate it and I can't say no to providing Emily with a better home. And to bring the boat to Dungeness, well, that will make life easier." Ed took a sip of his tea and continued, "Best we come and have a look at it, if that's all right with your grandfather."

"He'll be fine with that," Tom replied. "We'll be back on the two o'clock tide on Sunday, so say half-past four. Does that suit you?"

"Perfect," replied Emily. "I'll be so excited; I don't know how I'll think of anything else until I see it."

"That all sounds fair enough," Ed agreed

"Will you be able to come and look with us, Miss Tibbs?" Emily asked. "It takes another woman to see what needs doing."

"Emily, I'd very much like to but I'm going back to Ashford on the ten-fifteen."

"Of course, back home for Easter. It sounds funny saying that." Emily paused for a moment to reflect on her words. "I mean to say that I forget you have a home back in Ashford. I always think you belong here. Don't you think so, Tom?"

Alice was kept from hearing Tom's opinion on the matter, and he was given a reprieve from having to voice it, as it was Ed who replied to his wife: "Miss Tibbs has her young man back home in Ashford and a wedding in the summer."

"How silly, excuse my bad manners Miss Tibbs, I thought… I mean to say..." No one knew what Emily thought because she changed the subject, "More tea, Mr Barton… Tom?"

The sun was setting towards Rye as Alice and Tom walked back from Denge. It added a warmth to the grey shingle and made the sea a richer shade of blue. It was wonderful to be a part of improving someone's life and Alice felt a glow of contentment. As they reached the lighthouse, they paused before going their own way home, Tom along the coast towards the Pilot and Alice along the tracks to the schoolhouse.

"You'll be going home for Easter on Saturday," he said. "Two weeks back in Ashford. There will be blossom on the trees and daffodils in the gardens."

"Yes, I imagine there will be," Alice replied. "How odd, I hadn't really thought of it recently. How different it is to here, I mean."

"Perhaps you've become used to it."

"Perhaps I have, but it will be lovely to see the flowering cherry trees and spring bulbs; Mother has such a pretty display of tulips." Alice looked around at the shingle ground with its tough grass and tenacious little plants.

"Dungeness has a beauty of its own and in the

summer, we'll have our own little flowers, but perhaps you'll have to look harder for them, they'll be more subtle."

"I'll have plenty of time before I return home in July. And what about the broom, will that flower by then?"

"Yes, that will be in flower when you return and be bold enough. You'll see a bit of colour by late spring. Then you'll go back to the town to be married and be so busy you'll forget all about us."

"Oh no," Alice looked up at him, "I wouldn't do that, and I'll visit. Of course, I'll visit."

"Visiting isn't the same," he replied. "You won't be a part of it anymore."

"No, I don't suppose I will be."

"Time to move on," Tom said.

"Time to move on," Alice repeated thoughtfully.

Chapter Twenty-Five

Alice left Dungeness for Ashford on the following Saturday. As the wheels of the tank engine gathered pace, the light rains falling from low clouds were left hanging over the shingle headland. She passed through Lydd and by the time the train reached Appledore, the sky was blue with white wisps of cloud. From the grimy window, Alice looked out to appreciate the lush green fields and occasional group of playful lambs.

Soon she was nearing Ashford and the parish church with its turreted tower came into view; a cluster of Tudor, Georgian and Victorian buildings nestled around it. Set below the town, Alice could see Ashford's railway station and works and, to the right, her future home in New Town. The engine eased onto one of four tracks between the two platforms. Alice scanned the area under the deep, ornate canopies and soon spotted her parents who were, just as eagerly, looking for their daughter.

By the time the train came to a halt, Alice was already on her feet, holding onto her seat to steady herself. Then she was hauling her suitcase through the carriage doorway, where it was taken by Reverend Tibbs.

"Alice, it's been so long. All through this dreadful winter. Let me look at you." Her mother released Alice from her embrace and stood back to look at her. "I shall have to get used to your fringe, even though I saw it at

Christmas. You look a little older; it must be teaching all those children. You mustn't forget to cream your face at night."

"My dear, she must become older. Do not fuss so." Reverend Tibbs gave his daughter an affectionate pat on the arm. "Splendid to see you, my dear; we can't wait to hear all your news."

A porter hovered and was charged with the duty of carrying Alice's case to the pony and trap waiting patiently outside the station yard. They walked along the platform, out through the station gate and all the time Alice felt quite dazed by it all. Where was the fresh country air Ashford boasted? Here it was all smoke and steam, laced with pipe tobacco. So many people: the staff, those who had alighted, and those about to join the train. Such a noise, compared with the relative tranquillity of Dungeness, and such a diverse range of accents assaulting Alice's ears. She had not thought about it before, but the railway had attracted workers and visitors from all over the country.

Outside the station, the railway horse-bus was preparing to take travellers into the town. For Alice, it was a ride in the trap to the peace and quiet of the Willesborough rectory. With her father at the reins, they turned to the right, jostling for a place on the busy road between town and station. Men in cloth caps astride push bikes weaved their way around the carts, and boys darted out from nowhere, taking their chance amongst the traffic. A familiar Lion Brewery horse-drawn van passed them at a fair speed, causing the rector to mutter ungodly words under his breath. Alice noticed she was clenching her fists around the handles of her handbag, nervous at the pace of life back home in Ashford.

Thankfully, they skirted the town centre and reached the more peaceful Hythe Road to Willesborough village. As the white, weather-boarded windmill neared, the pony instinctively turned into Church Road. There was the spire of her father's church, St Mary the Virgin, and finally they turned into the rectory.

As before, Albert was due to come for afternoon tea. Now spring was here, Alice was hoping that he would agree to stroll over to New Town. He was sure to have heard by now which house was to be theirs and they could have a look at the outside. Perhaps during the week, Alice and her mother could go and introduce themselves to the current tenant and see inside.

There was a rap on the door and there he was looking just the same as always… but perhaps his hair was a little shorter, or maybe just slicked down in a different manner.

"Alice dearest, at last you are with us again." Albert held both her hands and gazed at her. "Home at last. How I have worried about you and the wisdom of you being so far from home."

"All is well, Albert. I'm sure this time away before we marry has been an adventure I can always look back on."

"Nevertheless, perhaps a position closer to home would have been wiser."

Stepping through into the dining room, Albert's attention was fully on her parents as they all went through the familiar motions of enquiries about work, family and observations about recent news. Alice became desperate to have word of her future home. It seemed as if every minute lasted an age, but she must just sit and wait for a moment of silence before she could ask about what must be the most interesting topic for them all. Finally, it was the rector who asked the all-important question:

"What news do you have on the house, Albert? Has Mr Baldwin set a retirement date yet?"

"Bad news, sir. Bad news indeed." Albert bowed his head slightly to portray the burden of telling. "I was told just this week that Mr Baldwin is to retire at the end of July, but his replacement comes from Manchester with a family of five children. His need for a house is greater than ours."

"That is bad luck and after all your hopes and expectations. Very disappointing." The rector shook his head in dismay and pushed his sandwiches aside for a moment whilst he reflected on the news.

Alice didn't speak. She had visualised it all: Daily life as a married woman would start when she stood at the front door to see Albert off in the morning; while he walked past the trees and across the green and she would watch him until he was out of sight, before returning to her housework. Later, she would walk to the local shop or the library with a basket under her arm. At the weekends, she might watch her husband work on the allotment, and they could have either his mother or her parents to afternoon tea. Alice had seen her life centred in a terraced house set on the green with the noise and bustle of the railway works in the background. What was she to picture now?

Her mother was talking. Alice heard the words but couldn't recall them. She forced herself to listen.

"...Might there be another opportunity? You deserve a house, Albert, they must see that. A good worker must surely have a house when he marries? Do you know of any others? Have you heard of any more being built, for that was the plan; they always intended to build more, you know..."

"There is a chance of a flat, but Mother says, and I must agree, that why would we live in a flat when she has a decent house with space for us all?"

There is a plan, Alice realised. *We are to live with Albert's mother. He has decided and not thought to ask me.* Her body felt heavy, crushed by the

231

disappointment. *Of course, it is a good plan and what most young couples expect, but it's not what I thought... I can't see it at all. We had plans: we were to decorate... choose new wallpaper. What role is there for me in a home where his mother already has all her routines in place, just as she likes them?*

When Albert left, two hours later, Alice had barely spoken. However, a plan had been made for the two of them to travel by train to Folkestone the next day. The weather looked good and a walk along the Leas with the chance of seeing across the sea to France was appealing. Alice forced a smile as Albert leaned forward and kissed her cheek in the hallway. She was determined that a walk on the clifftop and some fresh air would revive her spirits.

Sitting in her father's church the following evening, Alice reflected on what had been a very pleasant outing. It was all she could have hoped for when spending time with her handsome Albert, who was always attentive and courteous. Yet however much she told herself it had been the perfect day, a slight feeling of depression persisted.

Later in the week, Alice and her mother left the rector at home at his desk preparing the parish newsletter. They strolled into Ashford town, a walk of forty-five minutes along the rural road from Willesborough. Clumps of butter yellow primroses adorned the grass verges, and the trees were beginning to display tender green leaves.

"Your father needs some writing paper and envelopes," Mother had said earlier. "And it's Aunt Maud's birthday so I'd like to look in the William Giles' store to see if anything takes my fancy. I'm not forgetting your wedding dress either. We'll pick out some material and have Mrs Saunders make it up."

After half an hour they crossed the River Stour and

left the farmland behind them. Turning to the left they walked up East Hill with The Star pub, fine Georgian houses and substantial red brick walls on either side. Soon the tall houses became interspersed with shops as they entered the lower end of the High Street.

Their first stop was Headley's Print and Stationers, midway along the street. They stepped under the canopied entrance and into the shop. Alice loved the timeless order of paper, notebooks and envelopes on the dark wooden shelves. She inspected the ink-pens and pencils. This was a shop she had visited many times before with both parents as it was a favourite of her father's. On the spur of the moment, Alice chose a pen for Hazel. It would be lovely to return with a gift for her friend.

Next, mother and daughter went into William Giles', glass and china store. "You'll have a home of your own soon enough, Alice," her mother said as she veered towards the sets of crockery. "It's just a case of waiting. In the meantime, there is plenty to collect for your bottom drawer. How do you like this Spode Blue Italian pattern."

"I find it rather fussy," Alice replied with disinterest. "I'm not sure I want so much pattern on my dinner plate." She moved towards a different display, "This Wedgwood collection with the Mandarin border are nice, or perhaps the Etruria. A subtle pattern around the edge."

"Too fussy!" repeated Mrs Tibbs. "When I was setting up home, the more decoration the better."

Alice picked up more items, looked at the shape and the pattern then cast them back on the shelf, feeling no urge to begin a collection of china. She turned away from the displays. "Did you say a pot-pourri dish for Aunt Maud?"

"You'll have to decide on these things soon you know, Alice." Mrs Tibbs walked briskly towards the cut

233

glass ornaments display.

On leaving the shop, Mrs Tibbs made a beeline for her favourite material shop which was housed in one of the timber-framed Tudor buildings nestling under the shadow of the church. Her mind still on Alice's bottom drawer she headed towards the linens.

"French or Irish?" the enthusiastic mother asked her daughter.

"I... I... really don't mind," Alice replied.

Mrs Tibbs inspected some bales of material then instructed the assistant to cut off several yards of a French cotton with a high thread count. "We'll hem these in the evenings over the next week," she told Alice.

She then descended on the white and ivory silks, taking samples to the natural light at the windows to inspect the colour and quality.

"I wonder," Alice began, "... I wonder if perhaps a mauve or a pale pink... or even... or even a dove grey would be both pretty and more practical? I could use it again... perhaps make a few alterations."

"I don't really think... it's not what I was expecting. Not what I was expecting at all," Mrs Tibbs looked straight at Alice. "Let's look at the pattern books."

"Not too fussy, please Mother."

"Fussy! That word again. All brides want a fuss on their wedding day!"

Mother and daughter left the shop with a book of patterns to borrow and small samples of both ivory and rose pink. The cotton was to be delivered to their home by the end of the day.

"Now for something to eat," Mrs Tibbs announced and strode off leaving Alice to trail behind.

It was the afternoon of Easter Monday; Alice had been invited to have afternoon tea with Albert and his mother. Albert called for her and they walked around

234

the corner to his home. He lived with his mother, in a modern, orange-brick semi-detached house with a pretty bay window. His mother was fond of flowers and spent many hours a week tending the garden. As soon as a bloom was past its best, its head was snipped off, and no new growth could go untended as it was either cut into shape or trained into place. As Alice stepped up the garden path, she admired the tulips, daffodils and grape hyacinth. Around the front door the wisteria was yet to bloom for a couple of months.

Alice had never been further than the front parlour, which was reserved for Sundays and guests. How very strange that it seemed unlikely she would see any other part of the house until it became her home. She sat on a mahogany chair at the small table which stood in the bay window and surveyed the room. After tea, she would sit on the settee at Albert's side whilst his mother relaxed in the armchair

It was a pleasant place to sit and observe the comings and goings of the street outside. A writing slope was placed on a bookcase and Alice imagined that Mrs Havers often lifted the slope onto the table and sat there writing her letters. The table was covered with a dark red cloth and then a lace over-cloth. Curtains and a scalloped edge pelmet were also a dark red, this time in velvet. The fireplace, with its pretty tiles, perfectly framed the small fire in its grate. Walls, papered in a dark gold paisley pattern, were embellished with needlework pictures and decorative plates. The mantle above the fireplace displayed a carriage clock and the bookcase was adorned with figurines and vases

It was an attractive room which Mrs Havers kept in good order and of which she was rightly proud. Alice could see this would be a charming place to make her home but could not shift the slight feeling of depression settling upon her. How often would all those dainty ornaments need dusting, she wondered, and what would she have to write about when sitting at this very table as the new Mrs Havers?

"Alice dear, I had a notion that you and I could work on a cross stitch together, to celebrate your wedding," Mrs Havers suggested, as she poured the tea.

"That's a lovely idea," Alice replied. It really was very thoughtful of Albert's mother. "Perhaps we could walk to town in the week and choose the threads?"

"I'd like that very much," Mrs Havers smiled warmly at Alice. "I never had a daughter and I so look forward to spending time with you. When we are finished, Albert could frame it. He has quite a collection of woodworking tools in his shed now."

"A fair collection," Albert agreed.

The three of them continued to nibble on dainty sandwiches, scones and ginger cake. It was all very pleasant, and Alice hoped that she would enjoy learning to cook under the guidance of her new mother-in-law. But what else would she do beside the dusting, shopping and washing her delicate clothes? Most of the laundry was done by a local woman and a daily help did the sweeping and mopping. Would she help in the garden, or might she be able to work a few days a week? Alice broached the subject with Albert when his mother left them alone after tea.

"Albert, of course I want to do my share of chores and help your mother wherever I can, but there are only three of us and a daily help. Now we are not to have our own home perhaps I could help your mother and work as well?"

"Alice, bless you for wanting to educate young minds, but you see how Mother is looking forward to having your company, so we cannot deprive her." Albert patted Alice's arm tenderly.

"I just feel that I would like to do something useful," Alice persisted weakly.

236

"And so you will," Albert held her gaze with his blue eyes. "You will be marvellous company for mother and perhaps the two of you could do something beneficial to the community, such as helping the local people who are elderly or infirm. I am sure your father would know of families who would greatly benefit from having their shopping done for them or some company during the day."

"I'm sure he would," Alice agreed. "I need to feel useful."

"I was talking to Mother only this morning and we wondered about the wisdom of you returning to your teaching position. We no longer need your income to furnish our own home and Mother gets so lonely, you could be here, visiting daily and getting to know each other."

"Oh, I hadn't… I mean to say that…" Alice couldn't express her thoughts coherently. Not to go back to Dungeness she had at first, she was ashamed to admit, sneered upon and hated for its chilled sea mists and dreary grey landscape. But now it had become very much a part of her. She had realised beauty did not have to be in the form of apple blossom and swathes of wisteria. They were to be admired for their qualities, but charm came in different forms. The subtle grey tones of shingle ridges and the grey-blue of a stormy sky had their own wilder appeal.

Albert sat looking down at her, as someone might look at a sweet kitten or new-born lamb. "Of course, my darling, you are thinking of your commitment to the school and pupils, and I admire you for it. However, your greater loyalty is towards your family… your future family."

"Yes, I see," Alice replied.

"I am not saying a letter would suffice, no if you were to go to see Mrs Stubbs then that would show good manners and I am sure she will understand. She sounds like an eminently sensible woman. Yes, that is the thing to do."

"Yes, I imagine it would be," Alice agreed.

"Mother will be delighted and now we can look forward to Sunday afternoon walks or day trips all through the spring and summer." Albert's eyes shone and with his smartly slicked dark brown hair he looked so handsome gazing down at her. He lifted her hands to his lips, "Oh my love, how happy you make me."

Chapter Twenty-Six

"Lydd, Lydd. All alight for Lydd. Next stop Dungeness." The station master called out with all the importance he could muster. It may only be Lydd, but to him it was just as important as Paddington or Charing Cross.

Alice looked out through the grimy window at the smart little station. Containers of spring flowers sat against the warm orange brick of the long, low buildings with their slate topped roofs. A scallop edged canopy shaded the doorway and to either side was a row of arched sash windows. It was a fine building, lacking the worldly Italianate influences of Ashford, but rather pleasant, nonetheless.

She was alone in the one coach that was all the Lydd Railway Company deemed necessary to transport the people to and from this remote corner of Kent. However, on this bright, albeit breezy, April afternoon, Alice was sure to be joined by housewives who had travelled to Lydd for provisions and would now be returning to Dungeness. Eagerly she scanned the platform as best she could, given the build-up of soot on the windows, and was disappointed to see only the station master and his assistant.

It seemed that no one was going to accompany her on this last leg of the journey; it was to be just Alice. The coach doors had been slammed shut, the whistle had been blown and the flag waved, when the integrity of the staff at Lydd, and all the rules they stood for, were compromised by a latecomer. A shout alerted the

239

guard, who turned but could not bring himself to assist whoever disrespected the Lydd Railway Company timetable. He turned his attention back to the train, determined that nothing and no one would prevent the smooth operation of the service. But the young man flung himself at the door of the coach, grabbing and turning the small brass handle, then opening the door as the engine made those first slow turns of its great wheels. Belches of smoke were being released through the chimney as he threw himself into Alice's compartment.

"I just saved myself a long walk in this damned wind." His voice was cheerful but rough and, as he spoke, he flung himself down in the set of seats opposite Alice and placed a bag beside him. Dark blond curls were a little untidy, with no hat to keep them in place. He was freshly shaved though, sideburns neatly shaped. Grey eyes looked towards Alice and soft lines around them crinkled slightly as he smiled. His trousers and waistcoat were clean and of a decent fit, Alice observed. Not overly smart, but he was a fisherman and had no need to dress up like a city gent.

"Miss Tibbs, how did you enjoy your Easter holidays? I trust all was fine in Ashford; perhaps the weather was a little warmer?"

"The weather was fair, thank you, and as always it was good to see my family." Alice smiled back at the person who had irritated her so much on her arrival at Dungeness last autumn. He may be very different from the few men of her previous acquaintance, but her mind was broader now and she knew him to be a hard-working, respected member of the community here.

"Ed and Emily are settled now," Tom remarked. "She's so much happier and he's on the lifeboats."

"Do people accept him… forgive him?"

"Mostly they do, those who know him and see him for a decent fellow. He's a good sort, always willing to

240

help others and grateful for the help we've given him."

"I'm glad to hear it. He's a hard worker, and Emily too."

For a moment, Alice reflected on another time, on another journey from Ashford to Dungeness. It seemed like a lifetime ago, when she had arrived in the relentless wind and rain, only to stumble over the body of Emily Brooks. How lacking in life experience she had been and how fixed in her opinions. It seemed that the Alice who arrived six months ago was a different person, and in many ways she was.

The steam train passed the school and Alice looked over, hoping Hazel would be there when she arrived. She had missed the friendship of another young woman, having only her parents and Albert for company whilst she was at home. Hazel had decided to return to her family while Alice was away; she found it lonely being in the schoolhouse and away from the other cottages.

"Your last term," Tom stated. "Then back to Ashford with memories of the summer sun shining down on you."

"Oh, I don't think the sea mist and wind are that easily forgotten," Alice smiled. "Actually, it's not my last term though… I've written to Mrs Stubbs, and I am to stay on after the summer. In fact, I'll probably stay here for the summer and just visit my family in Ashford from time to time."

"And your… your marriage?"

"I think I've changed… I'm not the kind of woman Albert would want to marry." She paused, her cheeks colouring a little, and looked down at her hands and the indent showing where her engagement ring had been. "Neither do I believe that Albert would suit me."

Her companion didn't reply to this, perhaps unsure of how to respond. Commiserating with a young woman on the end of her engagement was beyond his

241

sphere of experience. So, they sat in silence for a moment, intent on looking out of the windows. The train slowed as it approached the station and gave a final shudder when it came to a halt.

Tom stood as the train came to a stop. Without a word, he reached for Alice's heavy suitcase, made his way to the door and opened it. Stepping out he placed her case on the platform and held the door open for her.

"Thank you." She looked up at him and went to put her hand on the case.

"I'll carry it to the schoolhouse for you," Tom said, his hand reaching the handle before hers. "It's very heavy."

They set off across the shingle, both still absorbed with their thoughts. For Alice, she saw the area afresh, as somewhere she would settle for the time being at least. She looked with new eyes at the variation in the tones of the grey-brown stones and at the fragile plants raising their heads now the sun was shining.

Rough grasses had an unusual rusty-red tinge to them as their seed-heads ripened, making an attractive carpet stretching in all directions. Pretty white flowers on grey-green stems risked reaching out to the sun on the desolate shingle-land. Alice found herself pausing to look closer at a delicate seed-head or to marvel at the brilliant blue spikes of viper's bugloss. Tulips and daffodils were all very pleasant, but here was a different form of beauty and it was just as engaging.

The companions passed a few comments, on safe subjects such as the weather or a distinctive bird flying by. Tom named some of the plants when Alice paused to study them. Alice apologised for taking her time and that the suitcase was so heavy.

At the schoolhouse door, Tom placed the case on the ground. "It's nice over Littlestone way, with tall houses overlooking the bay… and a decent path along the seafront," he began tentatively at first and paused before continuing, "…and a fine hotel where they do a nice afternoon tea, so I hear. The train goes there from Lydd and it's a pleasant stroll to the promenade."

Alice looked up at him and waited.

"So, I wondered… if perhaps next Saturday…?"

"That would be lovely," Alice replied.

"Great. Have a good week then and I'll see you… I'll knock for you at ten o'clock next Saturday."

"I'll look forward to it."

Tom turned away. After a few steps, he paused to wave, while he closed the gate in the picket fence surrounding the school. Then, with a grin on his face, he set off towards his wooden beach-front home.

THE END

About the Author

Emma loves to combine an interest in local history with creative writing. It is important to her that historical details are accurate to give readers an authentic insight into life on Romney Marsh, as well as creating memorable stories. Emma is keen to work with local artists and cover designers. She loves 'meet the author' events and selling books locally, enabling her to meet the readers.

Books
Reading order and publication dates

The Dungeness Saga (also featuring Lydd and Ashford) set in late Victorian times through to WW2:

Still Shining Bright* (2020): Cora and her daughter, Emily, are brought ashore to Dungeness by lifeboat. With no home or possessions, they rely on the kindness of strangers, and Cora must use her wit to survive.

Reckless Choices* (2021): A chance meeting on a train upsets Emily, while on the streets of Ashford someone lurks waiting to make trouble. As tensions brew within a close family, the young woman makes a rash choice.

Secrets of the Shingle (2016 & 2020): A mystery set on the wild, windswept wastes of the Dungeness peninsula in the 19th century and seen through the eyes of a naive young teacher.

Stranger on the Point (2018): Lily sets off to discover the remote coastal village her mother called home. A wrong turning takes her to a place where her arrival brings hope. The story of a determined young woman's quest to fulfil her worth, as shadows of WW1 live on.

The Artist's Gift (2019): This tells the story of a fictional young woman, widowed through the war and living amongst real life events during the Second World War. Inspired by the bombing of Lydd Church.

*Prequels to *Secrets of the Shingle*

Stand-alone novels:

A Place Called Hope (2005, reworked 2019): Set in the 16th century, this tells the story of two young women living through the decline of a remote settlement named Hope on Romney Marsh.

What the Monk Didn't See (2017 & 2021): The story of New Romney and the 1287 storm, which changed the fortunes of the town forever. As the storm breaks out, a monk climbs to the roof of the church tower. It is a superb vantage point, but what doesn't he see?

The Saxon Series introduces West Hythe, Lyminge and Aldington in 7th- century Anglo-Saxon times:

The Pendant Cross (2020): For a few days a year, the Sandtun (West Hythe) is used as a seasonal trading settlement. While they await the boats from Francia, friendships are made and hatred brews. Meanwhile, four monks travel by night carrying a precious secret.

The Sacred Stone (2021): An earthquake uncovers a Roman altar buried in the foundations of an old fort. An ambitious thane and his priest are determined to secure this prize, and their actions have repercussions on the people of Aldington.

The Dymchurch Series is set in Georgian times.

But First Maintain the Wall (2018): Harry is passing through the village when the seawall breaches and events force him to stay. As an outsider, he struggles to be accepted and a tentative friendship is forged with a young woman who seeks answers to her past.

The Whitsun Gallop (2022): On the day of the annual Whitsun Gallop, the people of Romney Marsh gather. It is a day to parade their best outfits, make merry, and wager on which gentleman jockey will glory. When the prize cup is stolen under the eyes of local dignitaries, a chain of events is set in place, rocking the secure world of Harry and Phoebe Farrers.

The Dymchurch Reckoning (2023):
A brutal encounter in the churchyard raises shockwaves beyond Dymchurch as the hunt for the killer begins and Harry Farrers finds himself in the midst of troubles caused by an old enemy.

For more details take a look at Emma's website:
www.emmabattenauthor.com

Printed in Great Britain
by Amazon